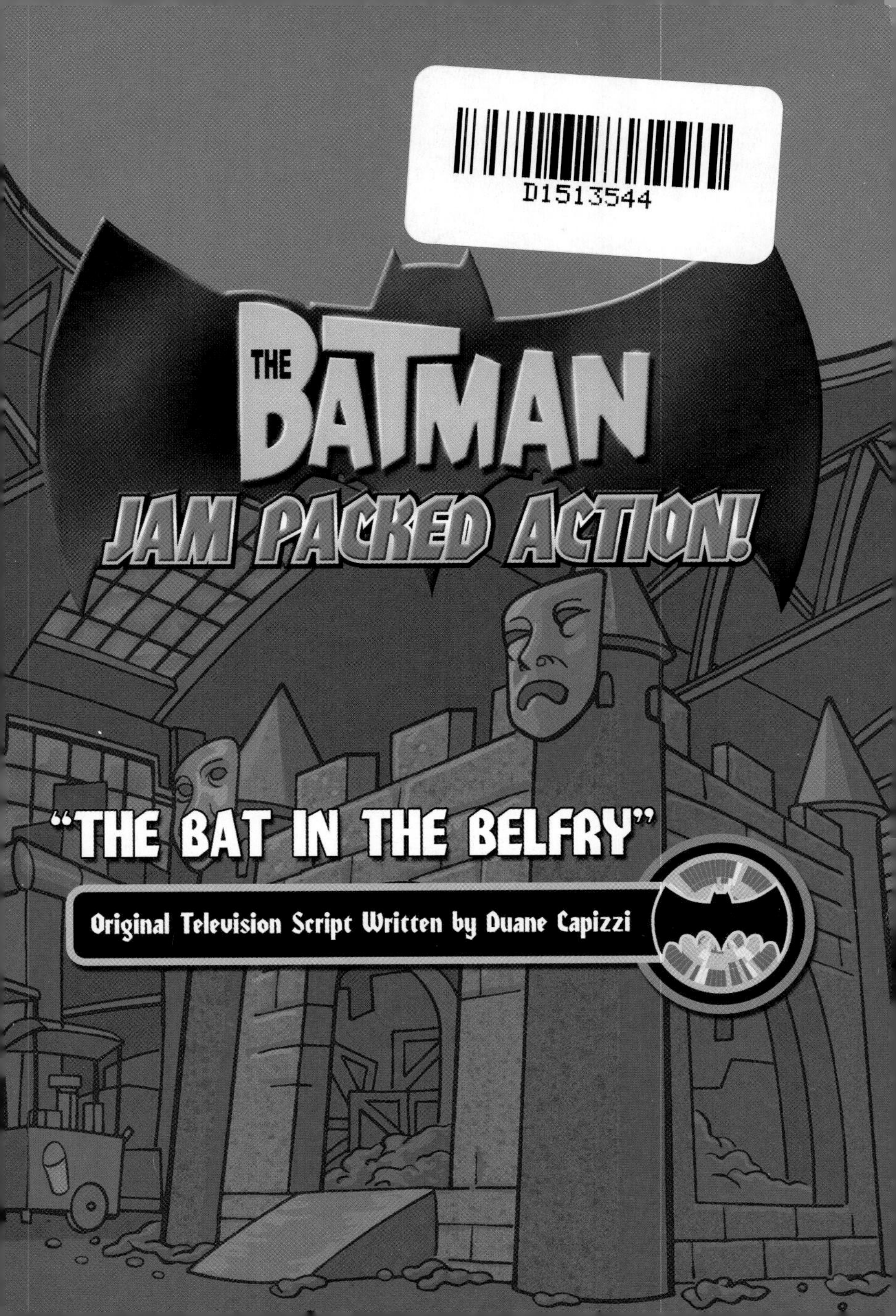
THE BATMAN
JAM PACKED ACTION!
"THE BAT IN THE BELFRY"
Original Television Script Written by Duane Capizzi

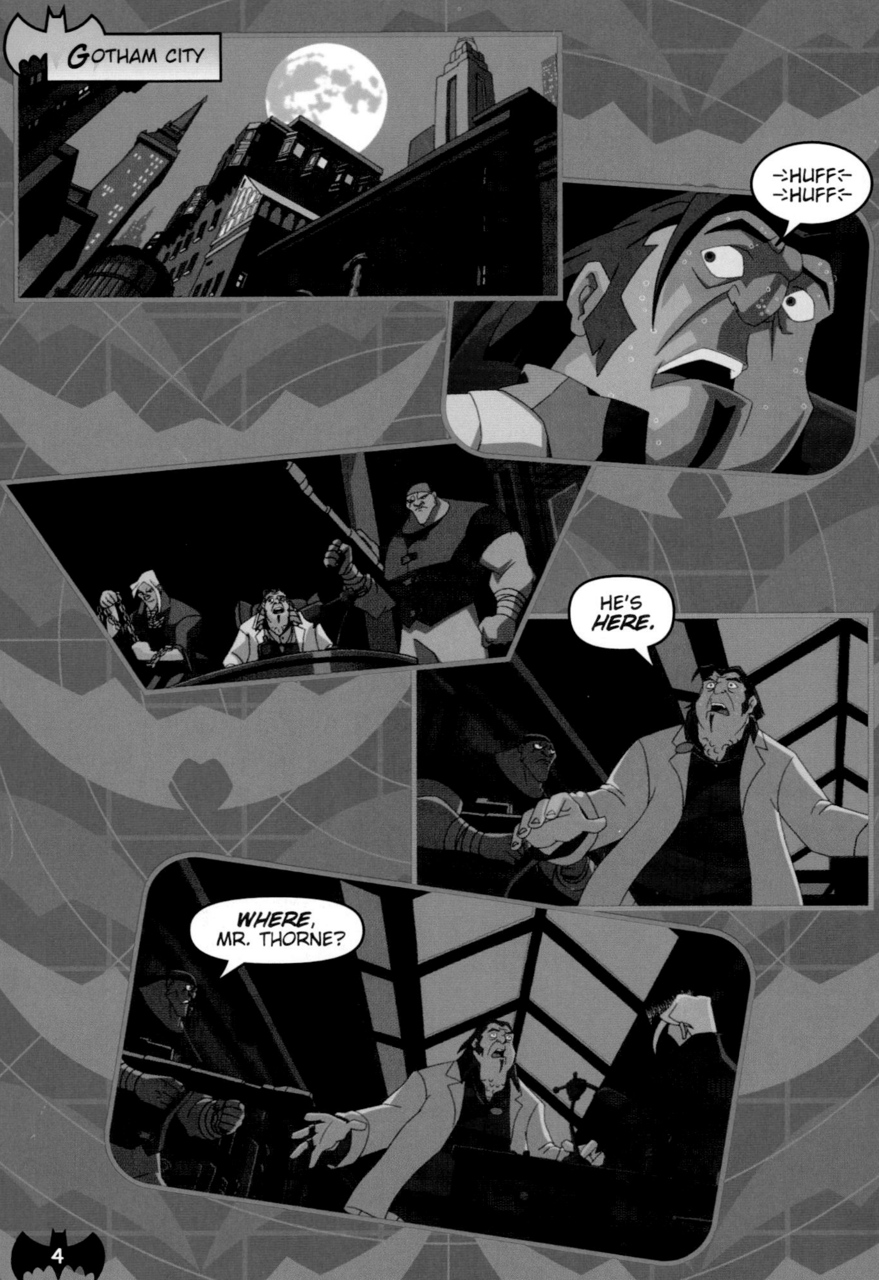
GOTHAM CITY
-HUFF-
-HUFF-
HE'S HERE.
WHERE, MR. THORNE?

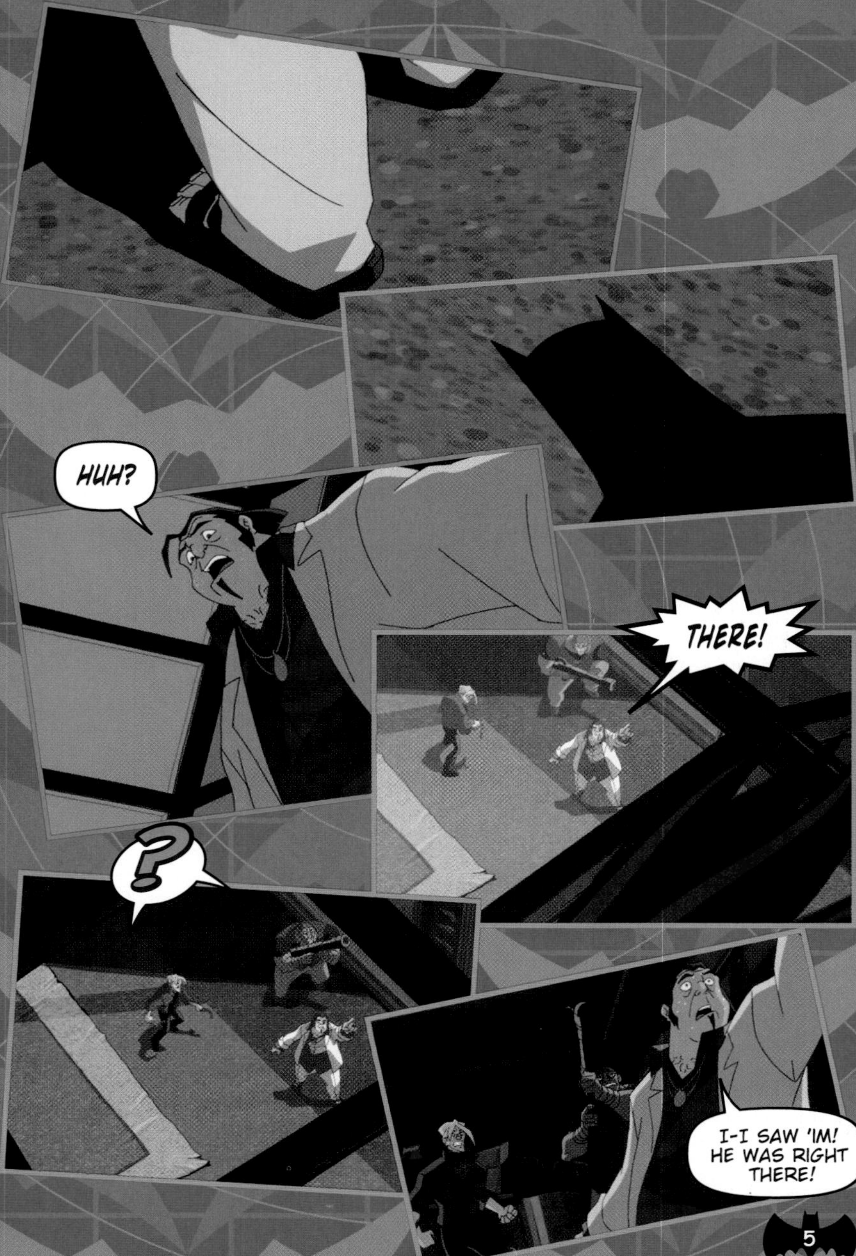
HUH?
THERE!
?
I-I SAW 'IM! HE WAS RIGHT THERE!

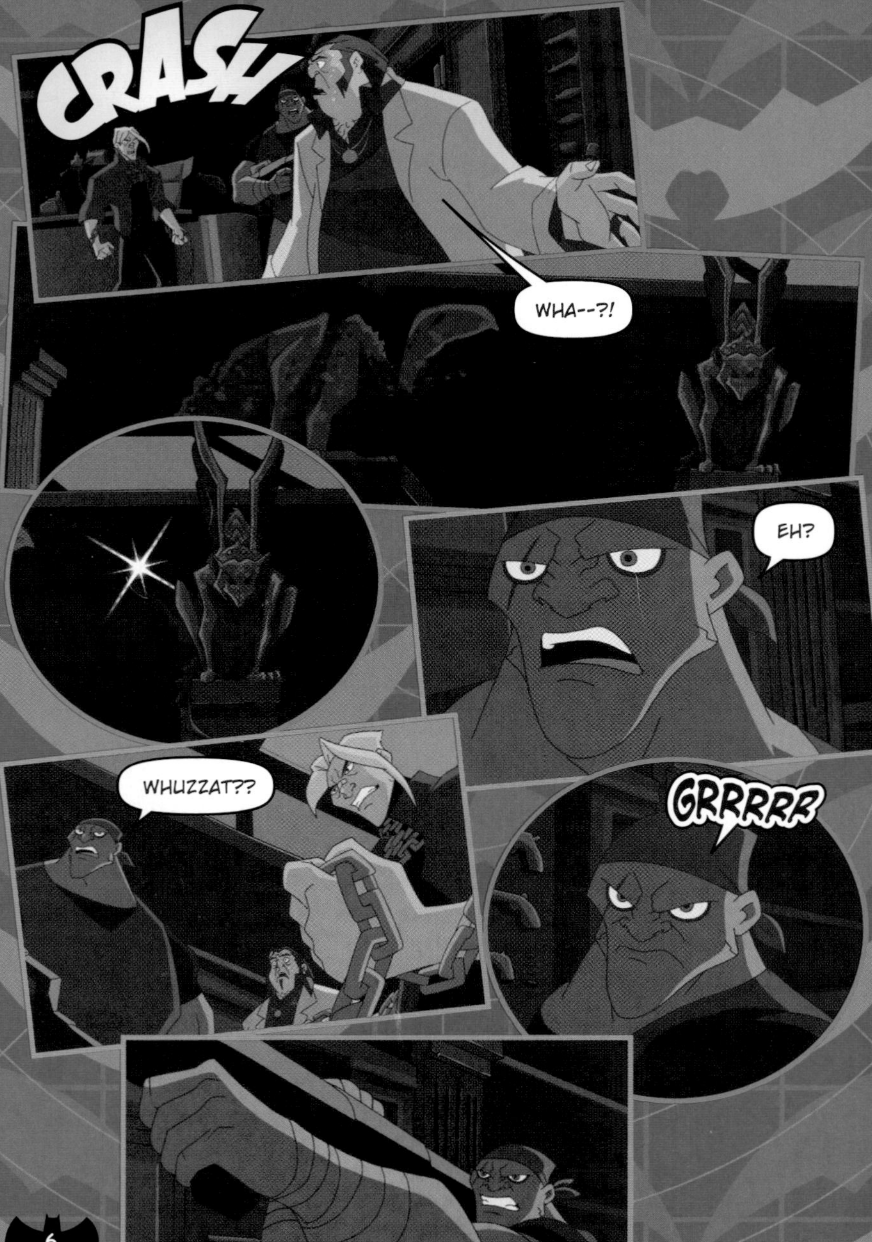
CRASH
WHA--?!
EH?
WHUZZAT??
GRRRRR

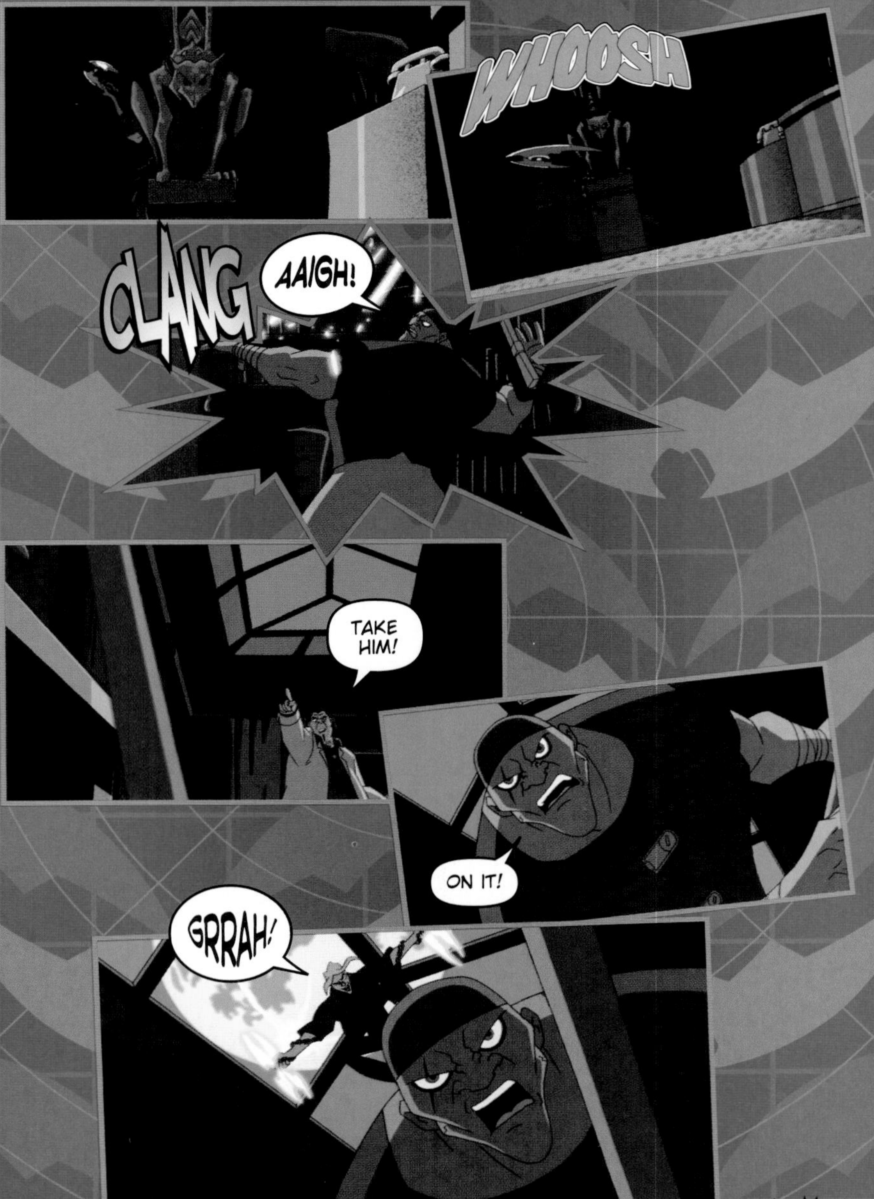
WHOOSH
CLANG
AAIGH!
TAKE HIM!
ON IT!
GRRAH!

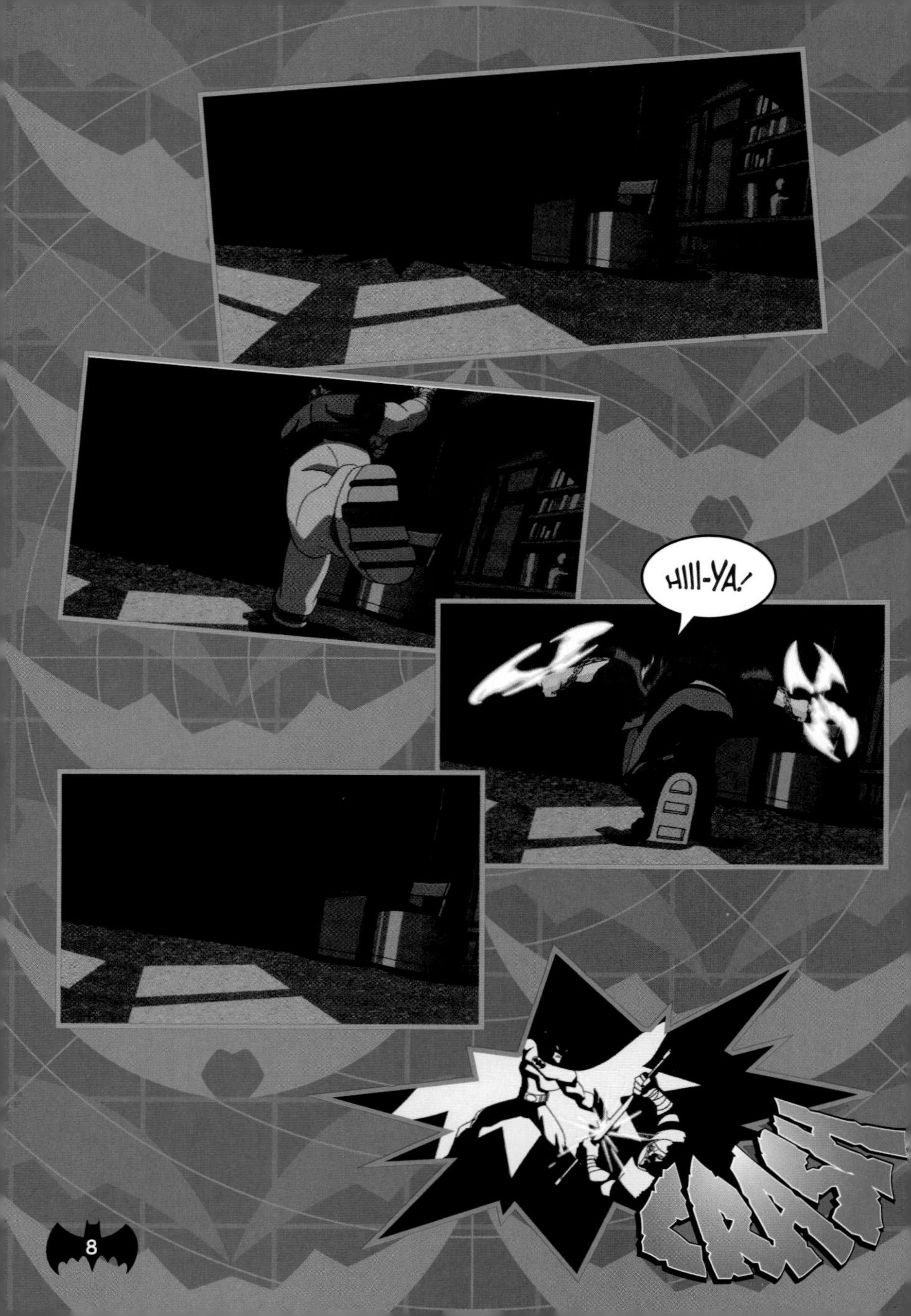
HIIII-YA!
CRASH

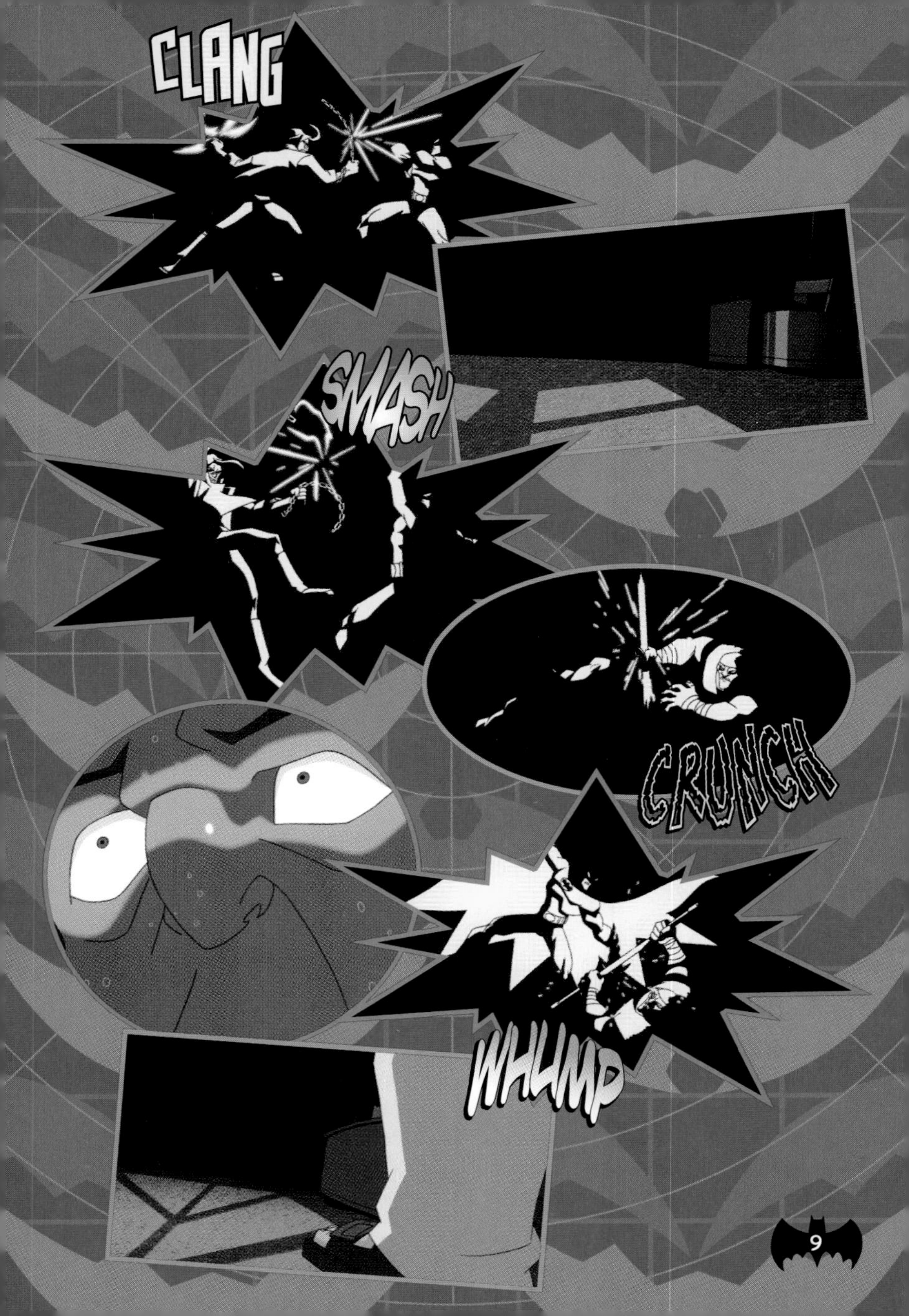
CLANG
SMASH
CRUNCH
WHUMP

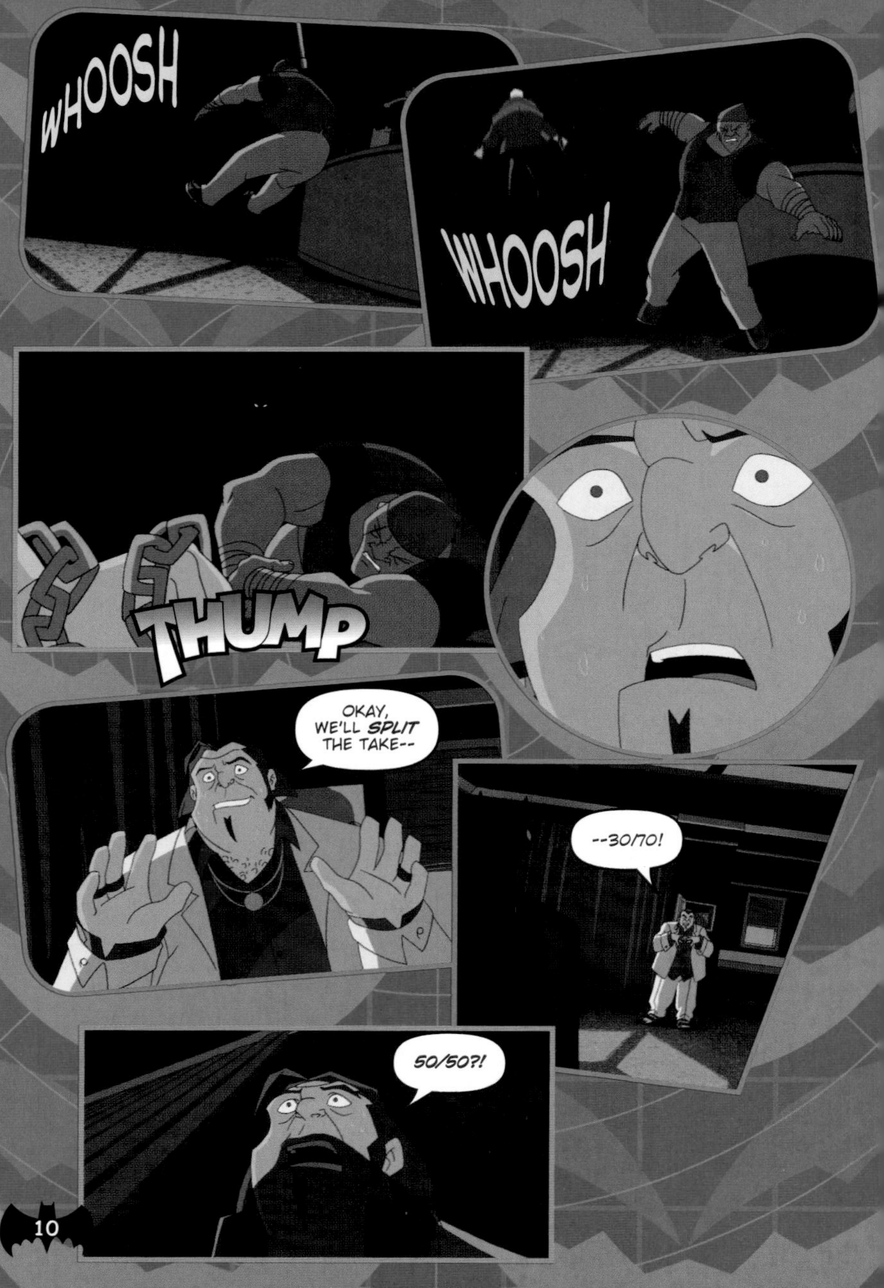
WHOOSH
WHOOSH
THUMP
OKAY, WE'LL SPLIT THE TAKE--
--30/70!
50/50?!

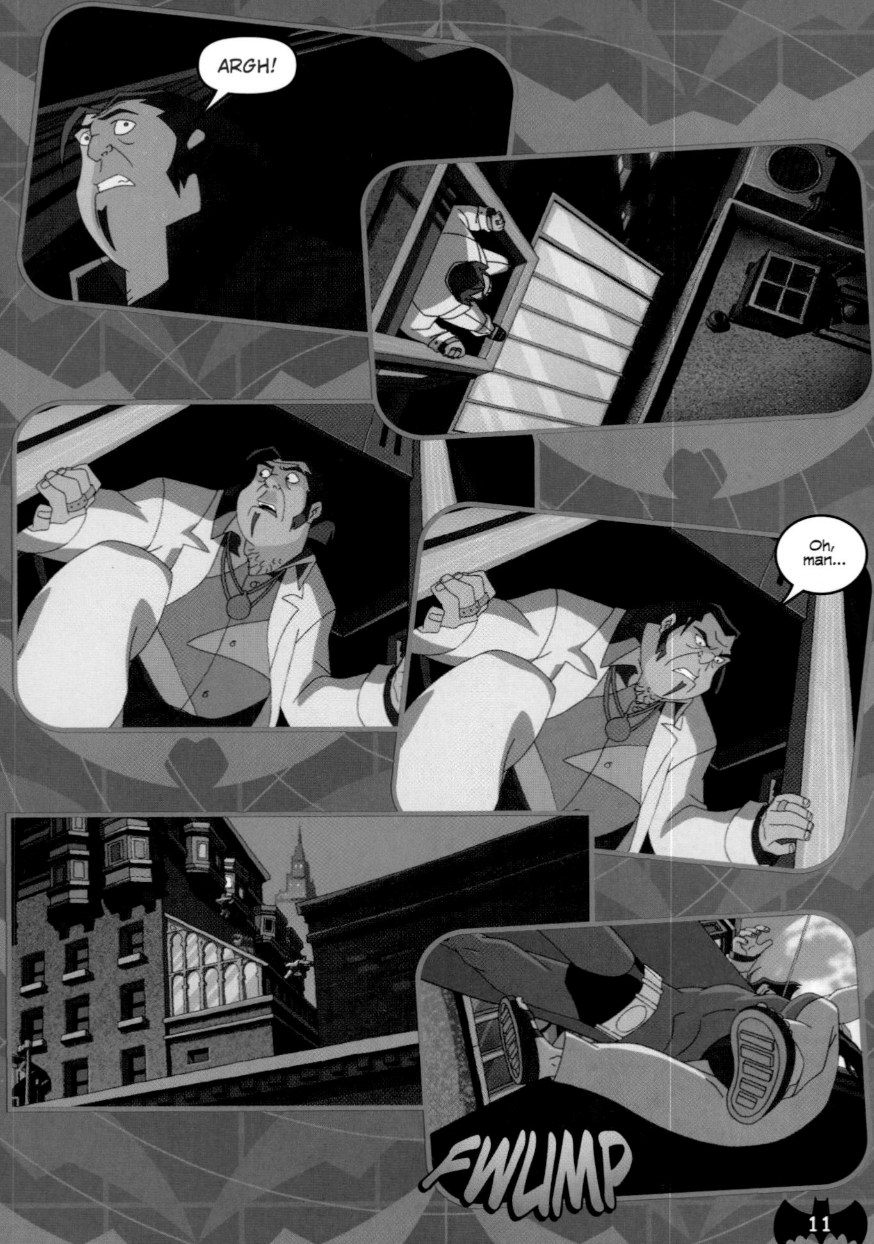
ARGH!
Oh, man...
FWUMP

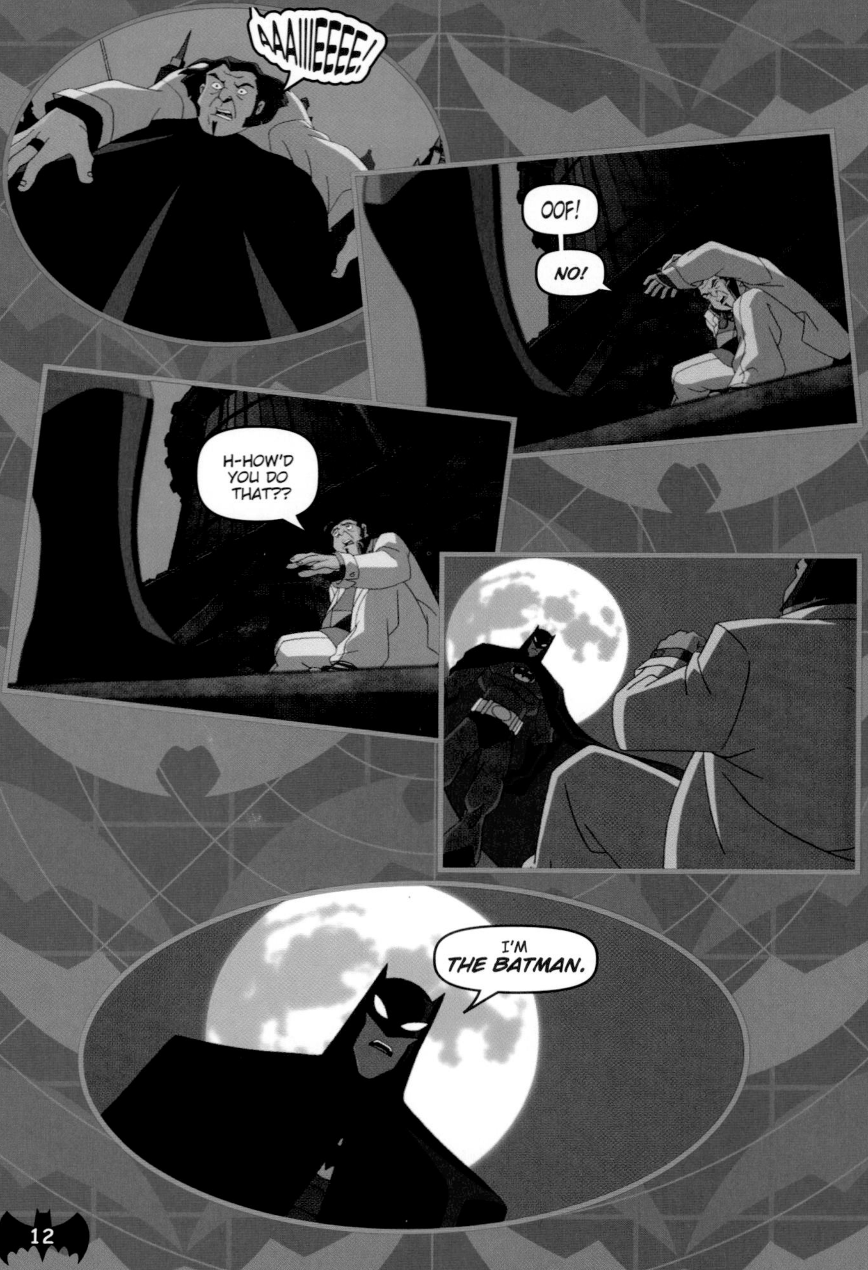
AAAIIIEEEE!
OOF!
NO!
H-HOW'D YOU DO THAT??
I'M THE BATMAN.

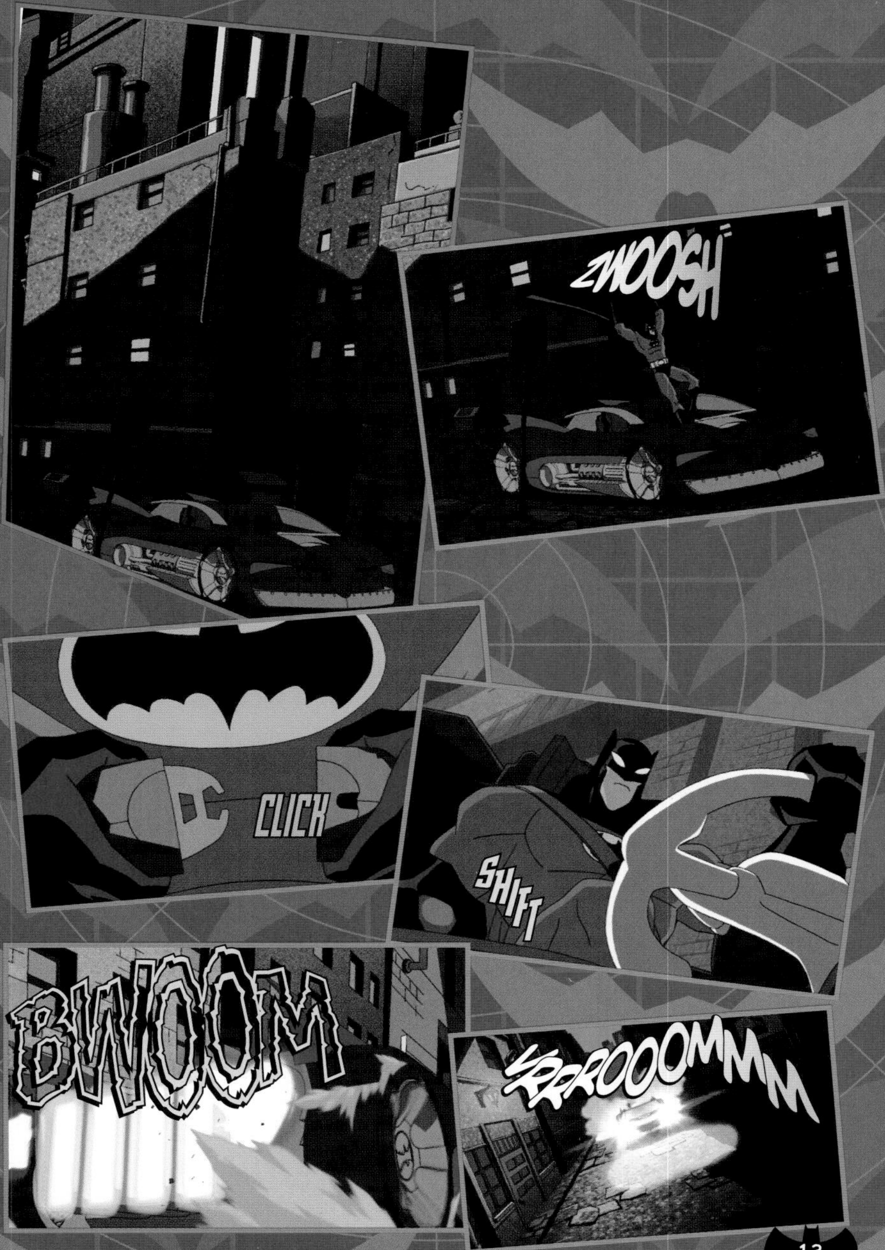
ZWOOSH
CLICK
SHIFT
BWOOM
VRRROOOOMMMM

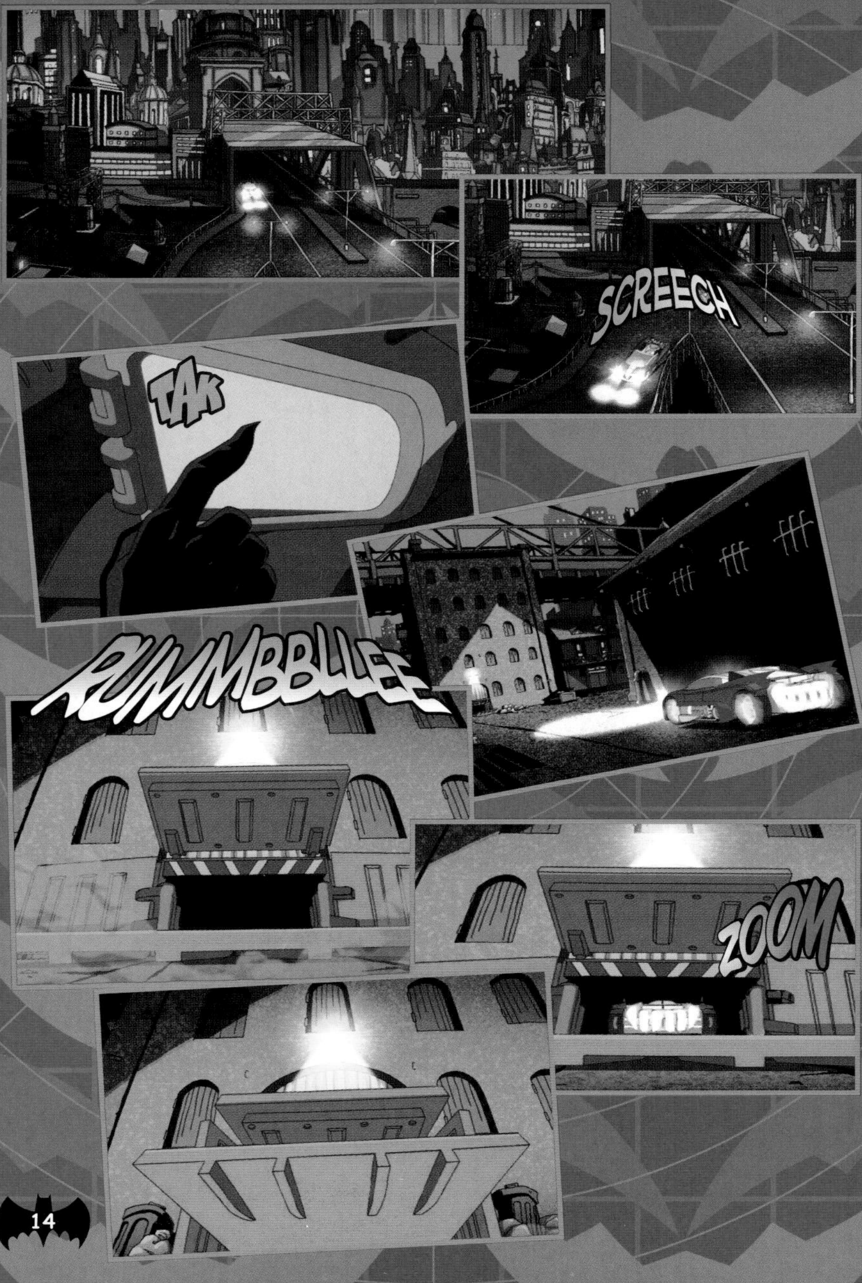
SCREECH
TAK
RUMMBBLLEE
ZOOM

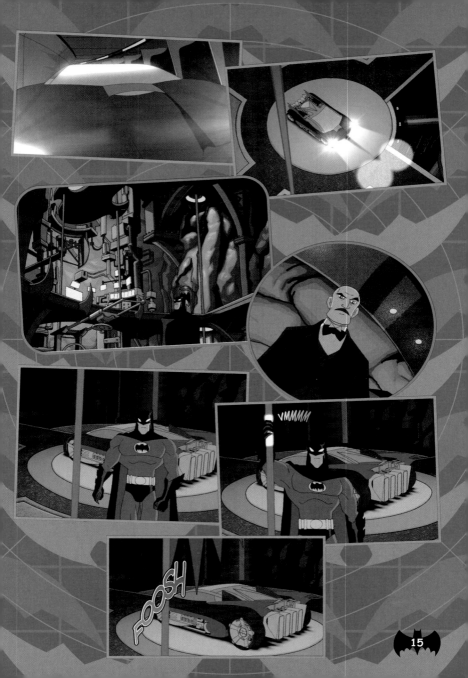

VMMMM

FOOSH

15

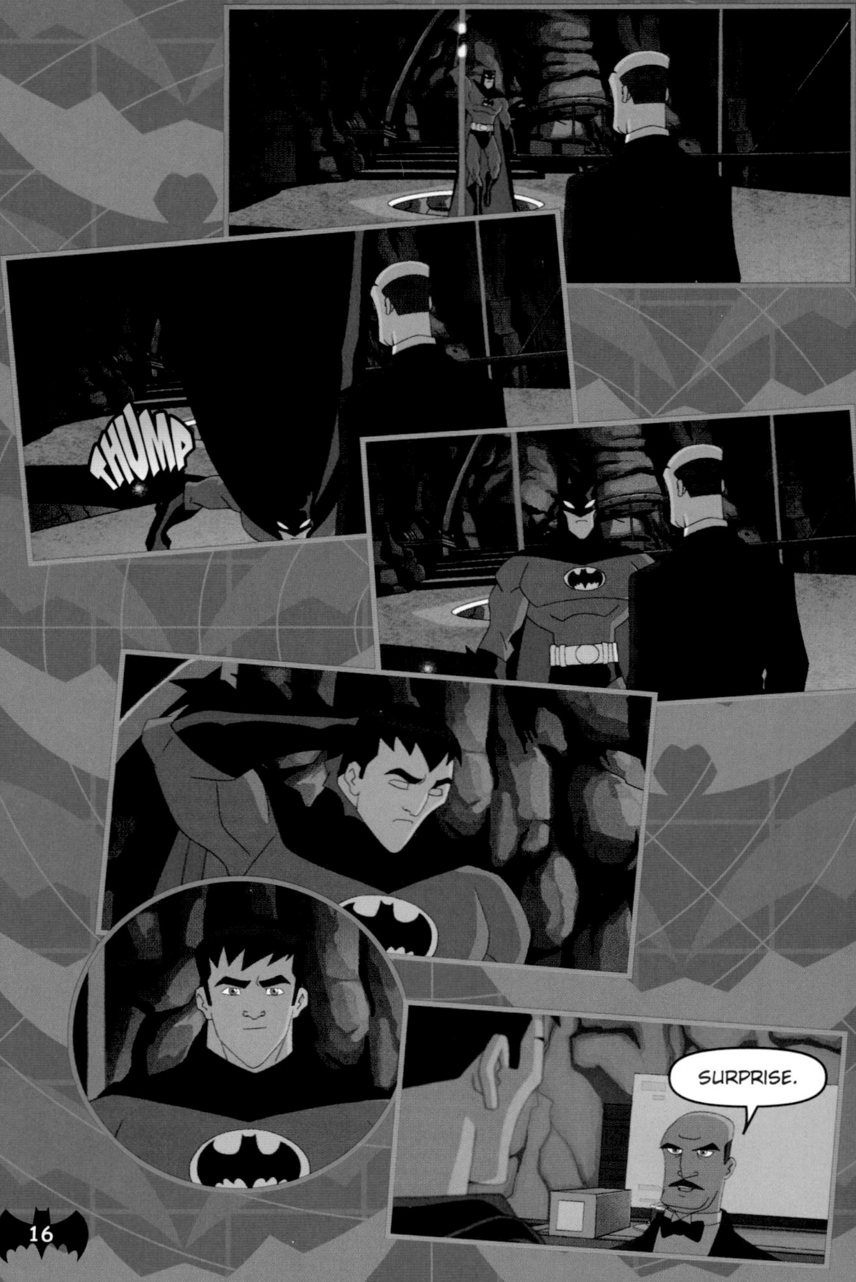
THUMP
SURPRISE.

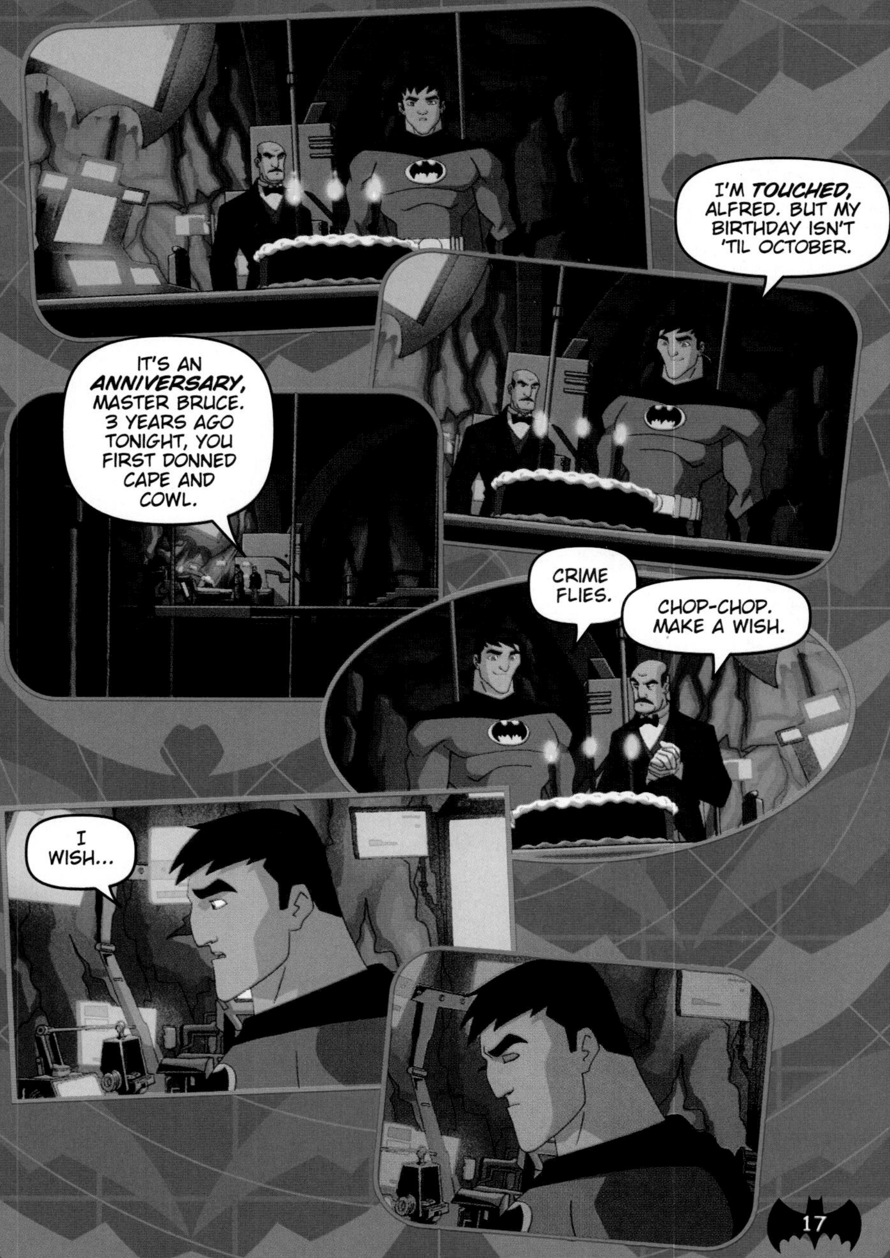
I'M *TOUCHED,* ALFRED. BUT MY BIRTHDAY ISN'T 'TIL OCTOBER.
IT'S AN *ANNIVERSARY,* MASTER BRUCE. 3 YEARS AGO TONIGHT, YOU FIRST DONNED CAPE AND COWL.
CRIME FLIES.
CHOP-CHOP. MAKE A WISH.
I WISH...

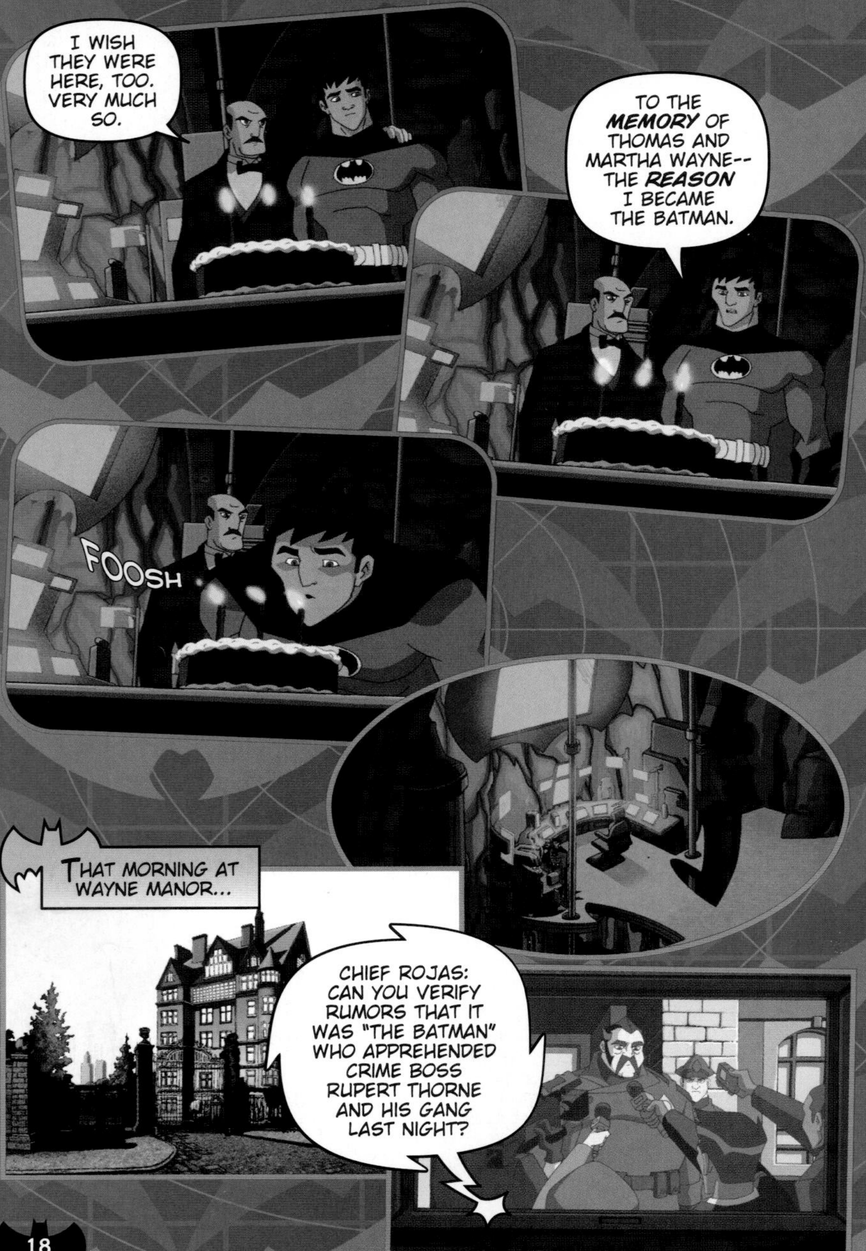

I WISH THEY WERE HERE, TOO. VERY MUCH SO.
TO THE *MEMORY* OF THOMAS AND MARTHA WAYNE-- THE *REASON* I BECAME THE BATMAN.
FOOSH
THAT MORNING AT WAYNE MANOR...
CHIEF ROJAS: CAN YOU VERIFY RUMORS THAT IT WAS "THE BATMAN" WHO APPREHENDED CRIME BOSS RUPERT THORNE AND HIS GANG LAST NIGHT?

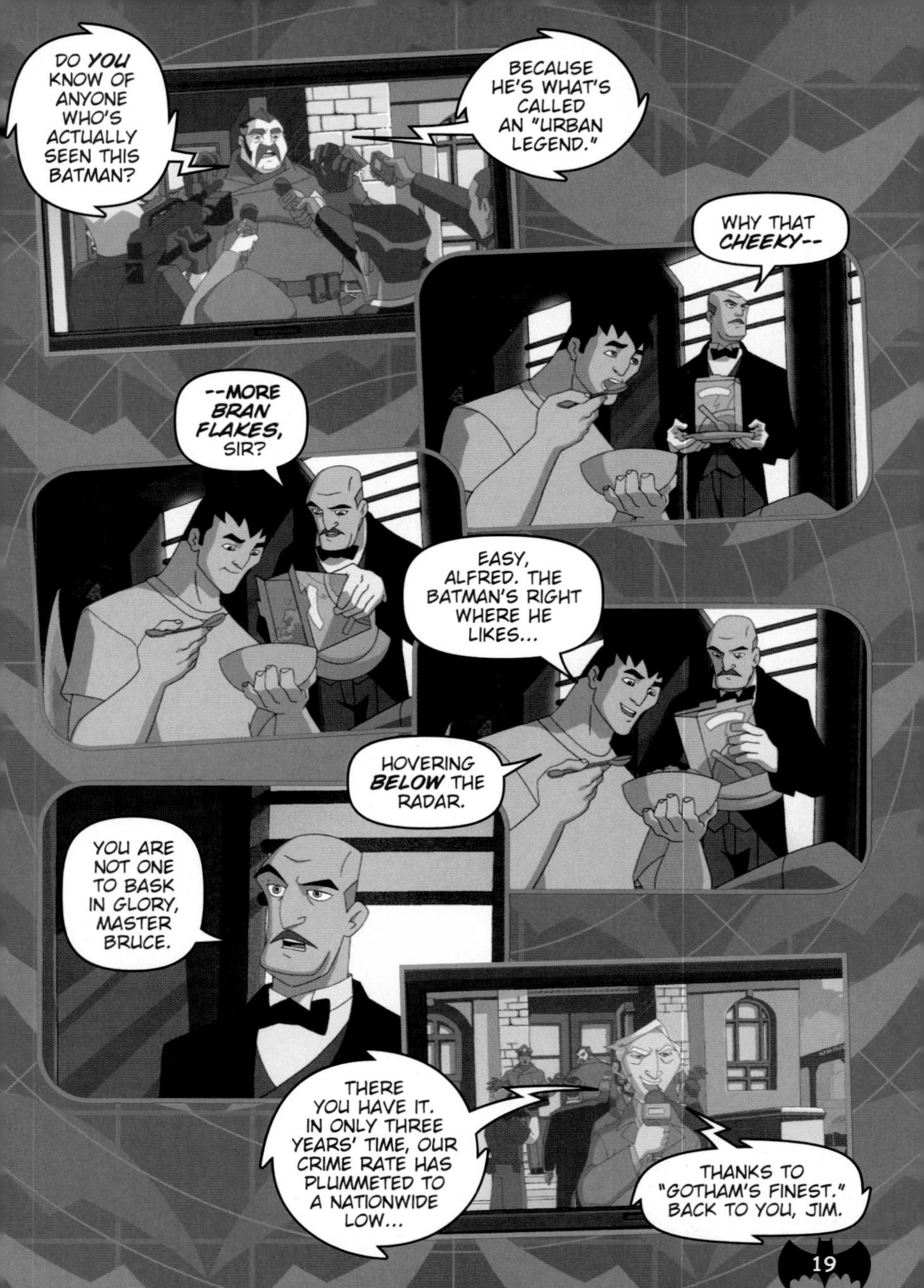
DO *YOU* KNOW OF ANYONE WHO'S ACTUALLY SEEN THIS BATMAN?
BECAUSE HE'S WHAT'S CALLED AN "URBAN LEGEND."
WHY THAT *CHEEKY*--
--MORE *BRAN FLAKES,* SIR?
EASY, ALFRED. THE BATMAN'S RIGHT WHERE HE LIKES...
HOVERING *BELOW* THE RADAR.
YOU ARE NOT ONE TO BASK IN GLORY, MASTER BRUCE.
THERE YOU HAVE IT. IN ONLY THREE YEARS' TIME, OUR CRIME RATE HAS PLUMMETED TO A NATIONWIDE LOW...
THANKS TO "GOTHAM'S FINEST." BACK TO YOU, JIM.

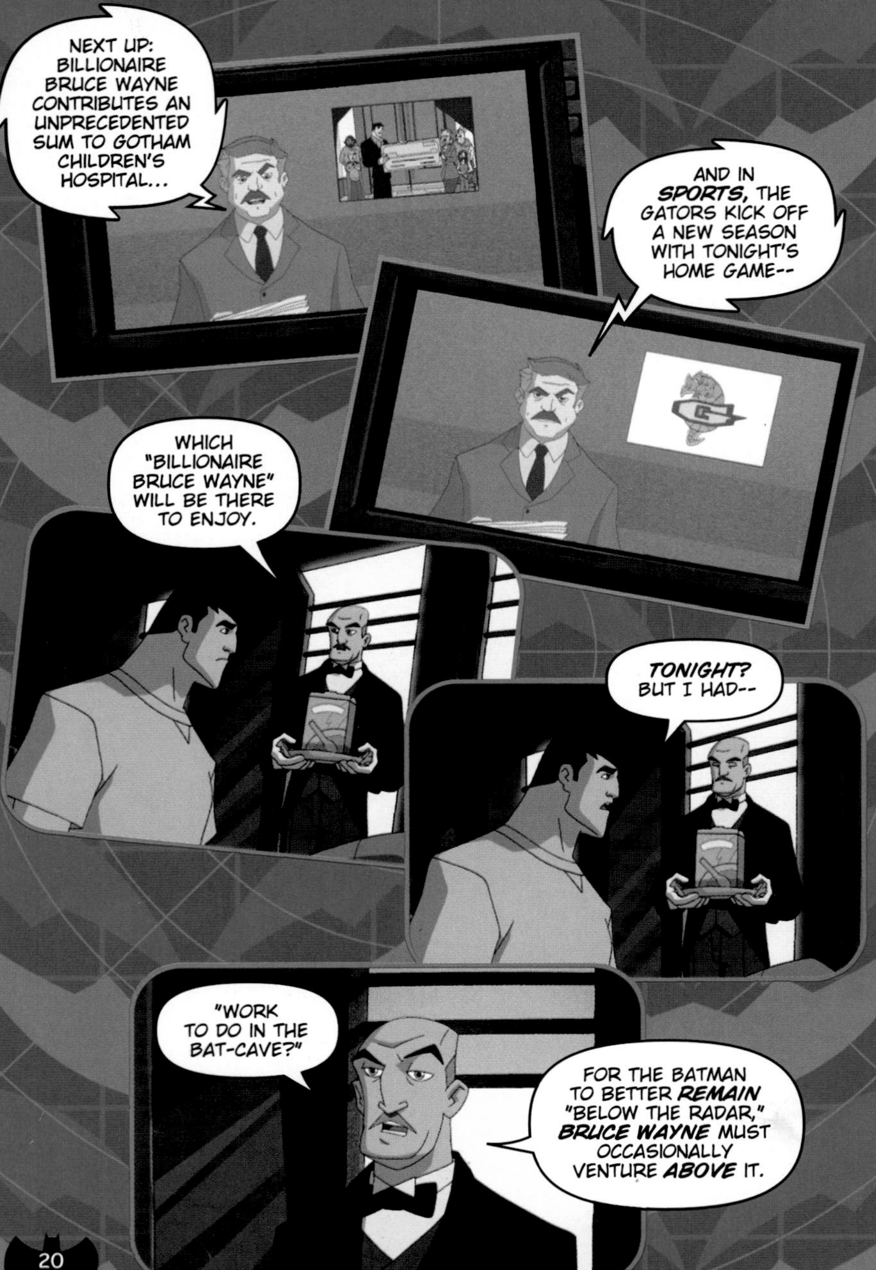
NEXT UP: BILLIONAIRE BRUCE WAYNE CONTRIBUTES AN UNPRECEDENTED SUM TO GOTHAM CHILDREN'S HOSPITAL...
AND IN SPORTS, THE GATORS KICK OFF A NEW SEASON WITH TONIGHT'S HOME GAME--
WHICH "BILLIONAIRE BRUCE WAYNE" WILL BE THERE TO ENJOY.
TONIGHT? BUT I HAD--
"WORK TO DO IN THE BAT-CAVE?"
FOR THE BATMAN TO BETTER REMAIN "BELOW THE RADAR," BRUCE WAYNE MUST OCCASIONALLY VENTURE ABOVE IT.

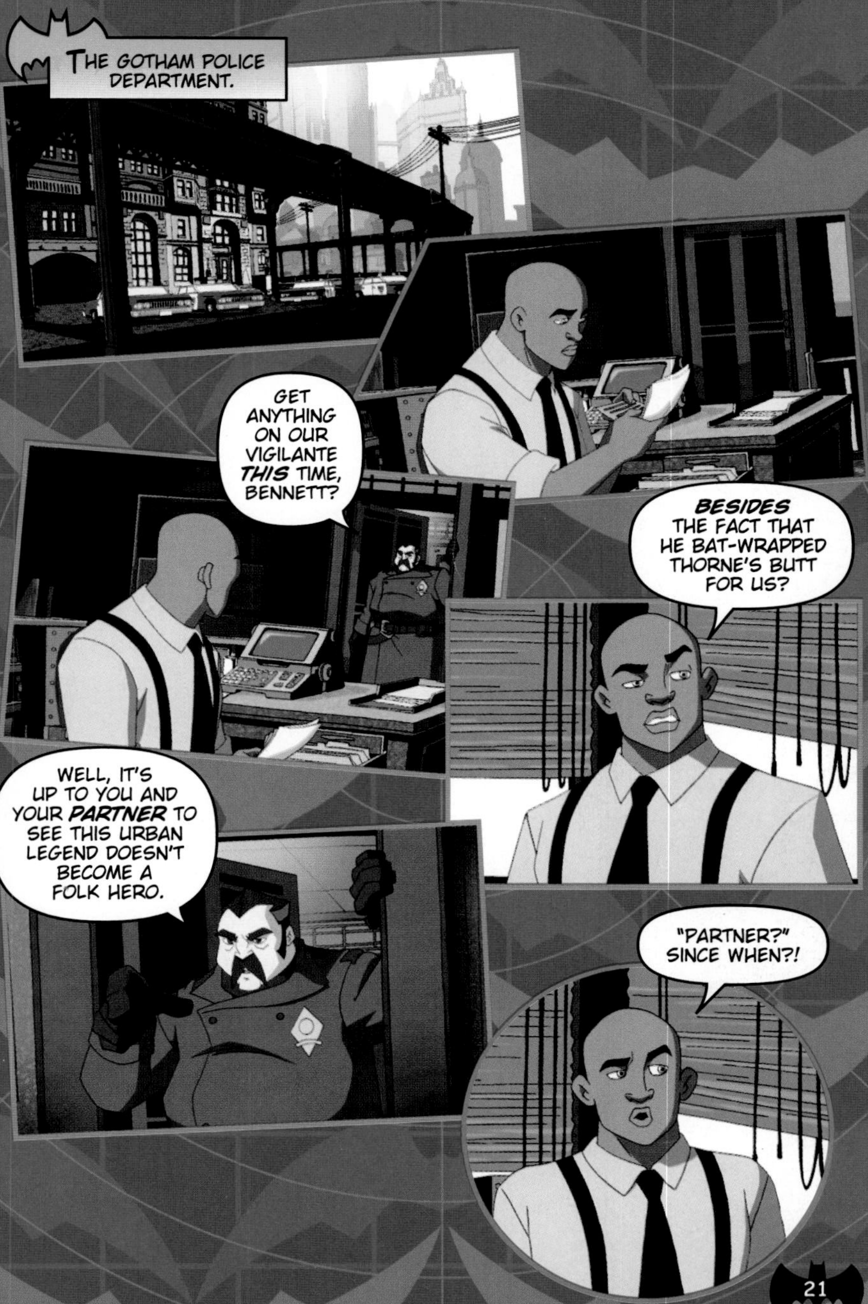
THE GOTHAM POLICE DEPARTMENT.
GET ANYTHING ON OUR VIGILANTE *THIS* TIME, BENNETT?
BESIDES THE FACT THAT HE BAT-WRAPPED THORNE'S BUTT FOR US?
WELL, IT'S UP TO YOU AND YOUR *PARTNER* TO SEE THIS URBAN LEGEND DOESN'T BECOME A FOLK HERO.
"PARTNER?" SINCE WHEN?!

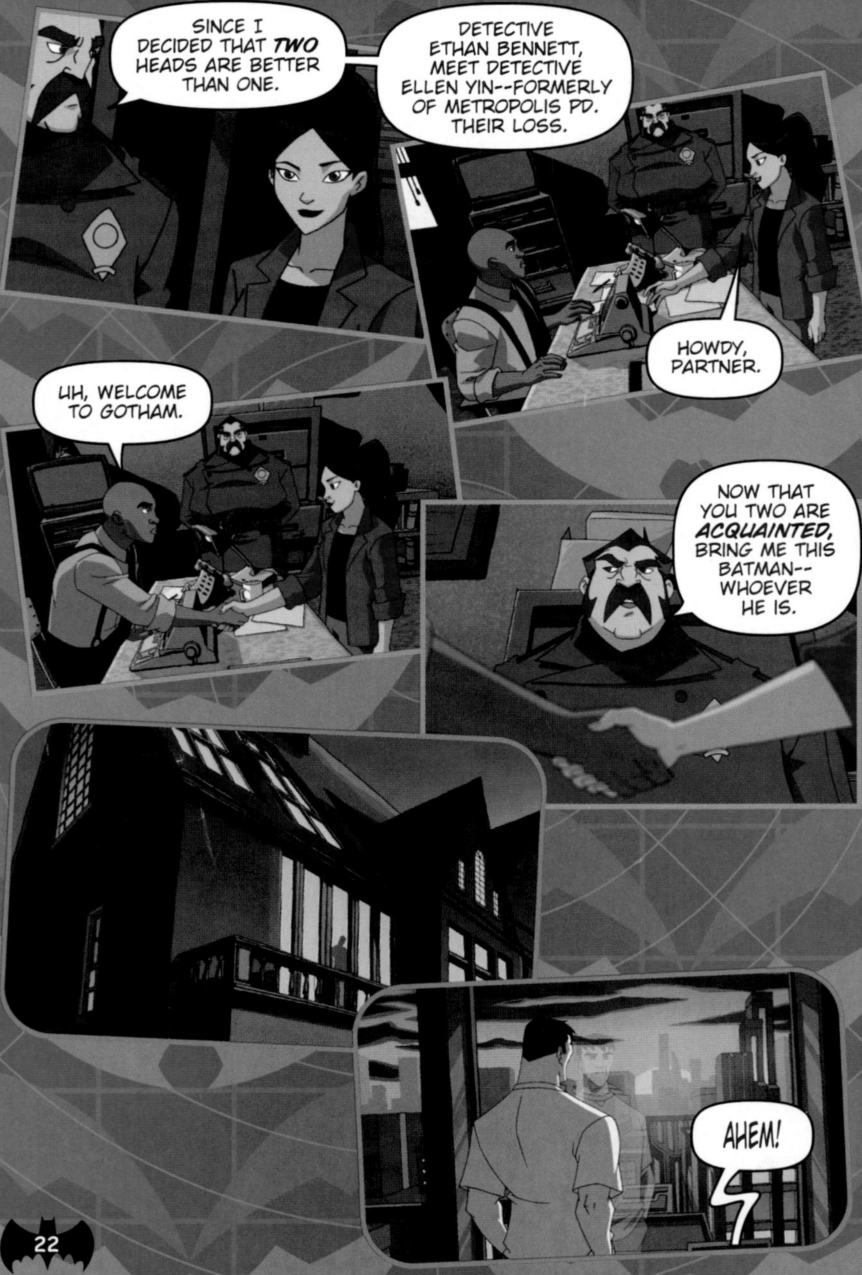
SINCE I DECIDED THAT **TWO** HEADS ARE BETTER THAN ONE.
DETECTIVE ETHAN BENNETT, MEET DETECTIVE ELLEN YIN--FORMERLY OF METROPOLIS PD. THEIR LOSS.
HOWDY, PARTNER.
UH, WELCOME TO GOTHAM.
NOW THAT YOU TWO ARE ***ACQUAINTED,*** BRING ME THIS BATMAN--WHOEVER HE IS.
AHEM!

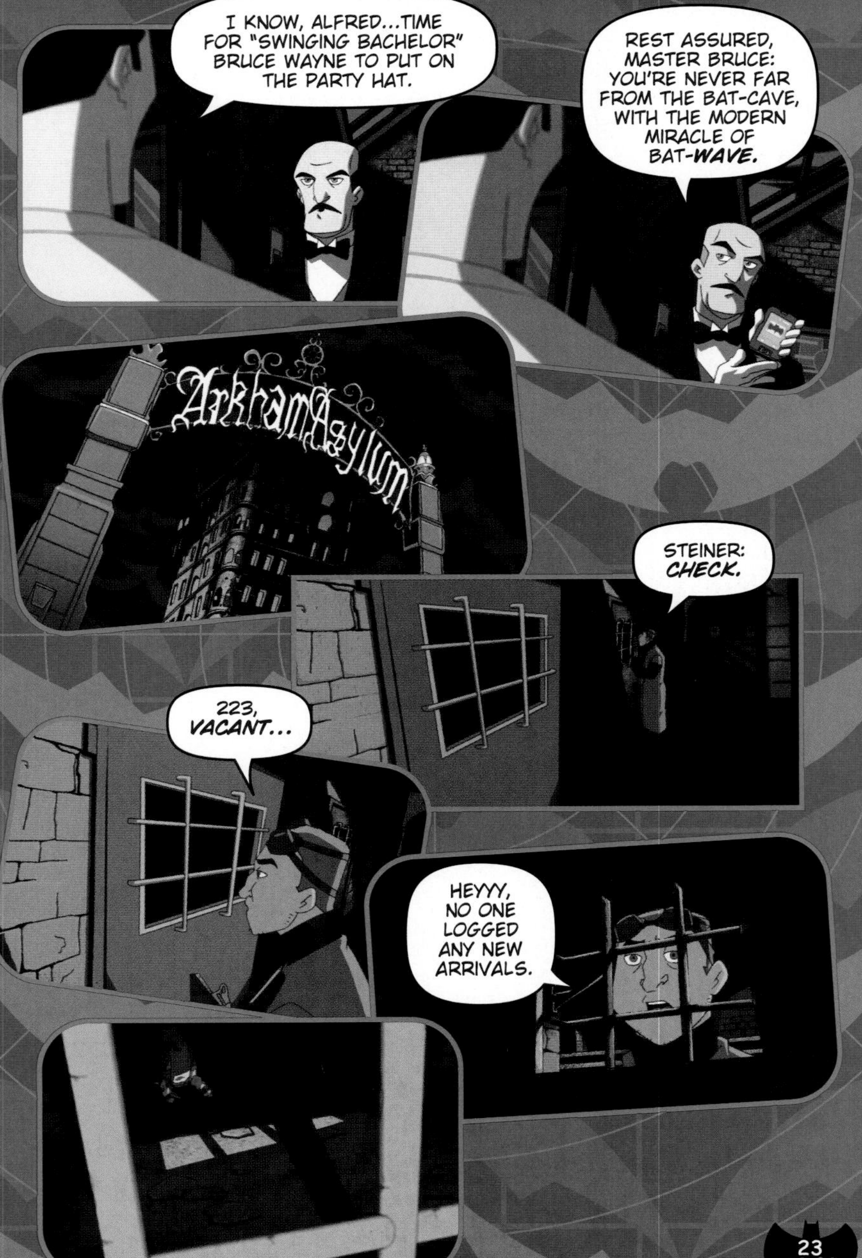
I KNOW, ALFRED...TIME FOR "SWINGING BACHELOR" BRUCE WAYNE TO PUT ON THE PARTY HAT.
REST ASSURED, MASTER BRUCE: YOU'RE NEVER FAR FROM THE BAT-CAVE, WITH THE MODERN MIRACLE OF BAT-*WAVE.*
Arkham Asylum
STEINER: *CHECK.*
223, *VACANT...*
HEYYY, NO ONE LOGGED ANY NEW ARRIVALS.

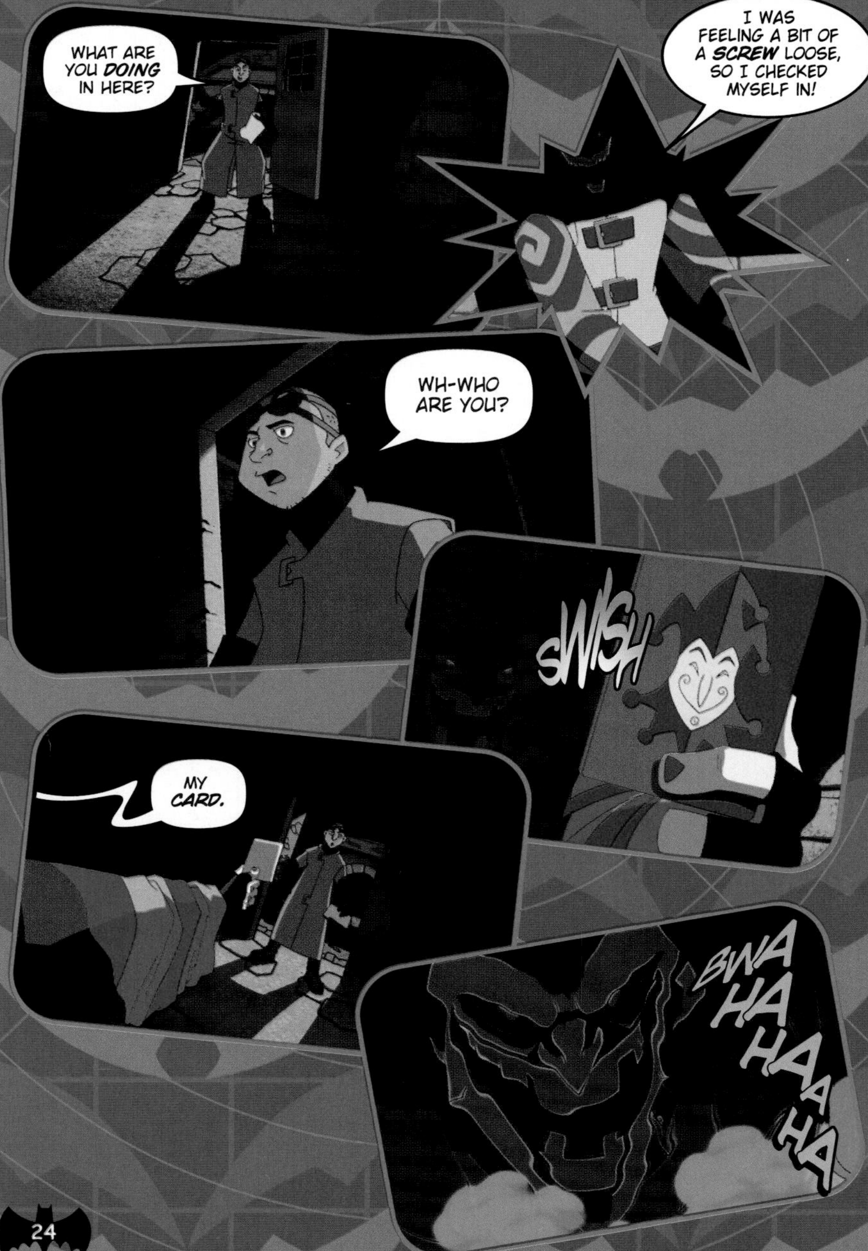
WHAT ARE YOU *DOING* IN HERE?
I WAS FEELING A BIT OF A *SCREW* LOOSE, SO I CHECKED MYSELF IN!
WH-WHO ARE YOU?
SWISH
MY *CARD.*
BWA HA HA HA HA HA

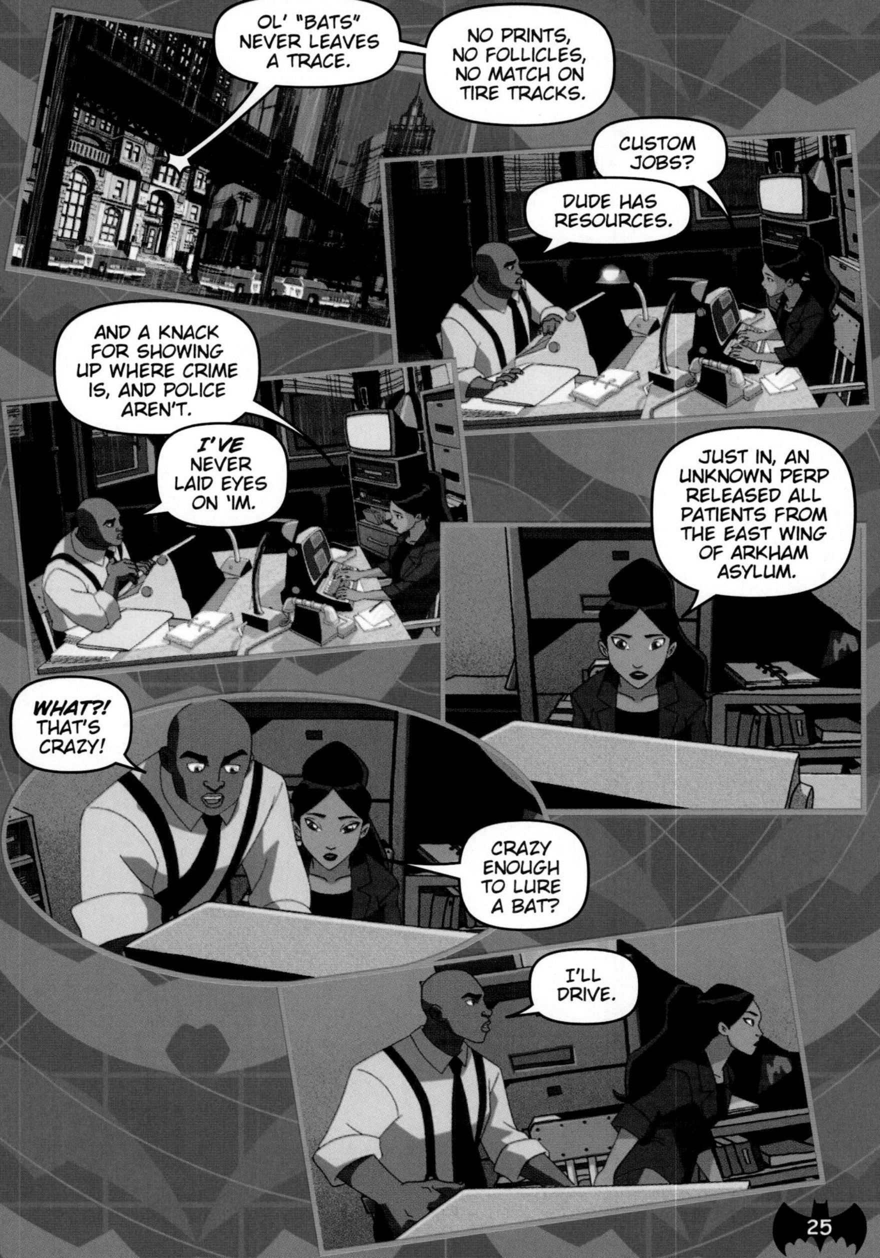
OL' "BATS" NEVER LEAVES A TRACE.
NO PRINTS, NO FOLLICLES, NO MATCH ON TIRE TRACKS.
CUSTOM JOBS?
DUDE HAS RESOURCES.
AND A KNACK FOR SHOWING UP WHERE CRIME IS, AND POLICE AREN'T.
I'VE NEVER LAID EYES ON 'IM.
JUST IN, AN UNKNOWN PERP RELEASED ALL PATIENTS FROM THE EAST WING OF ARKHAM ASYLUM.
WHAT?! THAT'S CRAZY!
CRAZY ENOUGH TO LURE A BAT?
I'LL DRIVE.

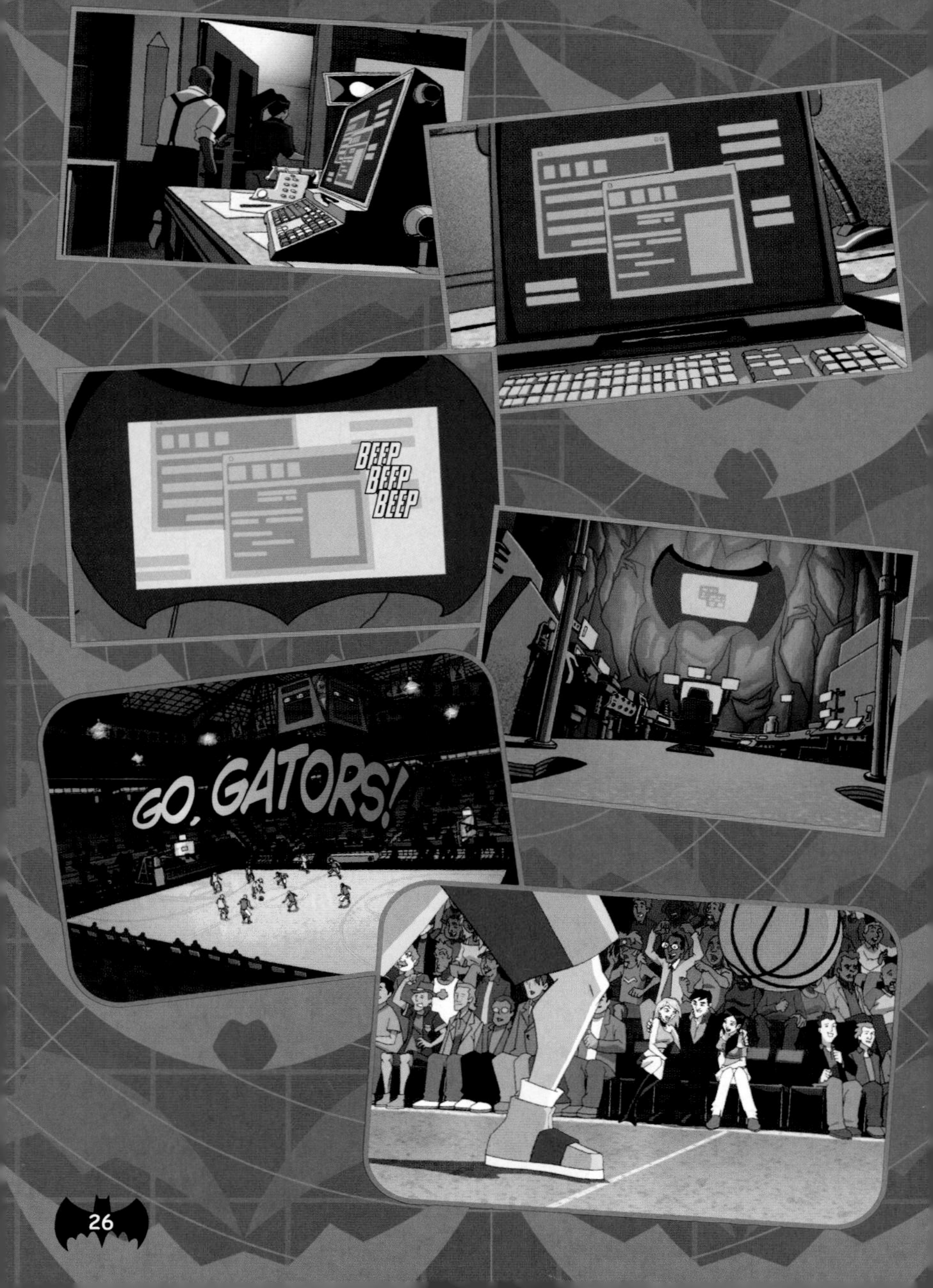
BEEP
BEEP
BEEP
GO, GATORS!

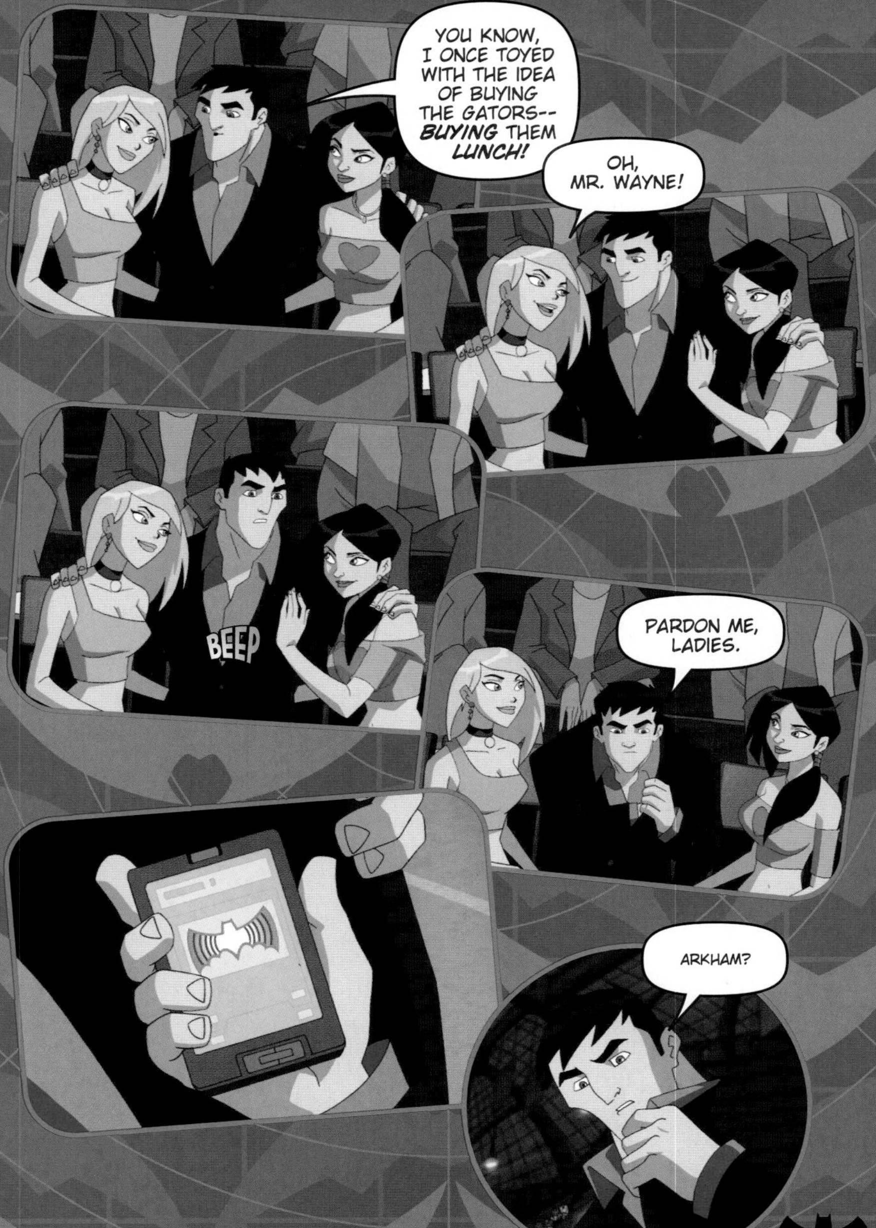
YOU KNOW, I ONCE TOYED WITH THE IDEA OF BUYING THE GATORS-- *BUYING* THEM *LUNCH!*
OH, MR. WAYNE!
BEEP
PARDON ME, LADIES.
ARKHAM?

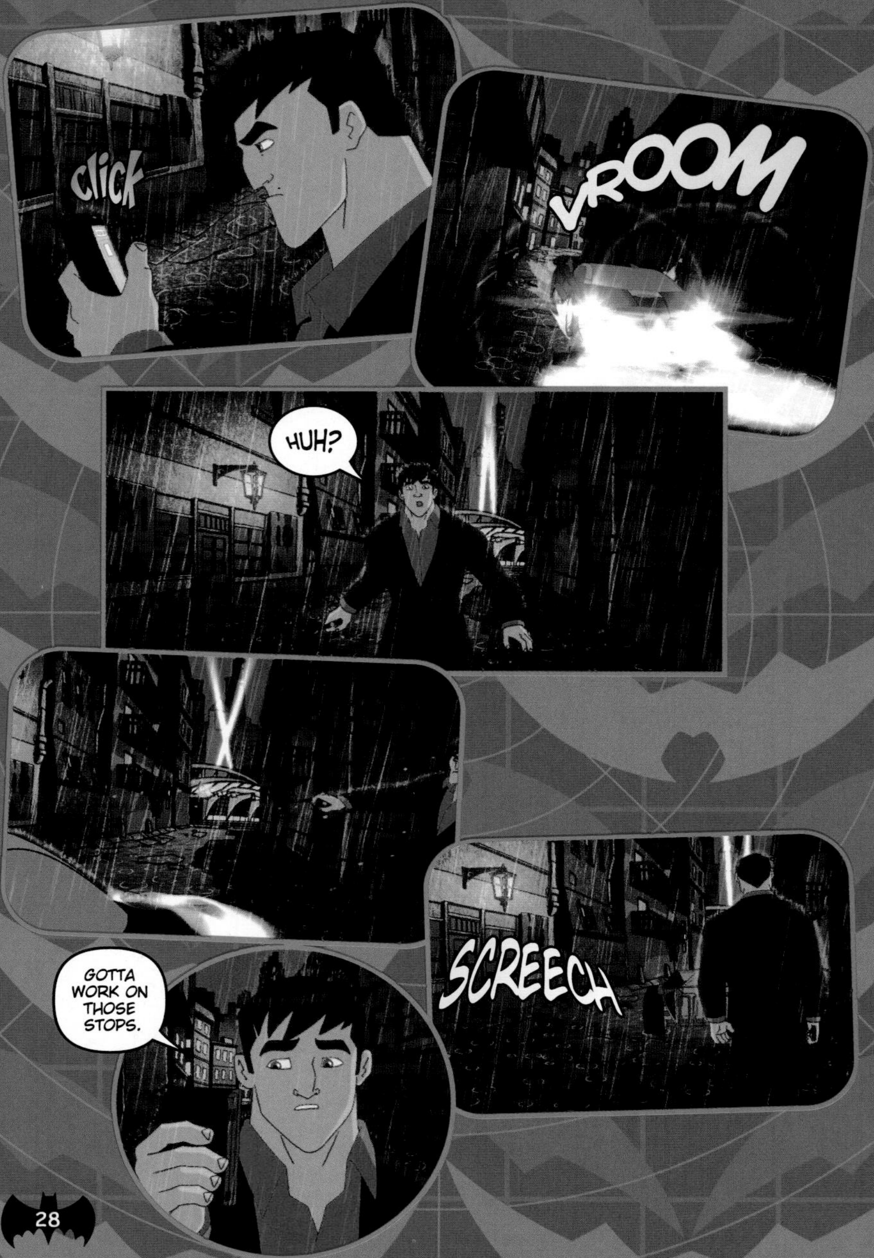
CLICK
VROOM
HUH?
SCREECH
GOTTA WORK ON THOSE STOPS.

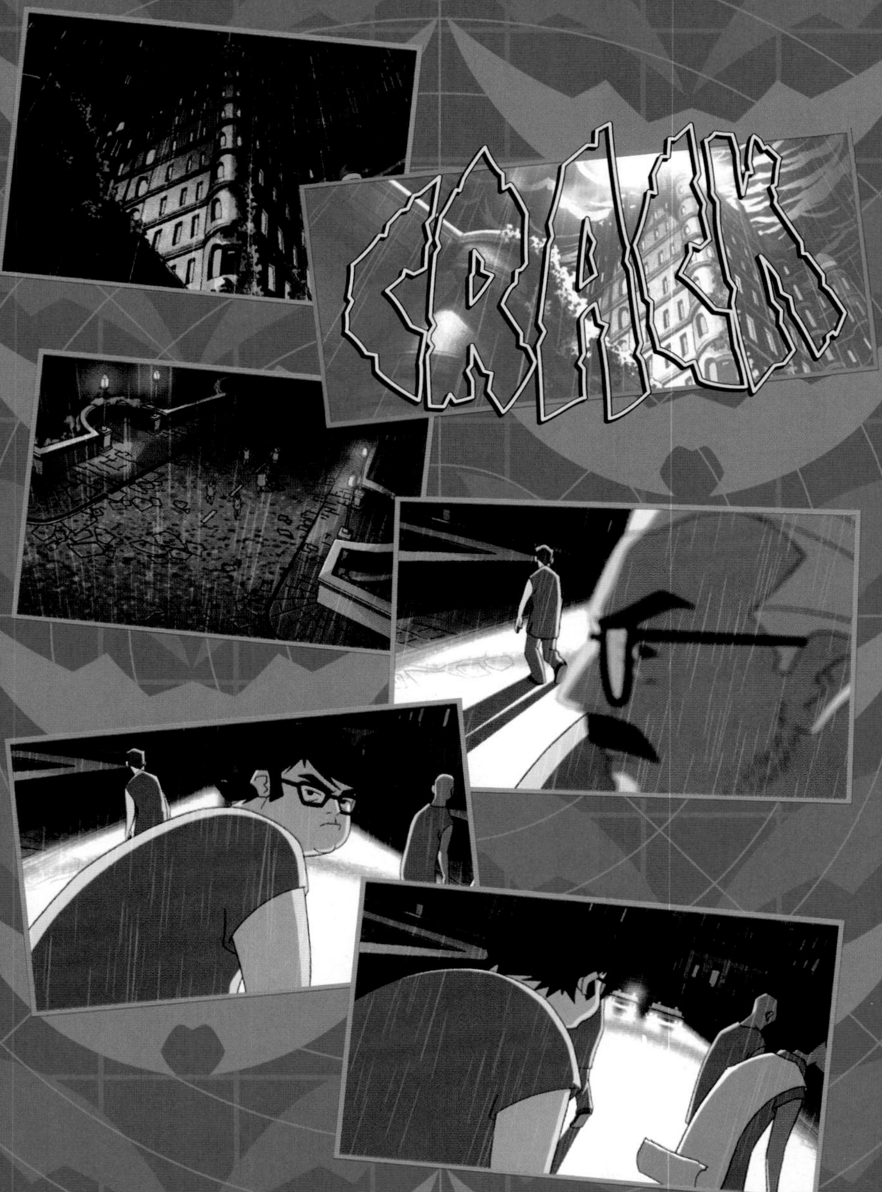
CRACK

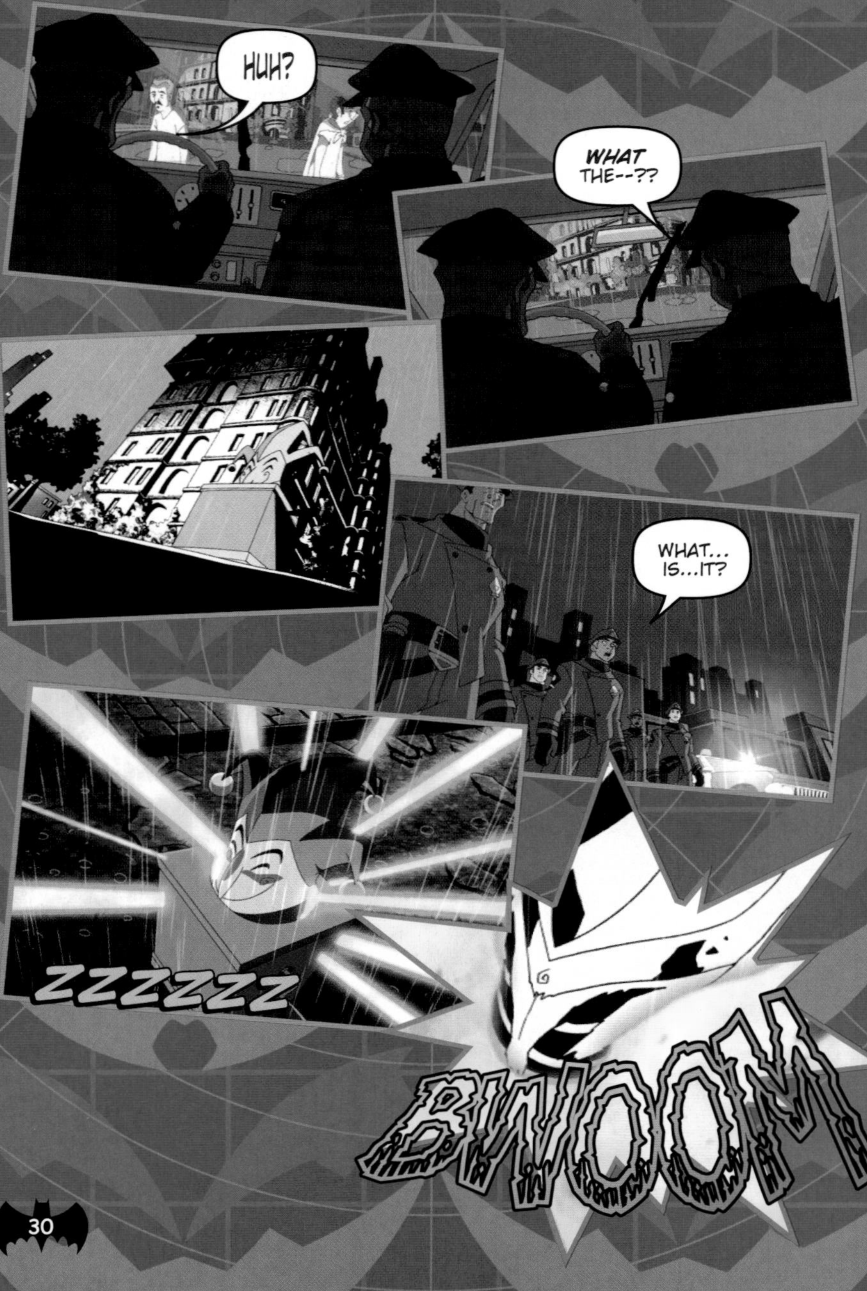
HUH?
WHAT THE--??
WHAT... IS...IT?
ZZZZZZZ
BWOOM

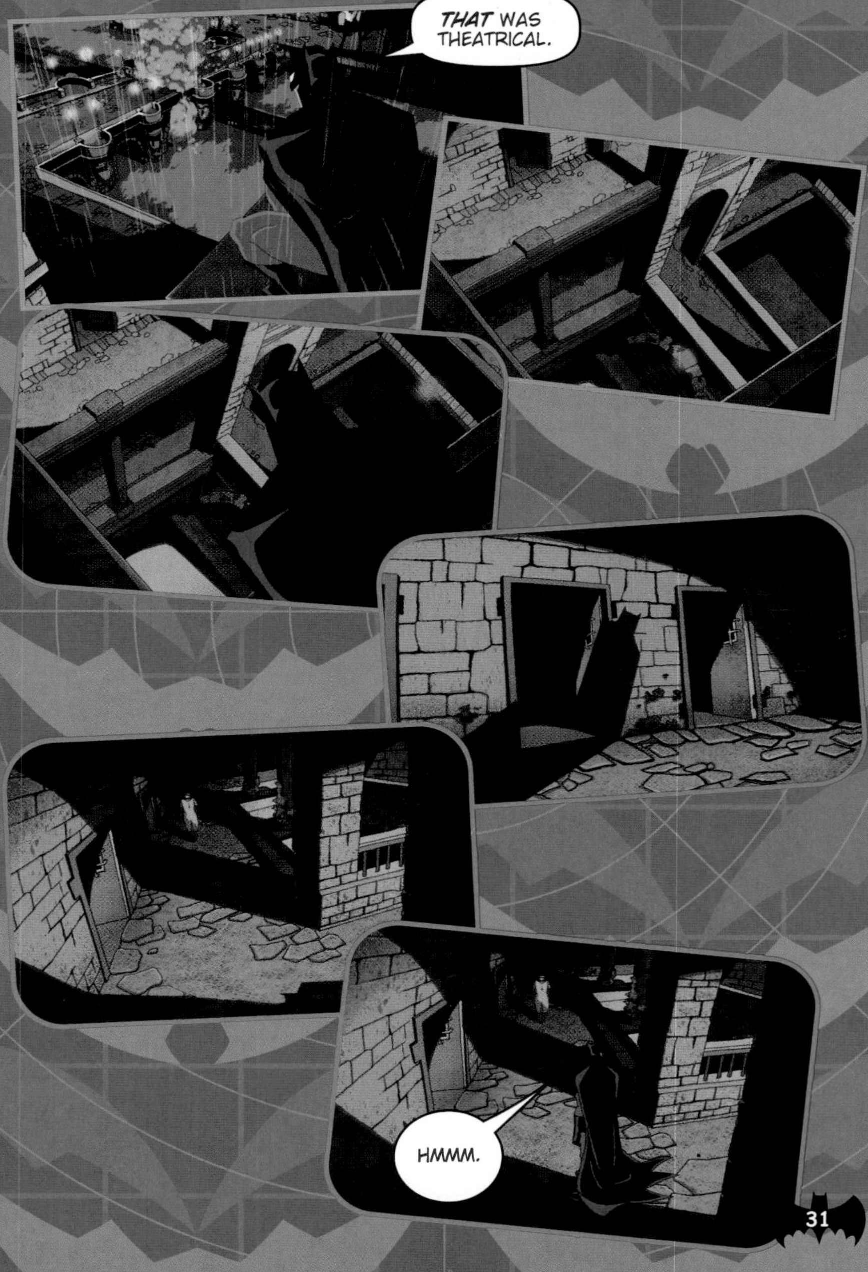
THAT WAS THEATRICAL.
HMMM.

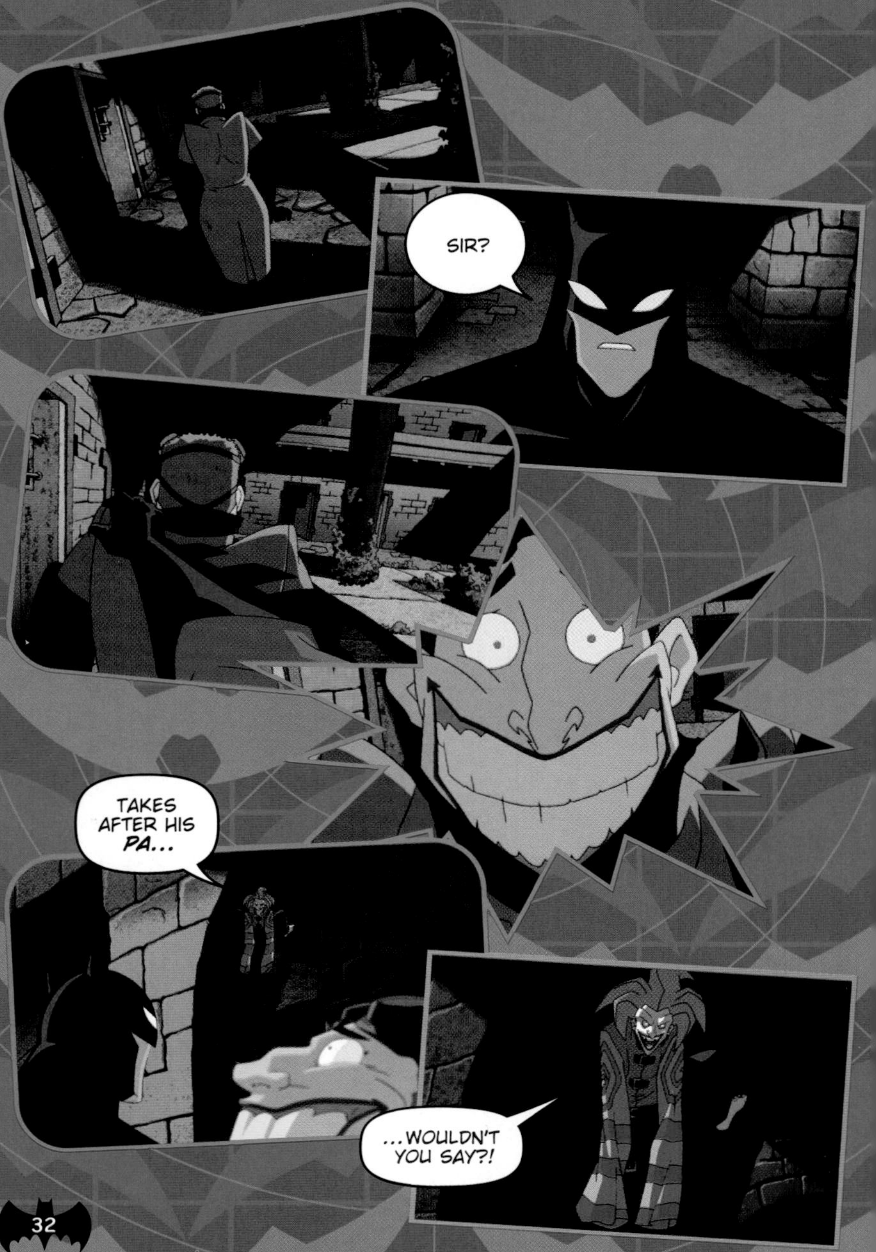
SIR?
TAKES AFTER HIS *PA*...
...WOULDN'T YOU SAY?!

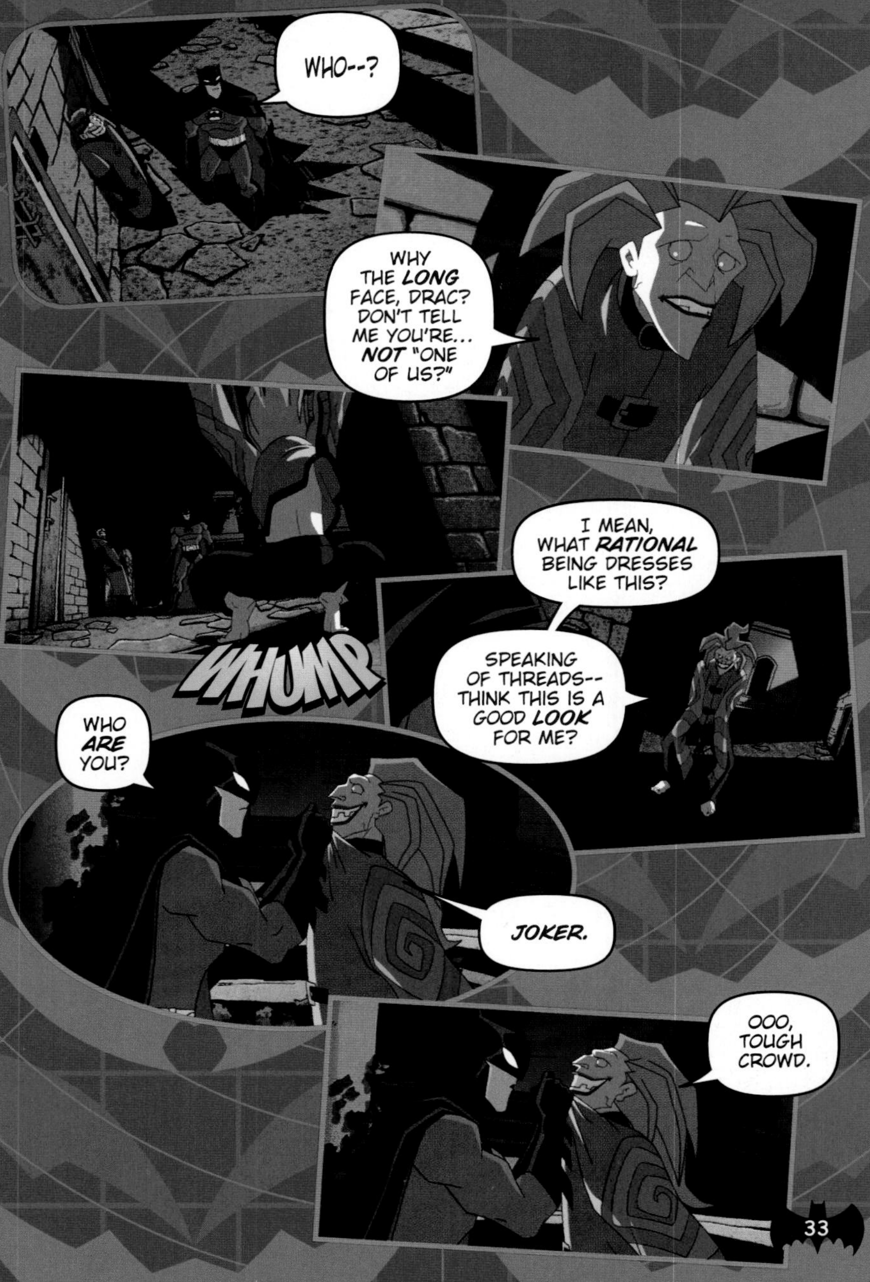
WHO--?
WHY THE LONG FACE, DRAC? DON'T TELL ME YOU'RE... NOT "ONE OF US?"
WHUMP
I MEAN, WHAT RATIONAL BEING DRESSES LIKE THIS?
SPEAKING OF THREADS-- THINK THIS IS A GOOD LOOK FOR ME?
WHO ARE YOU?
JOKER.
OOO, TOUGH CROWD.

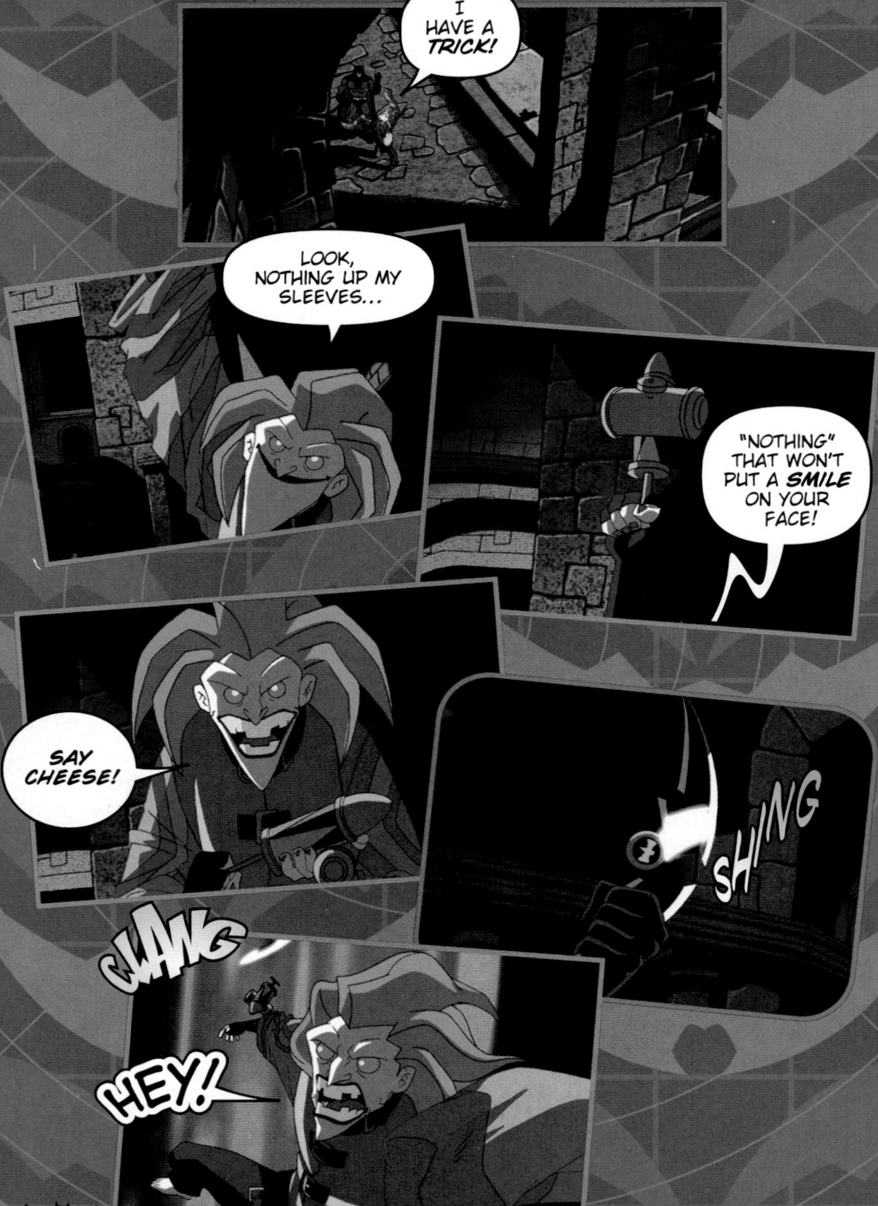
I HAVE A *TRICK!*
LOOK, NOTHING UP MY SLEEVES...
"NOTHING" THAT WON'T PUT A ***SMILE*** ON YOUR FACE!
SAY CHEESE!
SHING
CLANG
HEY!

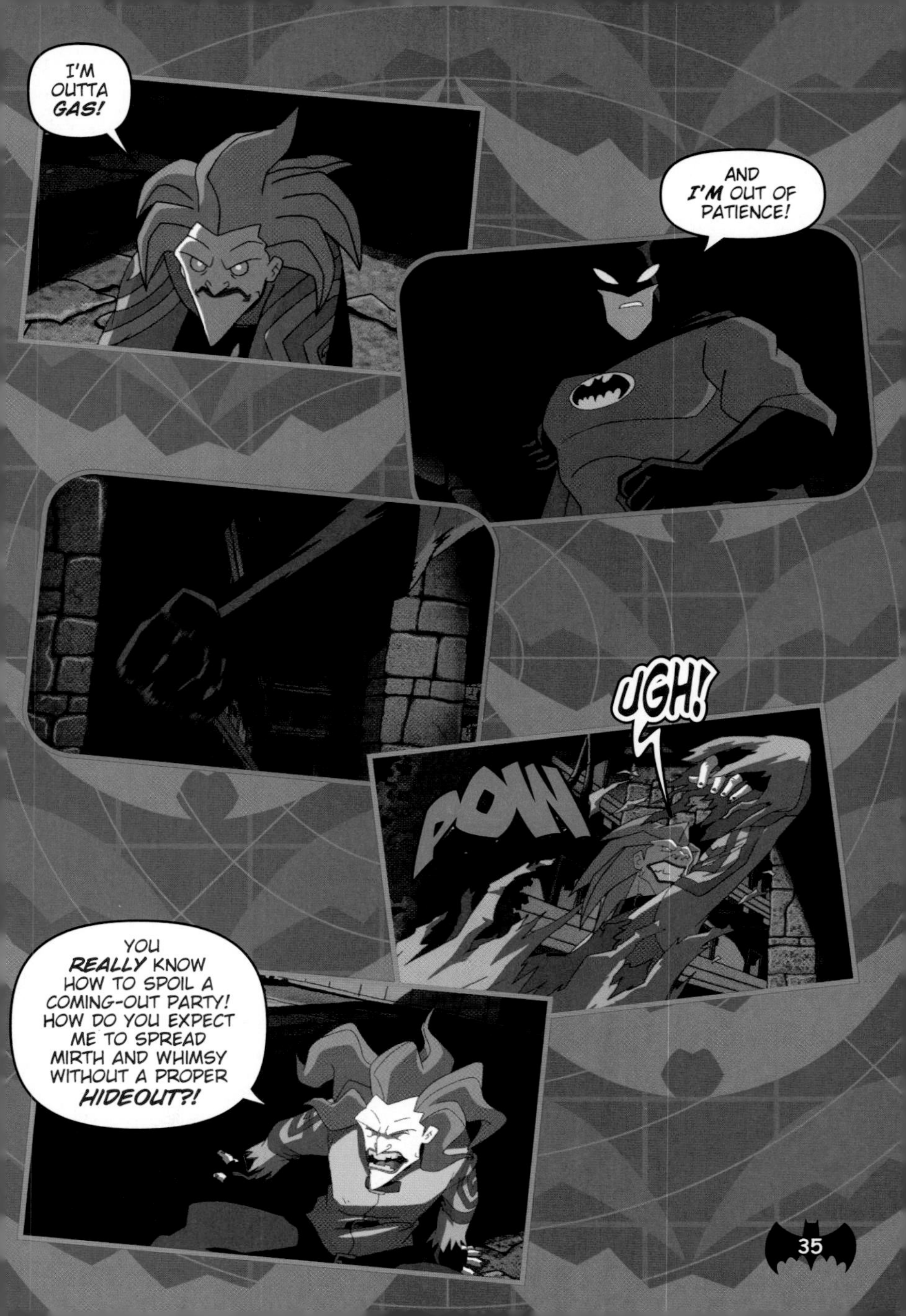
I'M OUTTA GAS!
AND I'M OUT OF PATIENCE!
UGH!
POW
YOU REALLY KNOW HOW TO SPOIL A COMING-OUT PARTY! HOW DO YOU EXPECT ME TO SPREAD MIRTH AND WHIMSY WITHOUT A PROPER HIDEOUT?!

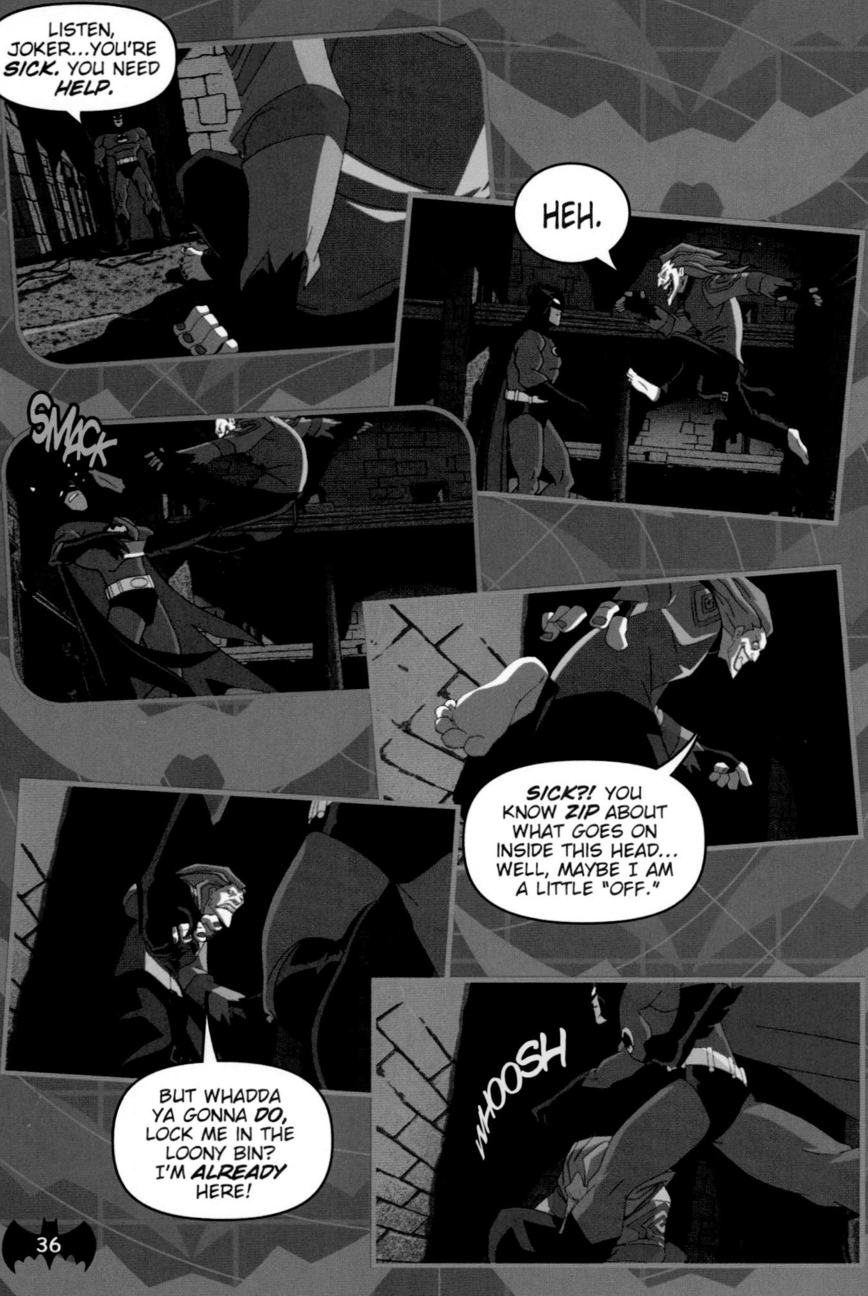

LISTEN, JOKER...YOU'RE SICK. YOU NEED HELP.
HEH.
SMACK
SICK?! YOU KNOW ZIP ABOUT WHAT GOES ON INSIDE THIS HEAD... WELL, MAYBE I AM A LITTLE "OFF."
BUT WHADDA YA GONNA DO, LOCK ME IN THE LOONY BIN? I'M ALREADY HERE!
WHOOSH

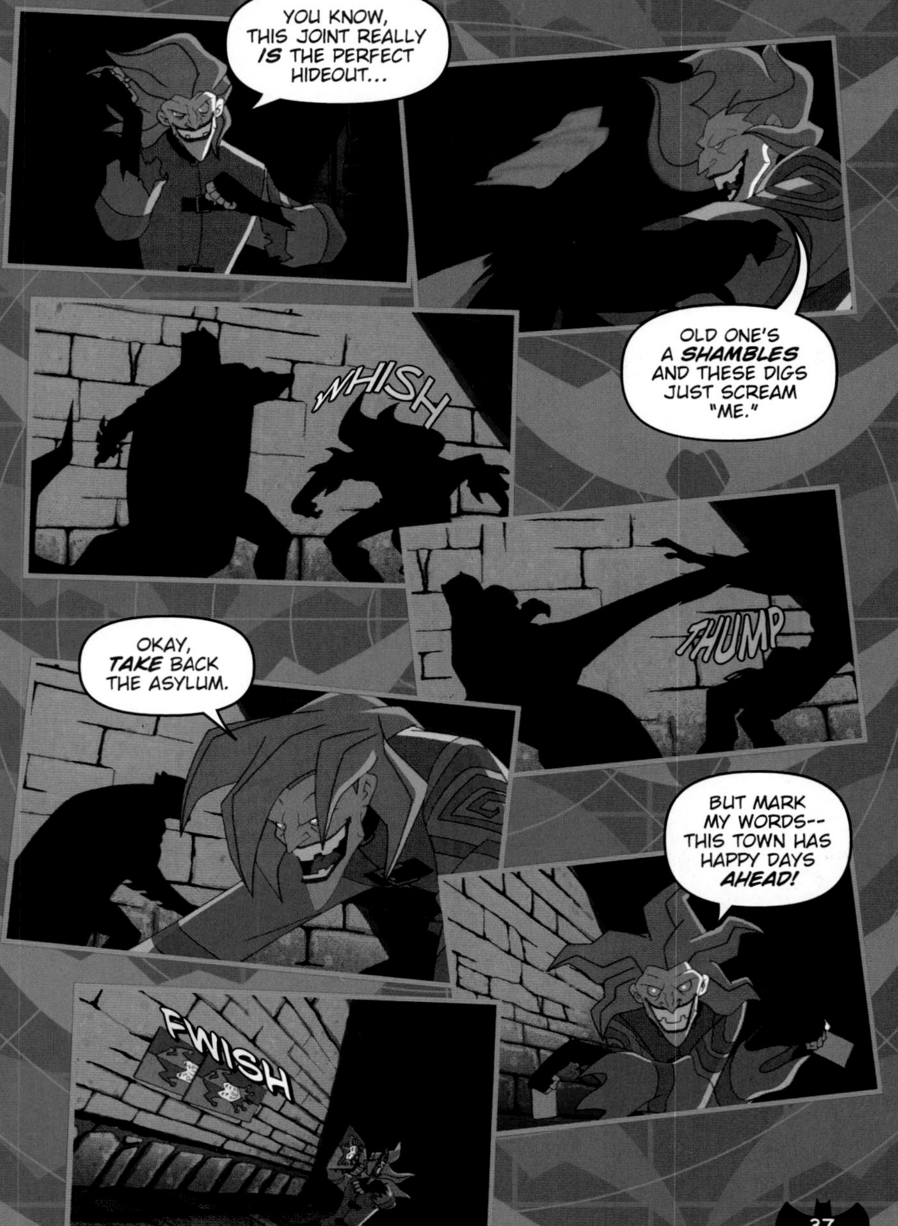

YOU KNOW, THIS JOINT REALLY *IS* THE PERFECT HIDEOUT...
OLD ONE'S A ***SHAMBLES*** AND THESE DIGS JUST SCREAM "ME."
WHISH
THUMP
OKAY, ***TAKE*** BACK THE ASYLUM.
BUT MARK MY WORDS-- THIS TOWN HAS HAPPY DAYS ***AHEAD!***
FWISH

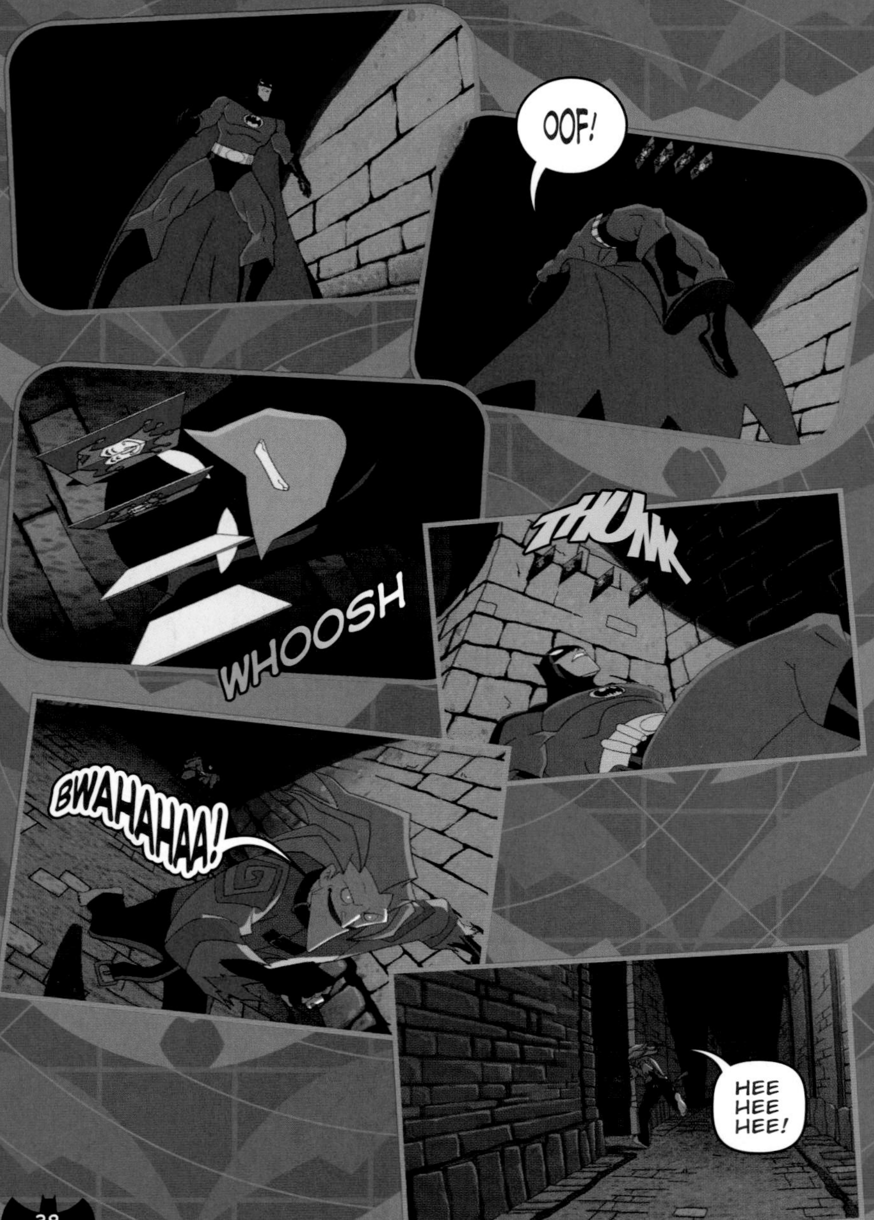

OOF!
WHOOSH
THUNK
BWAHAHAA!
HEE HEE HEE!

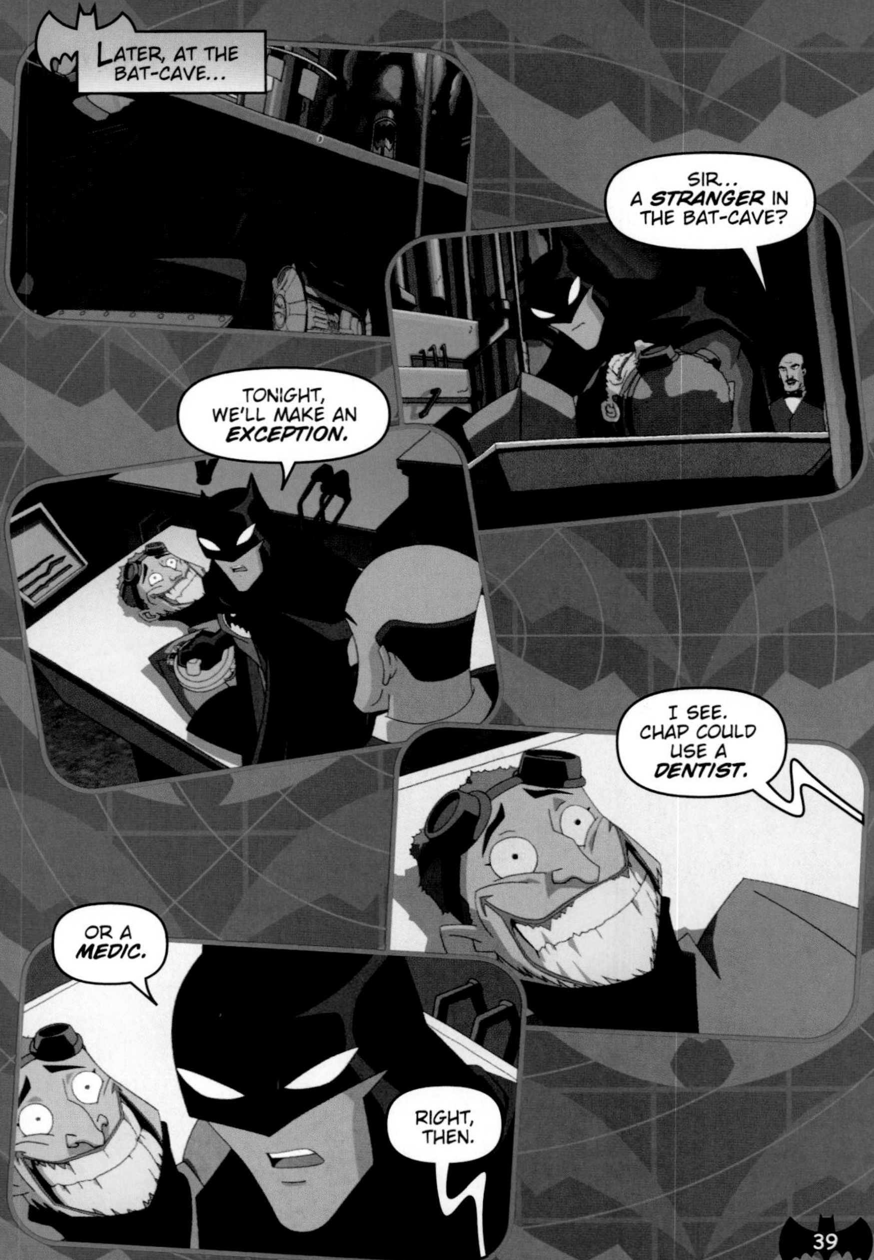
LATER, AT THE BAT-CAVE...
SIR... A STRANGER IN THE BAT-CAVE?
TONIGHT, WE'LL MAKE AN EXCEPTION.
I SEE. CHAP COULD USE A DENTIST.
OR A MEDIC.
RIGHT, THEN.

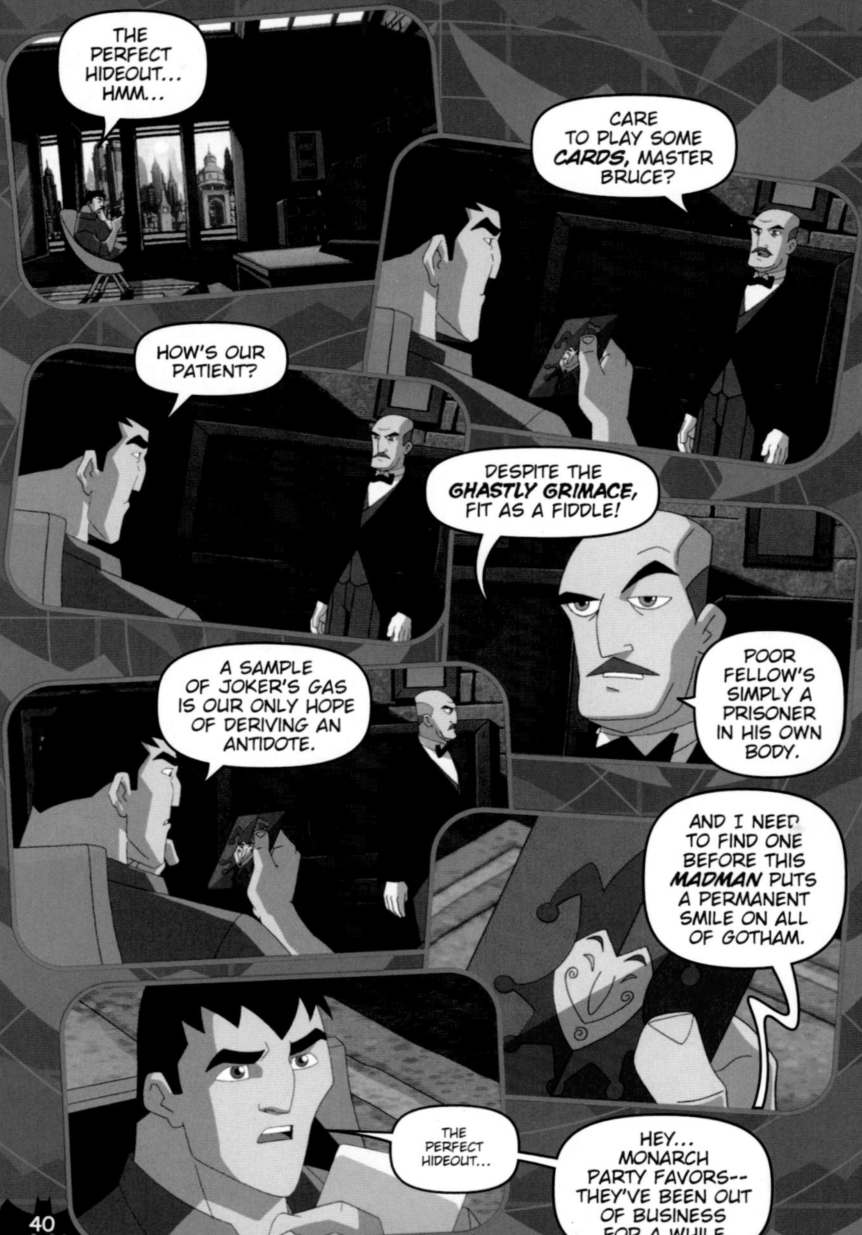
THE PERFECT HIDEOUT... HMM...
CARE TO PLAY SOME CARDS, MASTER BRUCE?
HOW'S OUR PATIENT?
DESPITE THE GHASTLY GRIMACE, FIT AS A FIDDLE!
POOR FELLOW'S SIMPLY A PRISONER IN HIS OWN BODY.
A SAMPLE OF JOKER'S GAS IS OUR ONLY HOPE OF DERIVING AN ANTIDOTE.
AND I NEED TO FIND ONE BEFORE THIS MADMAN PUTS A PERMANENT SMILE ON ALL OF GOTHAM.
THE PERFECT HIDEOUT...
HEY... MONARCH PARTY FAVORS-- THEY'VE BEEN OUT OF BUSINESS FOR A WHILE.

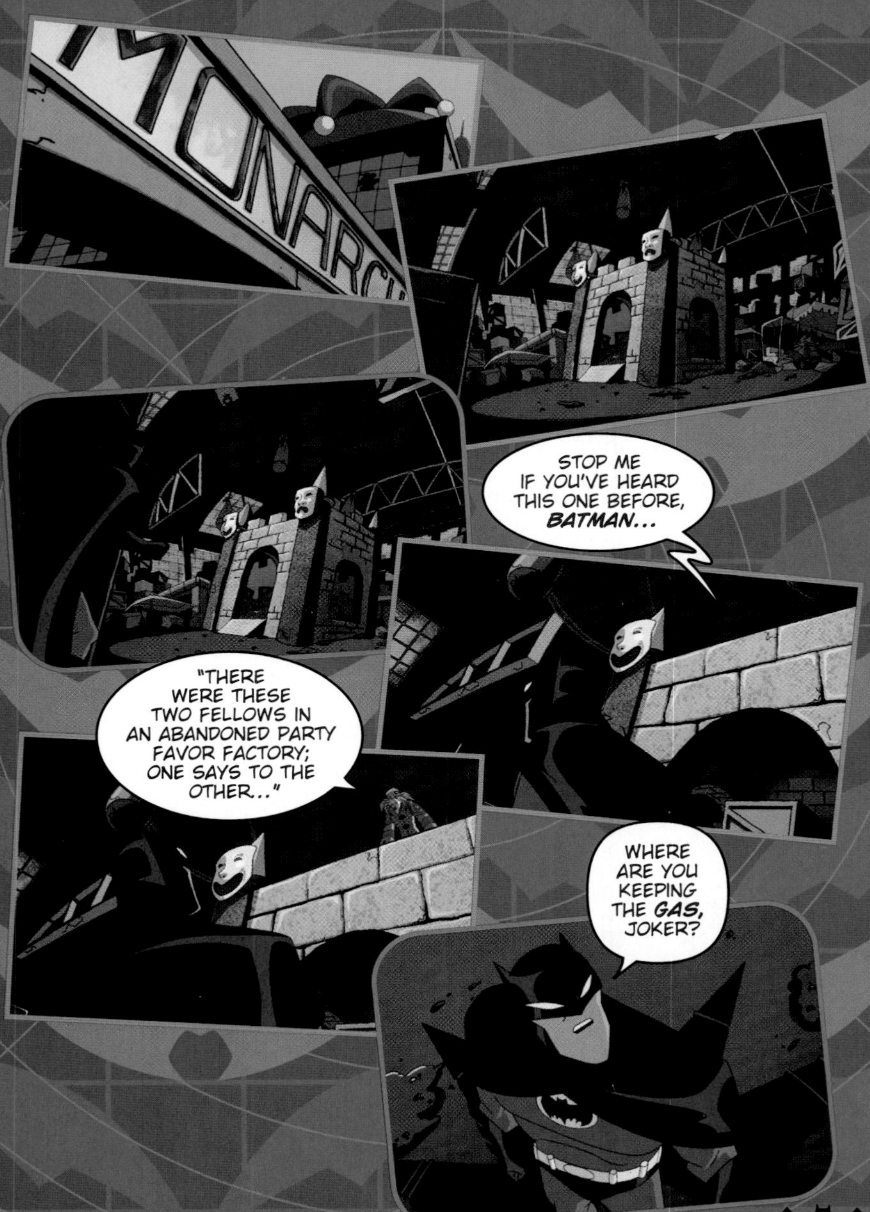
MONARC
STOP ME IF YOU'VE HEARD THIS ONE BEFORE, ***BATMAN...***
"THERE WERE THESE TWO FELLOWS IN AN ABANDONED PARTY FAVOR FACTORY; ONE SAYS TO THE OTHER..."
WHERE ARE YOU KEEPING THE ***GAS,*** JOKER?

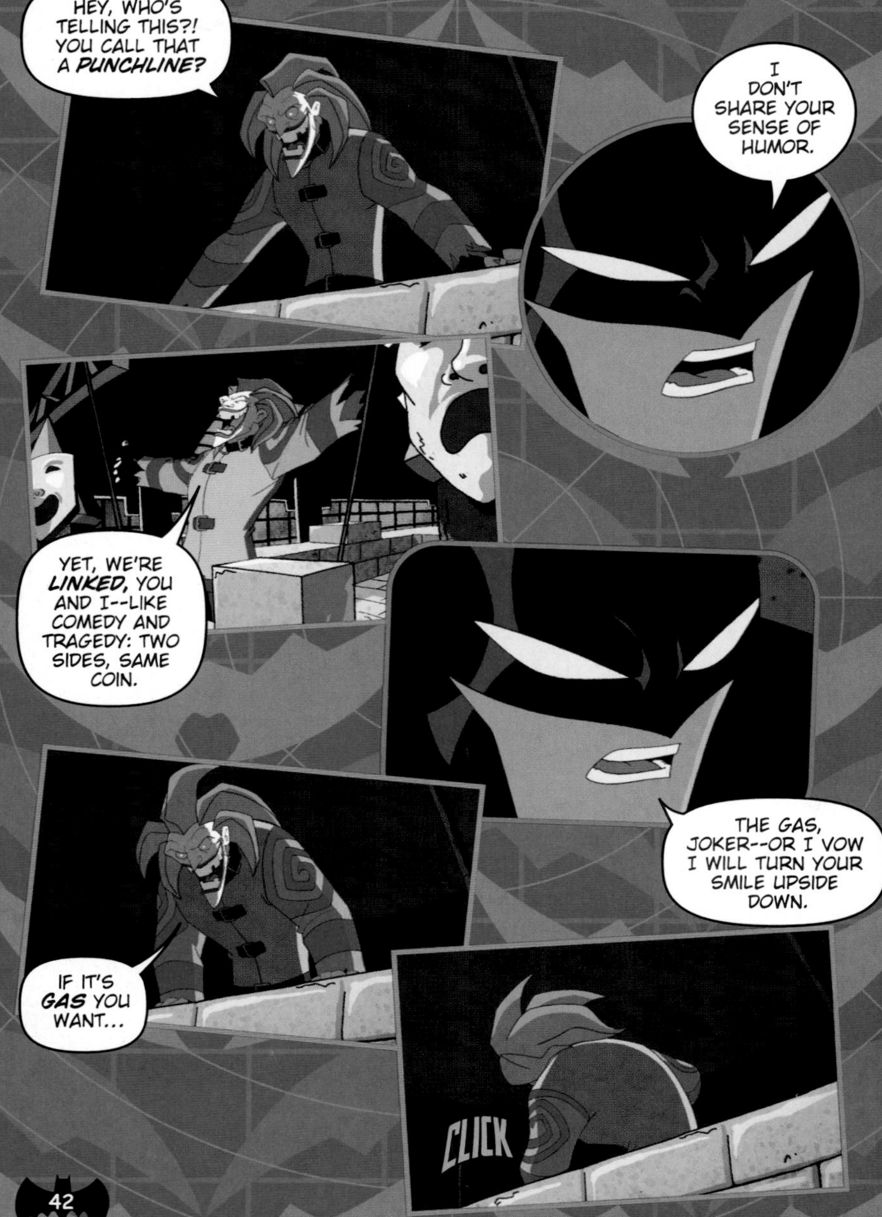
HEY, WHO'S TELLING THIS?! YOU CALL THAT A PUNCHLINE?
I DON'T SHARE YOUR SENSE OF HUMOR.
YET, WE'RE LINKED, YOU AND I--LIKE COMEDY AND TRAGEDY: TWO SIDES, SAME COIN.
THE GAS, JOKER--OR I VOW I WILL TURN YOUR SMILE UPSIDE DOWN.
IF IT'S GAS YOU WANT...
CLICK

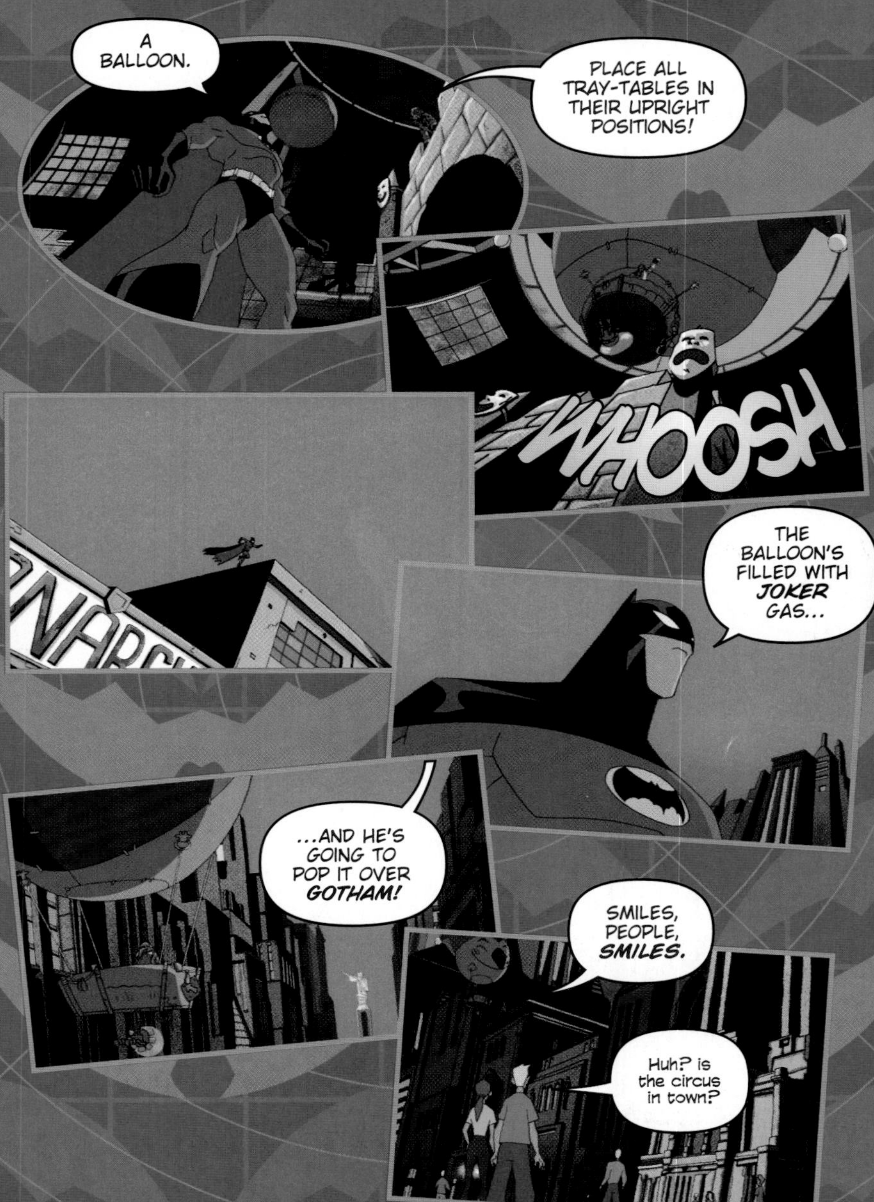

A BALLOON.
PLACE ALL TRAY-TABLES IN THEIR UPRIGHT POSITIONS!
WHOOSH
THE BALLOON'S FILLED WITH ***JOKER*** GAS...
...AND HE'S GOING TO POP IT OVER ***GOTHAM!***
SMILES, PEOPLE, ***SMILES.***
Huh? is the circus in town?

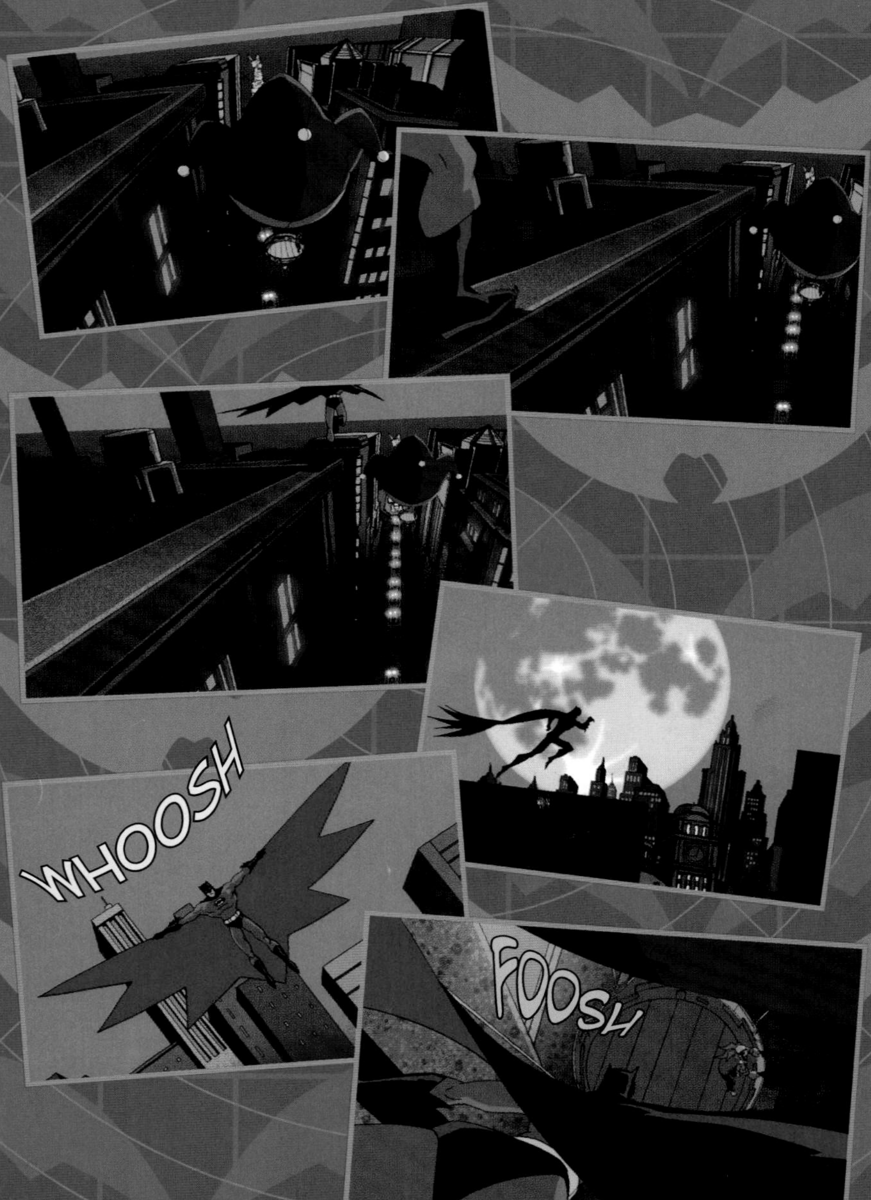
WHOOSH
FOOSH

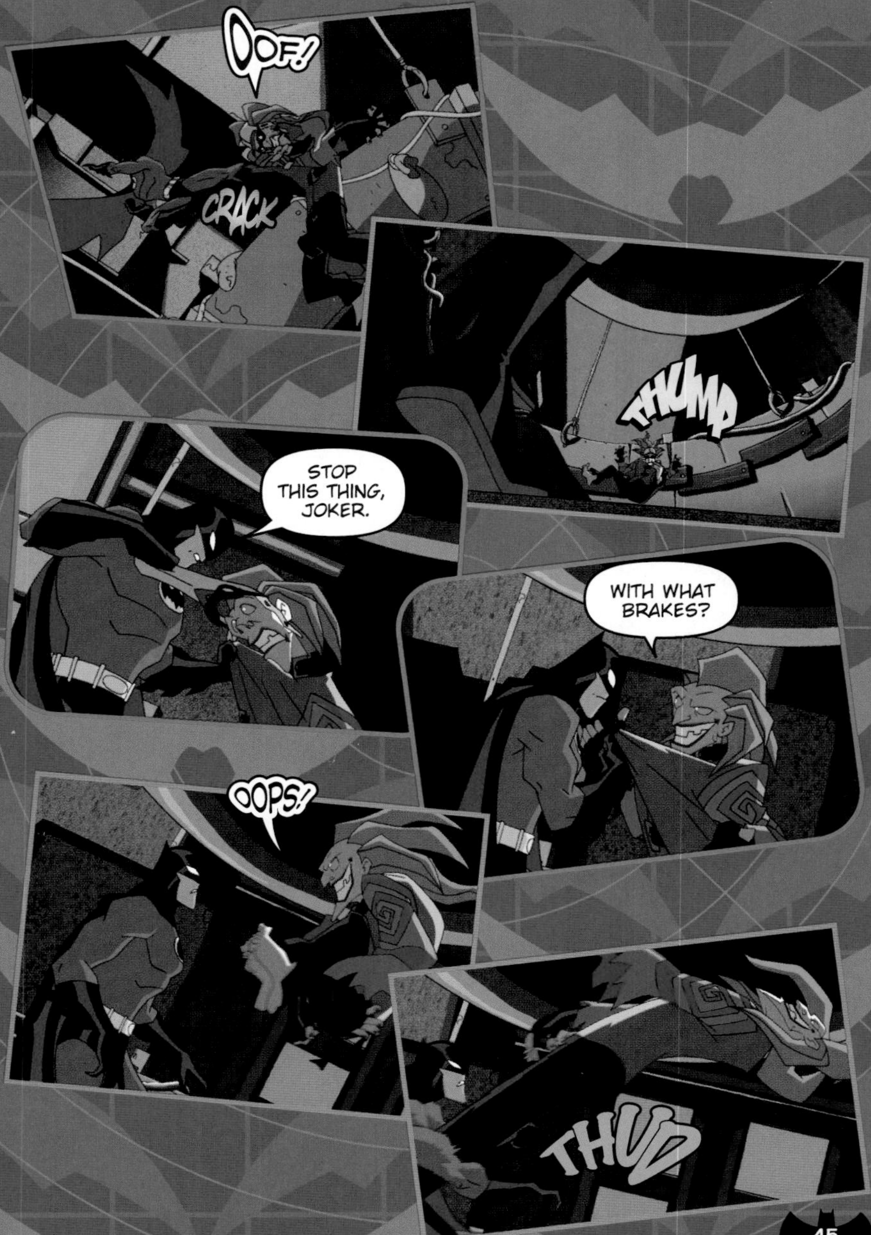

OOF!
CRACK
THUMP
STOP THIS THING, JOKER.
WITH WHAT BRAKES?
OOPS!
THUD

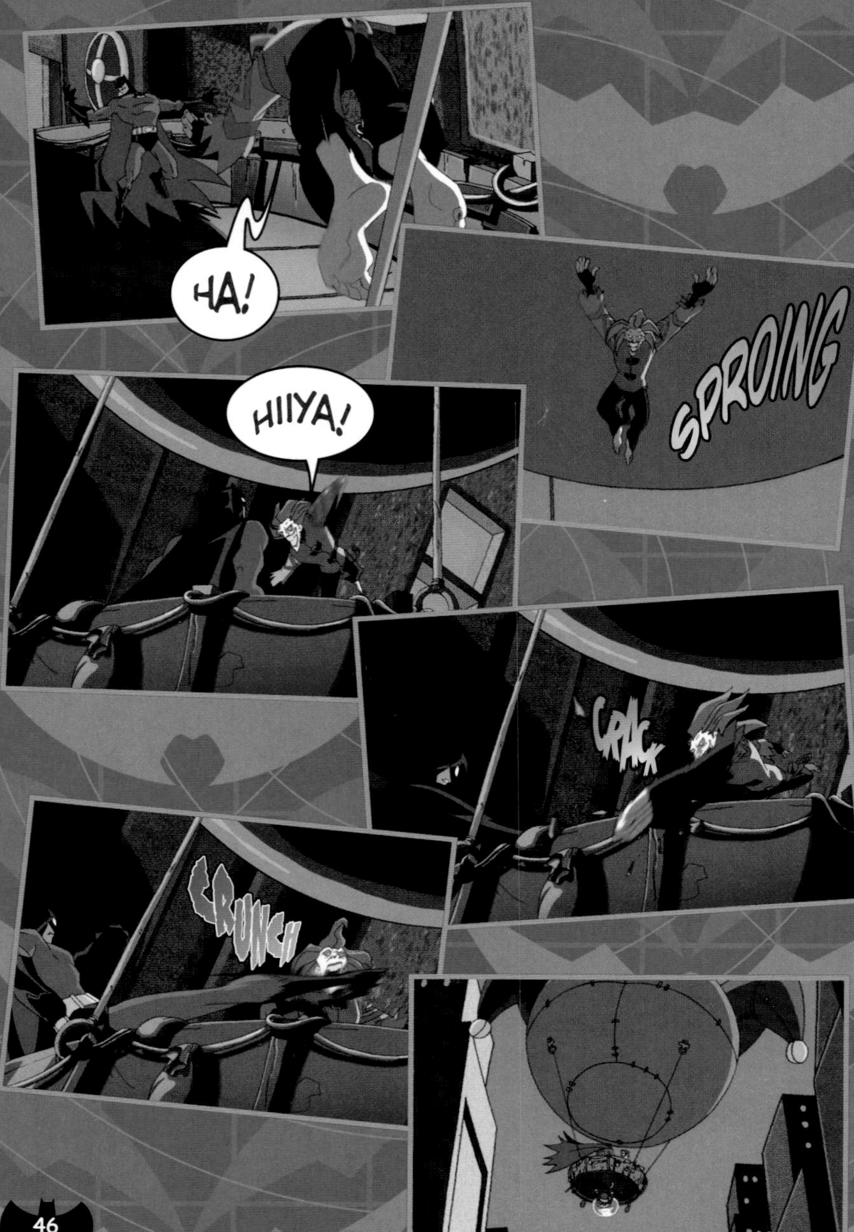
HA!
SPROING
HIIYA!
CRACK
CRUNCH

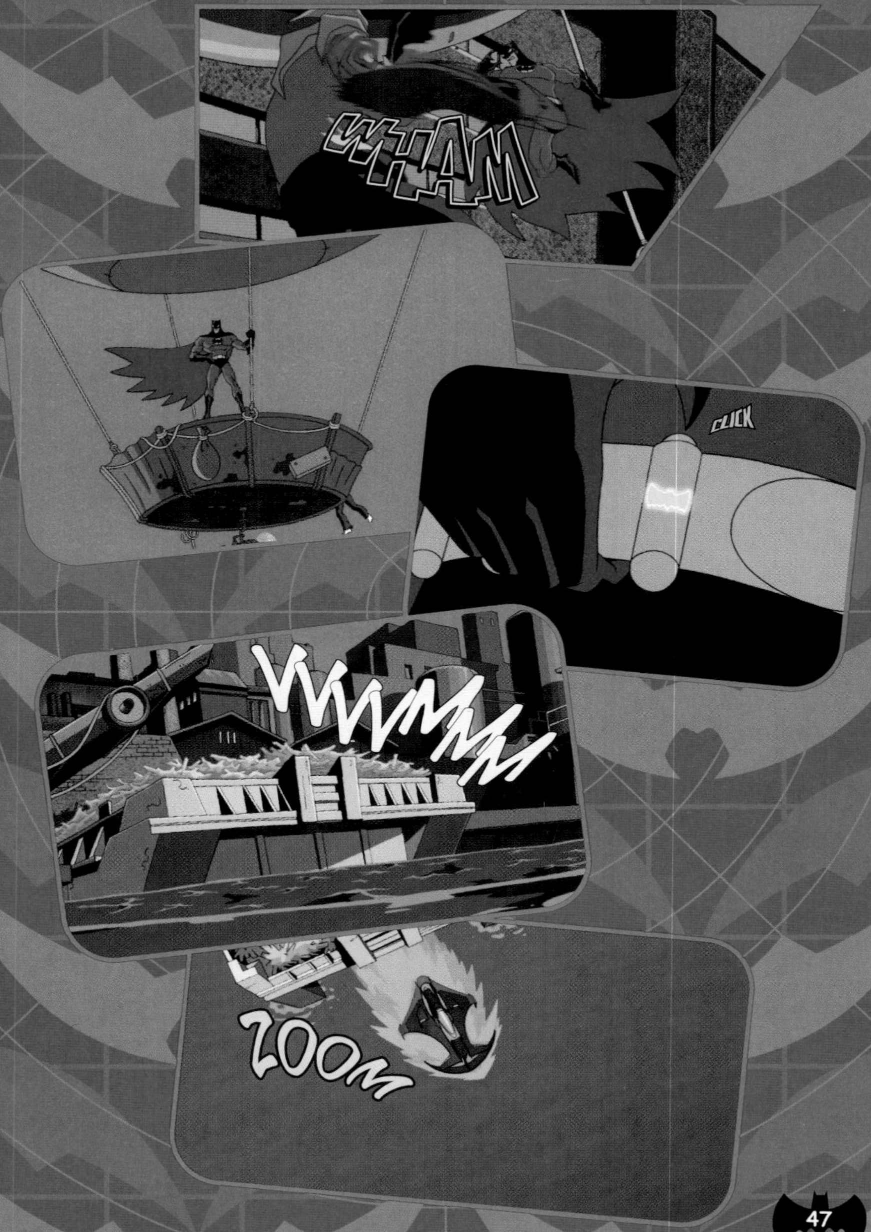
WHAM
CLICK
VVVVMMMM
ZOOM

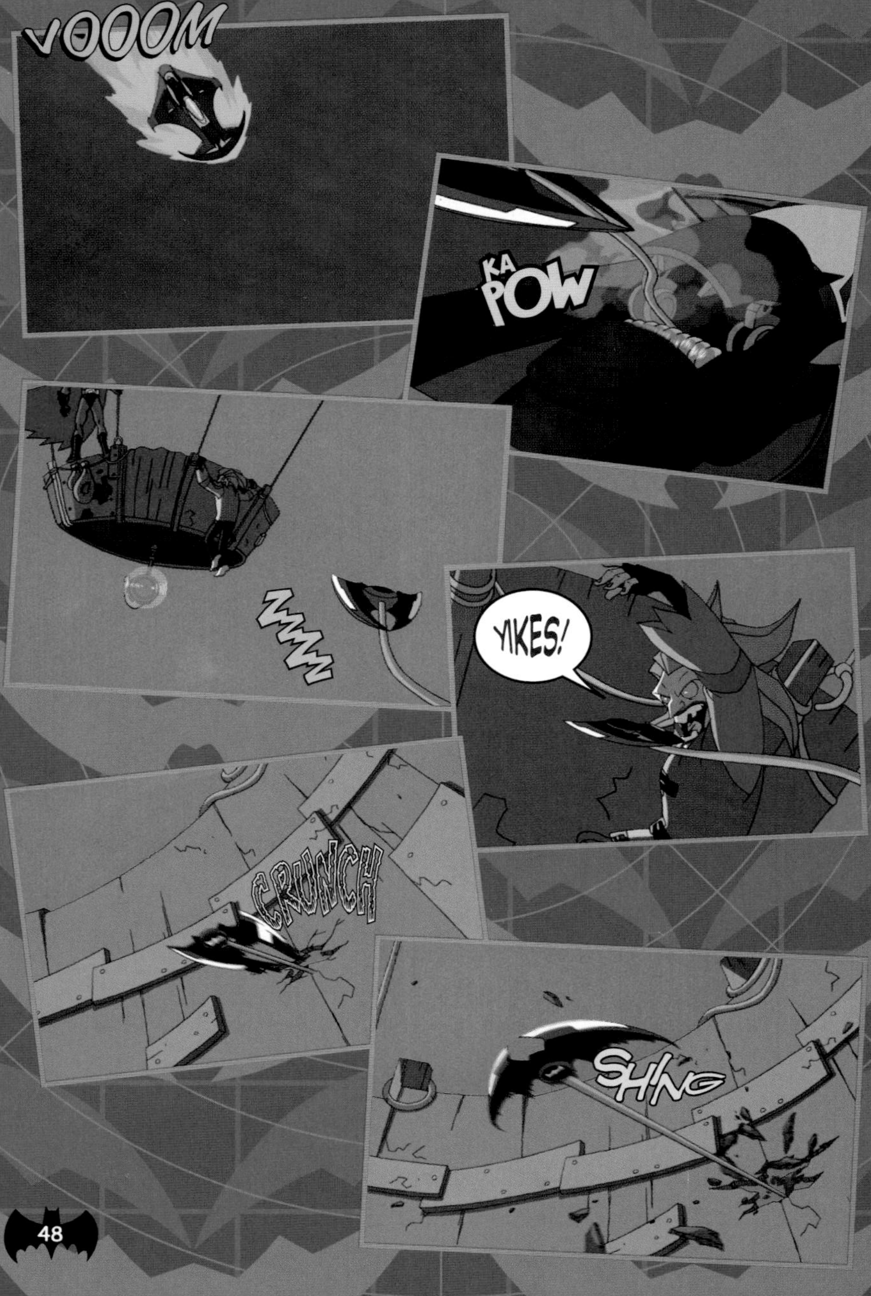
VOOOM
KA POW
ZZZZ
YIKES!
CRUNCH
SHING

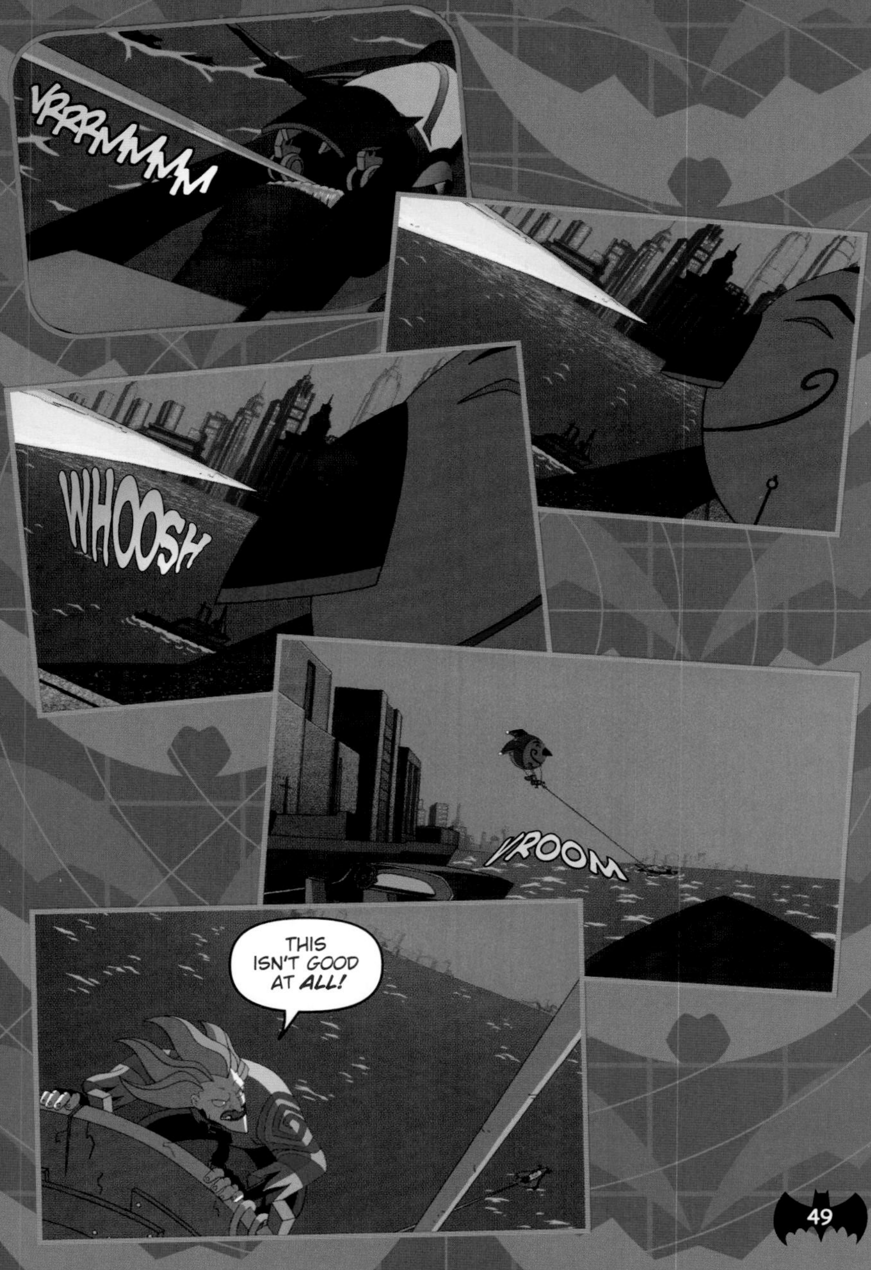

VRRRMMMM
WHOOSH
VROOM
THIS ISN'T GOOD AT ALL!

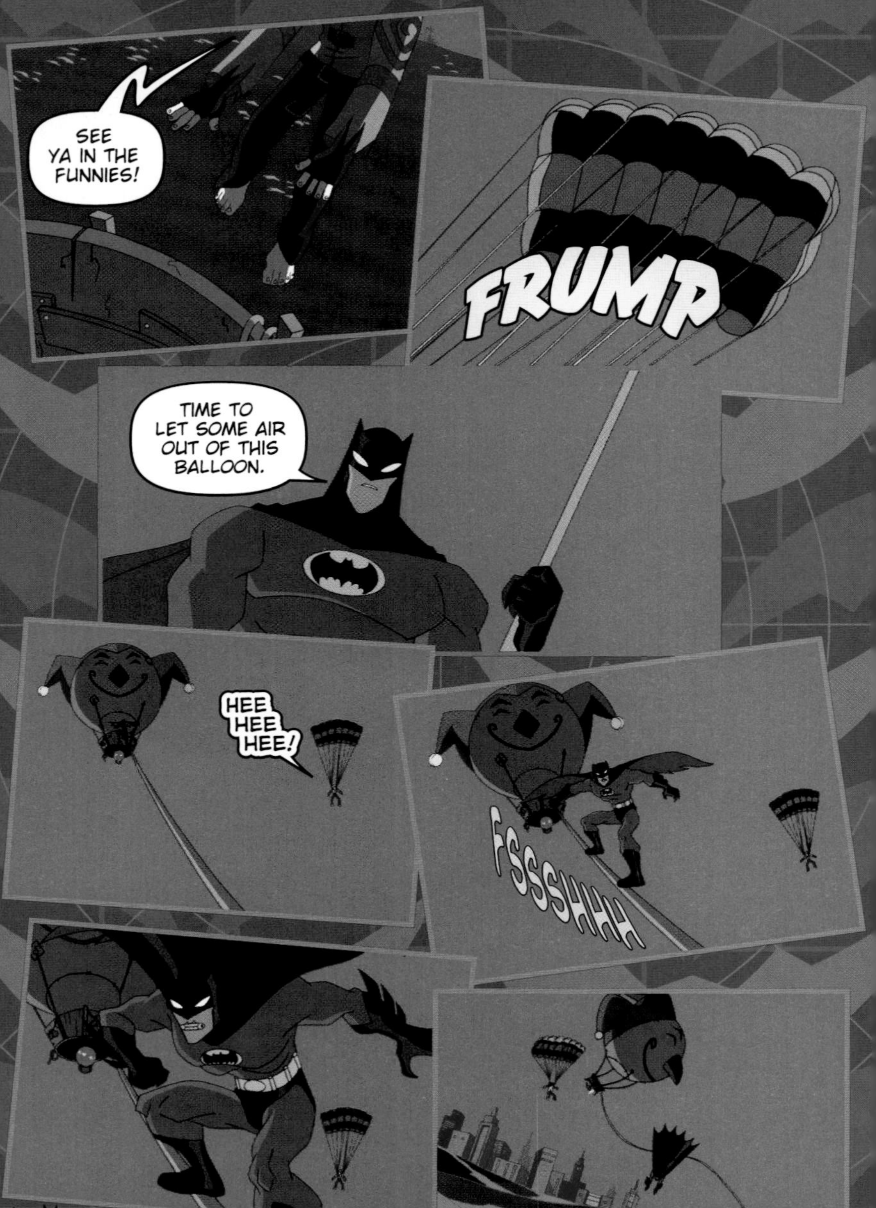
SEE YA IN THE FUNNIES!
FRUMP
TIME TO LET SOME AIR OUT OF THIS BALLOON.
HEE HEE HEE!
FSSSHHHH

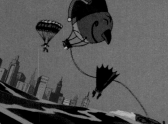

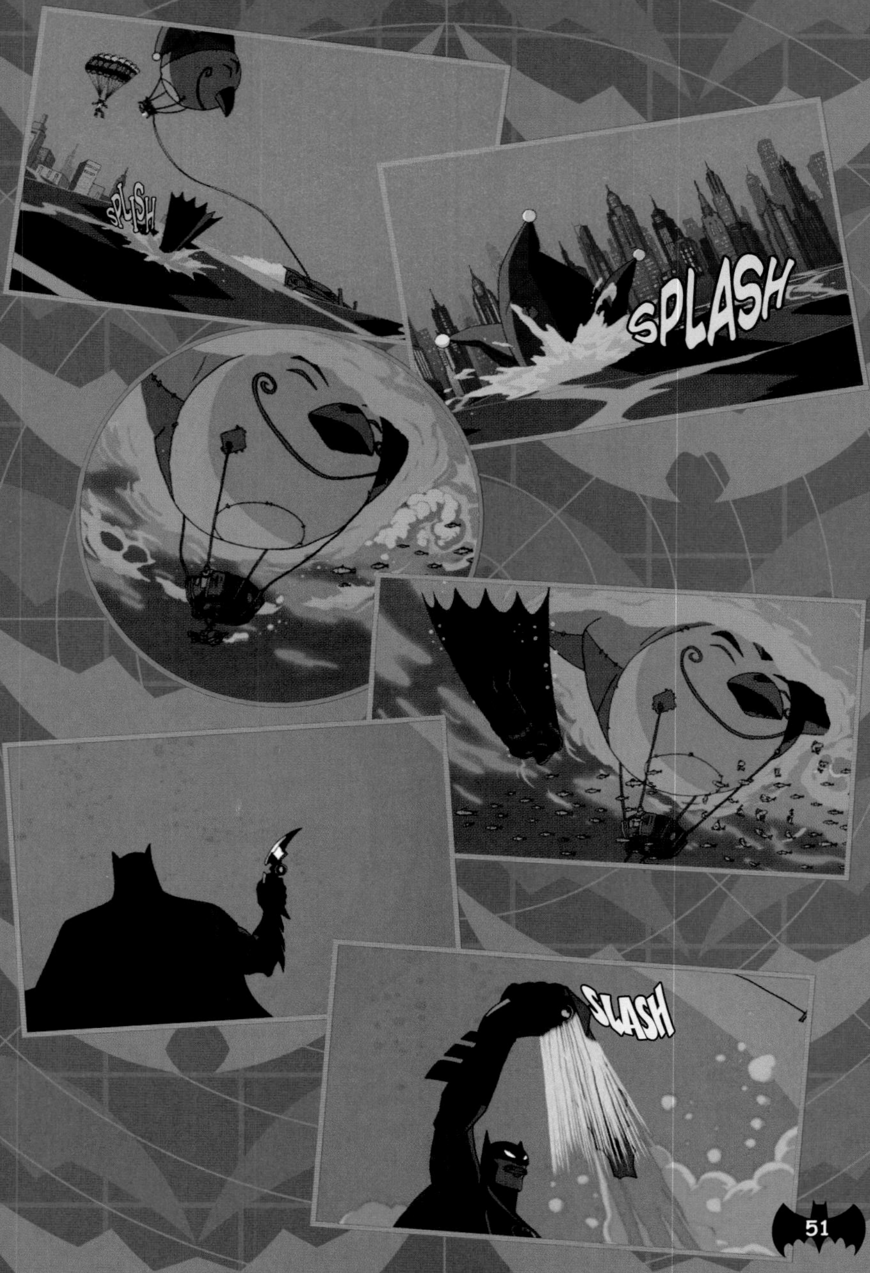
SPLISH
SPLASH
SLASH

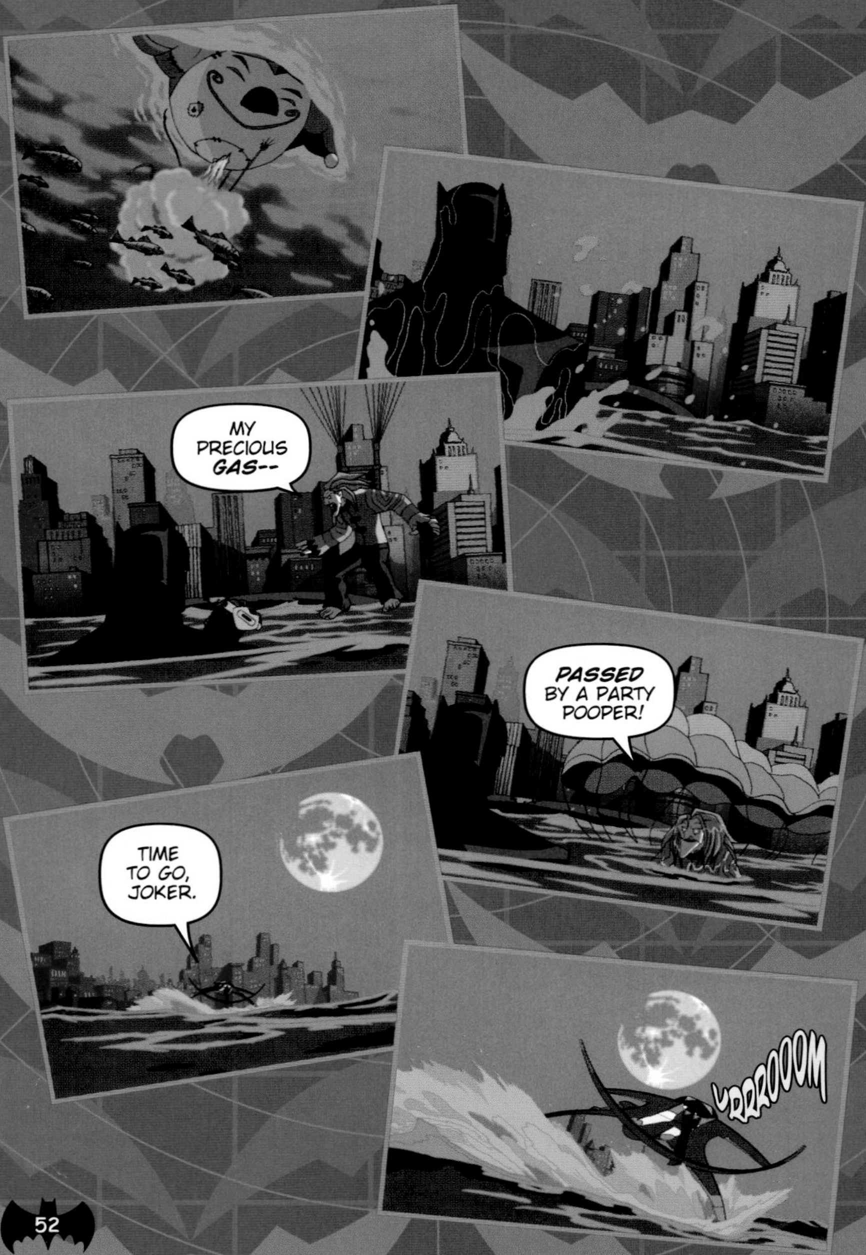
MY PRECIOUS GAS--
PASSED BY A PARTY POOPER!
TIME TO GO, JOKER.
URRROOOM

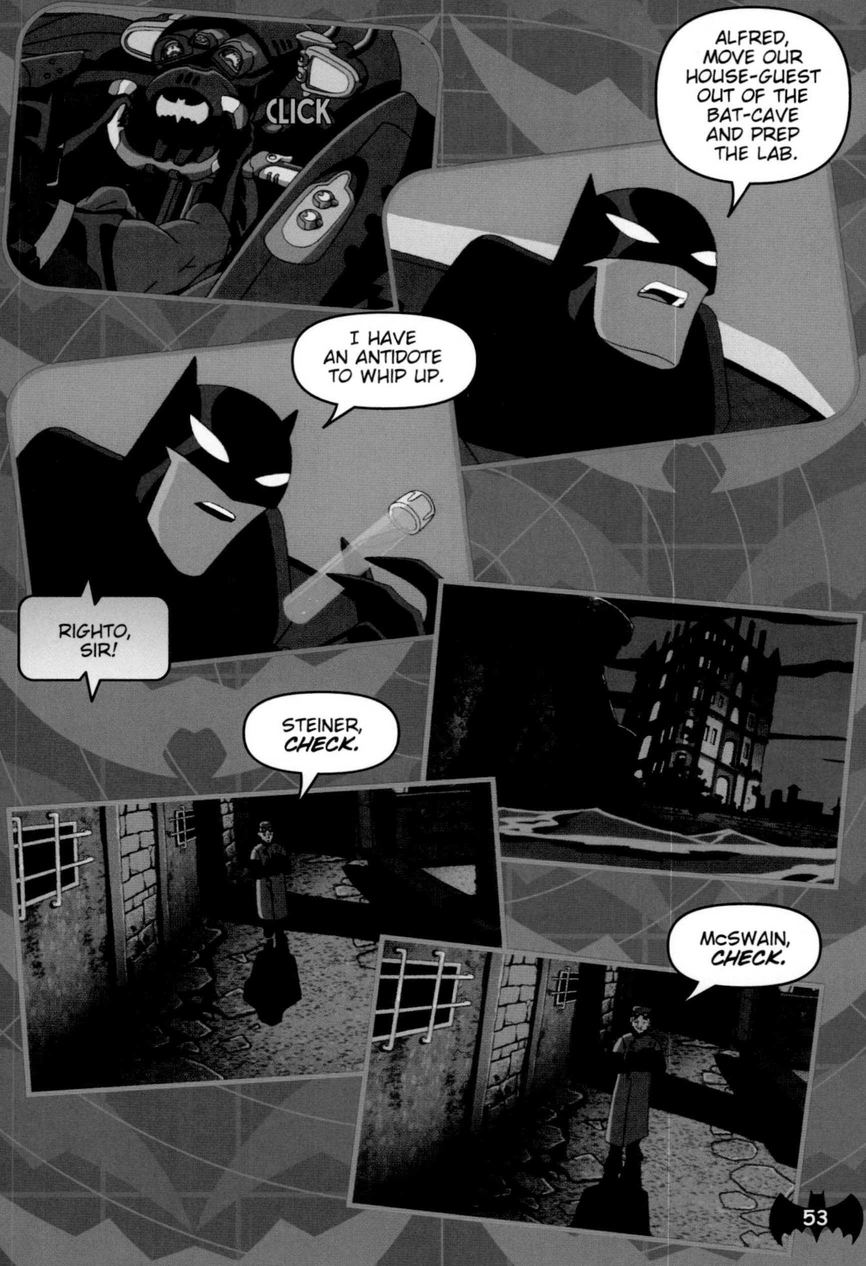

CLICK
ALFRED, MOVE OUR HOUSE-GUEST OUT OF THE BAT-CAVE AND PREP THE LAB.
I HAVE AN ANTIDOTE TO WHIP UP.
RIGHTO, SIR!
STEINER, *CHECK.*
McSWAIN, *CHECK.*

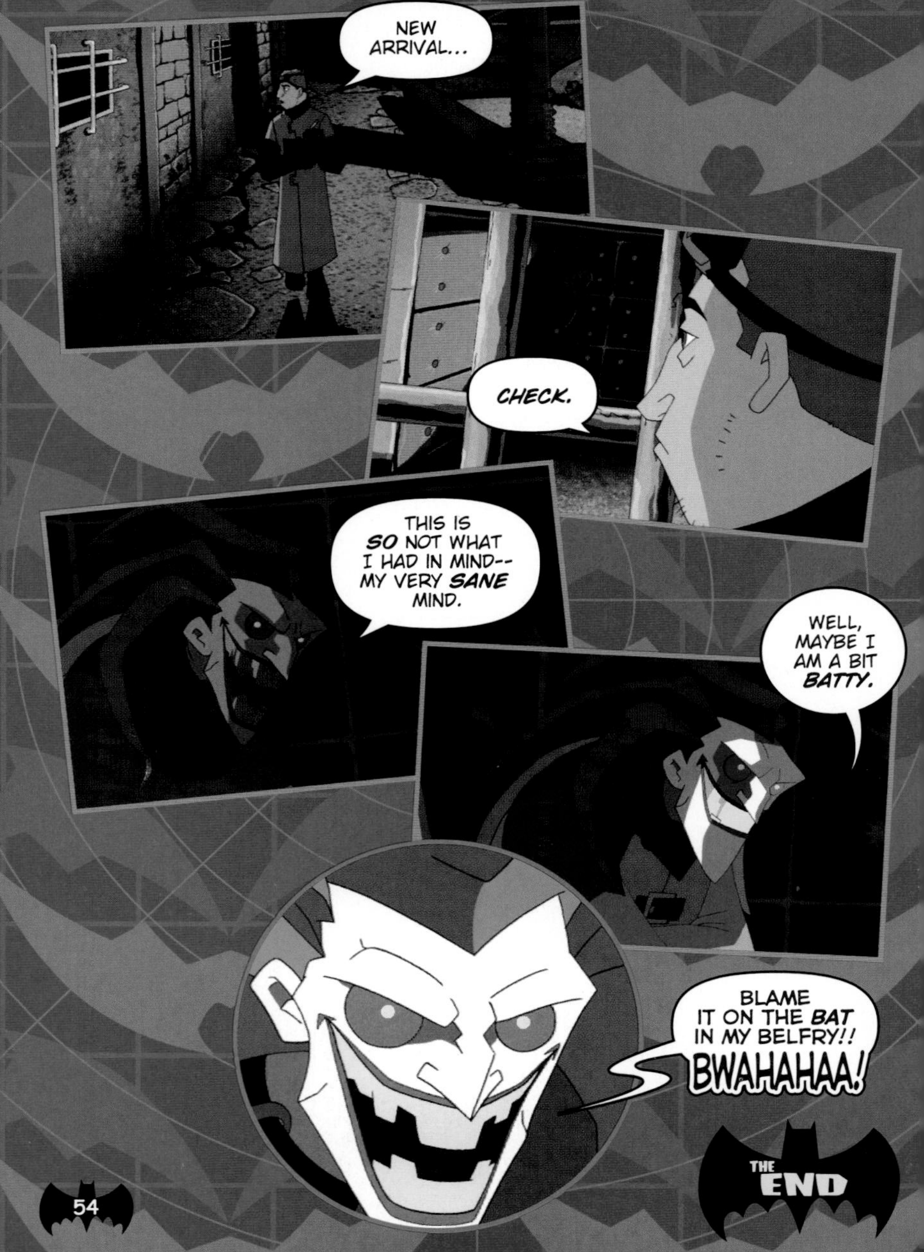
NEW ARRIVAL...
CHECK.
THIS IS SO NOT WHAT I HAD IN MIND--MY VERY SANE MIND.
WELL, MAYBE I AM A BIT BATTY.
BLAME IT ON THE BAT IN MY BELFRY!!
BWAHAHAA!
THE END

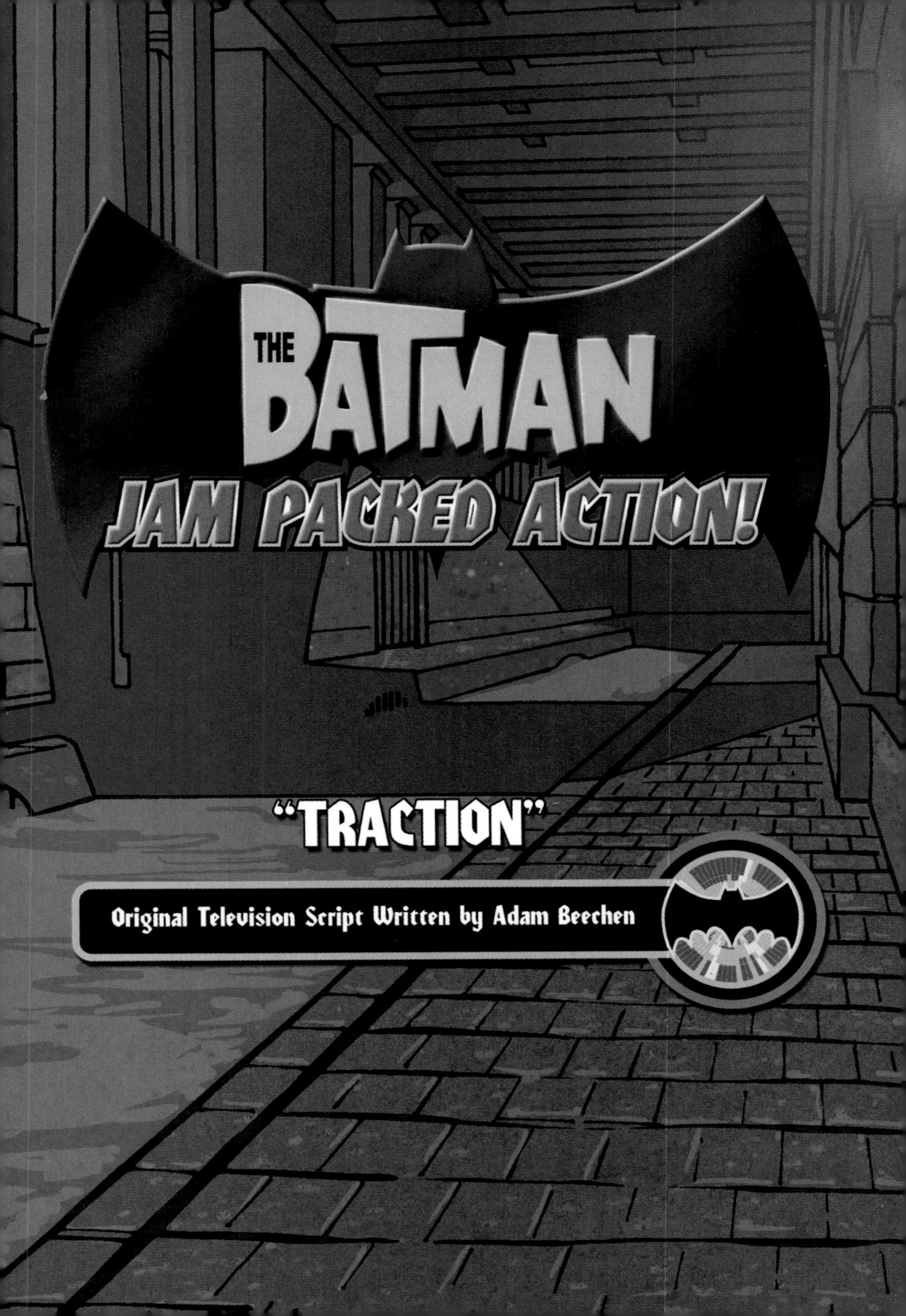
THE BATMAN
JAM PACKED ACTION!
"TRACTION"
Original Television Script Written by Adam Beechen

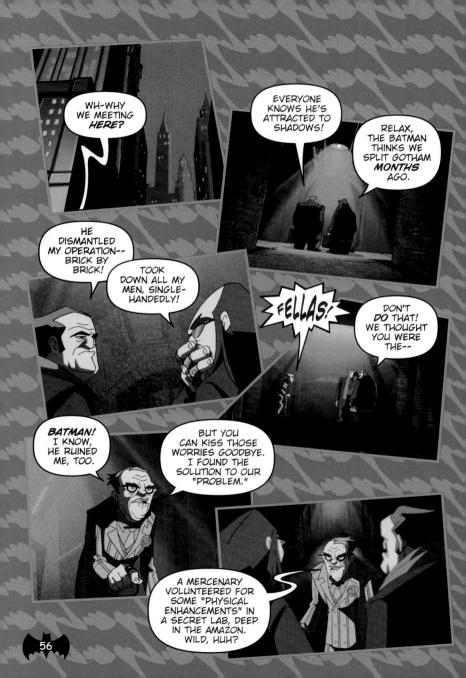

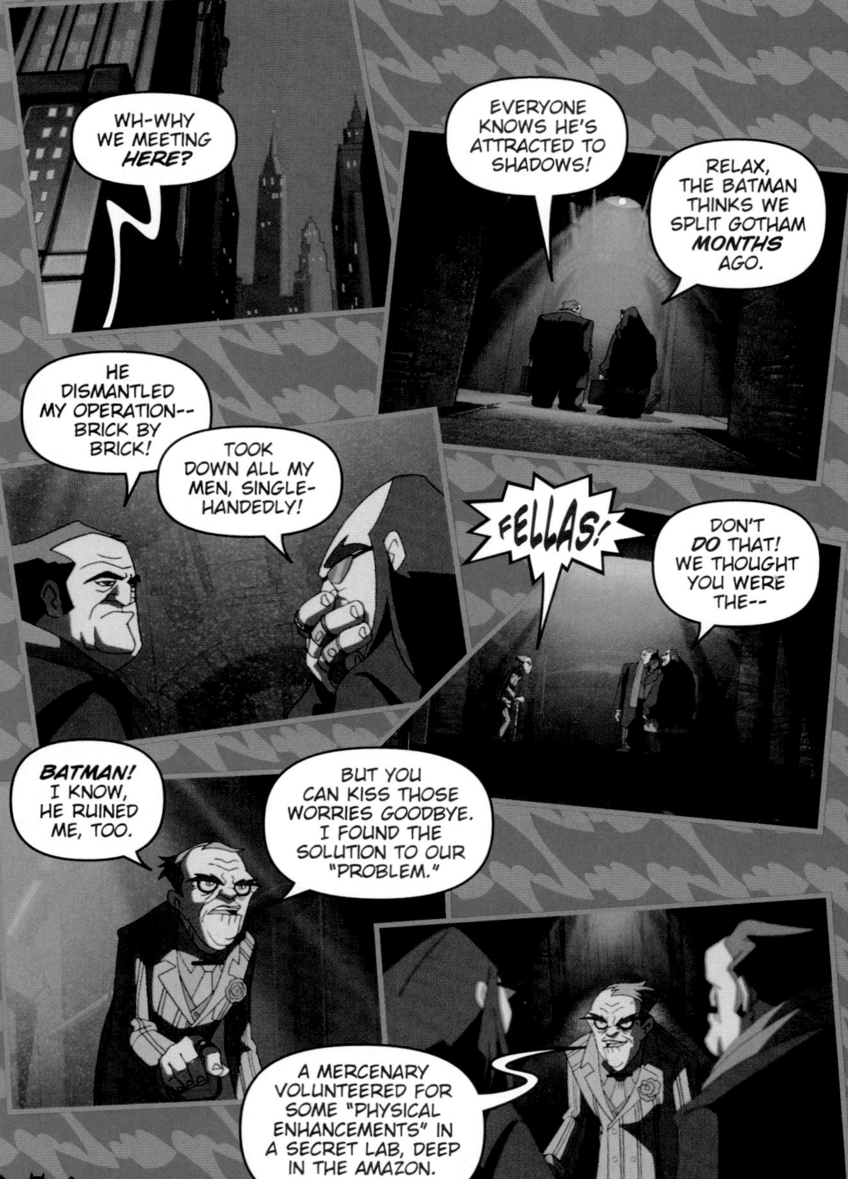
WH-WHY WE MEETING *HERE?*
EVERYONE KNOWS HE'S ATTRACTED TO SHADOWS!
RELAX, THE BATMAN THINKS WE SPLIT GOTHAM *MONTHS* AGO.
HE DISMANTLED MY OPERATION-- BRICK BY BRICK!
TOOK DOWN ALL MY MEN, SINGLE-HANDEDLY!
FELLAS!
DON'T *DO* THAT! WE THOUGHT YOU WERE THE--
BATMAN! I KNOW, HE RUINED ME, TOO.
BUT YOU CAN KISS THOSE WORRIES GOODBYE. I FOUND THE SOLUTION TO OUR "PROBLEM."
A MERCENARY VOLUNTEERED FOR SOME "PHYSICAL ENHANCEMENTS" IN A SECRET LAB, DEEP IN THE AMAZON. WILD, HUH?

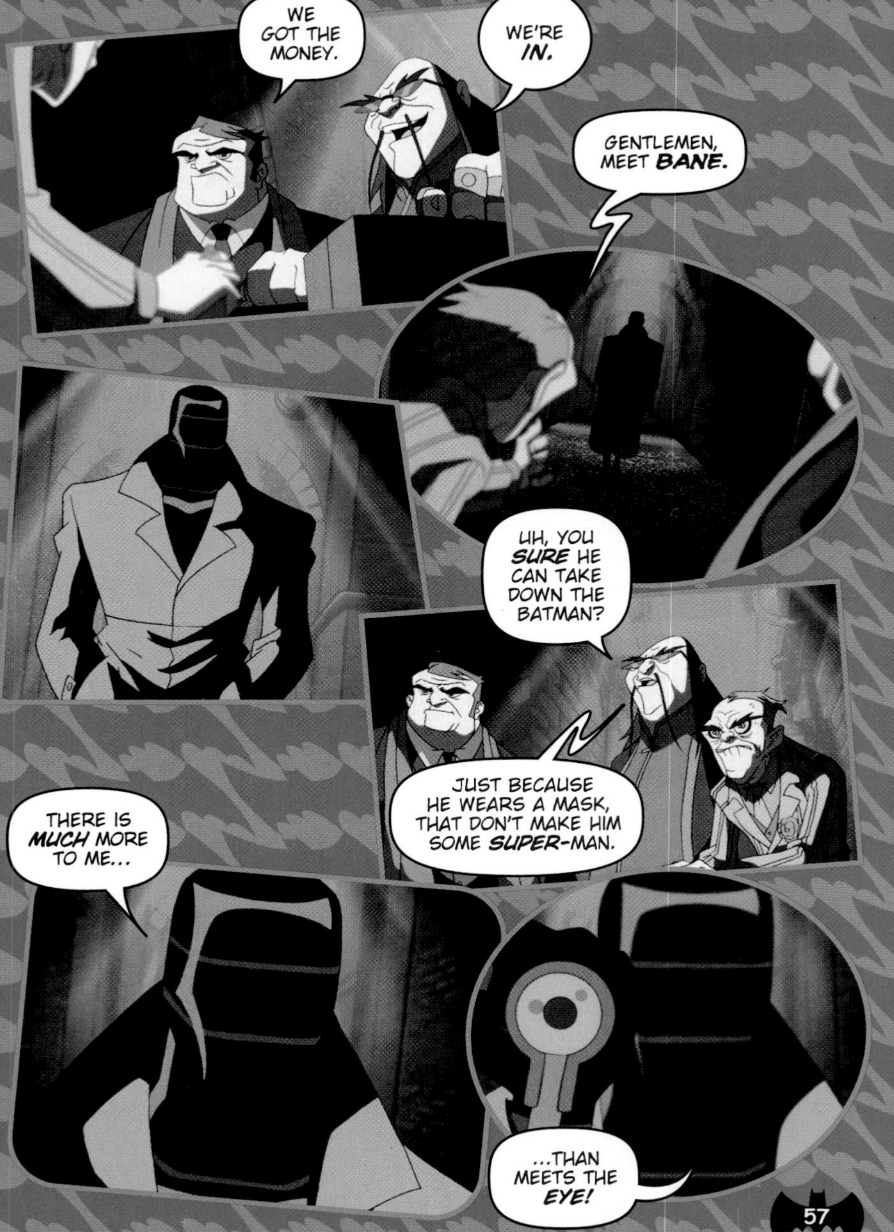
WE GOT THE MONEY.
WE'RE *IN.*
GENTLEMEN, MEET **BANE.**
UH, YOU ***SURE*** HE CAN TAKE DOWN THE BATMAN?
JUST BECAUSE HE WEARS A MASK, THAT DON'T MAKE HIM SOME ***SUPER***-MAN.
THERE IS ***MUCH*** MORE TO ME...
...THAN MEETS THE ***EYE!***

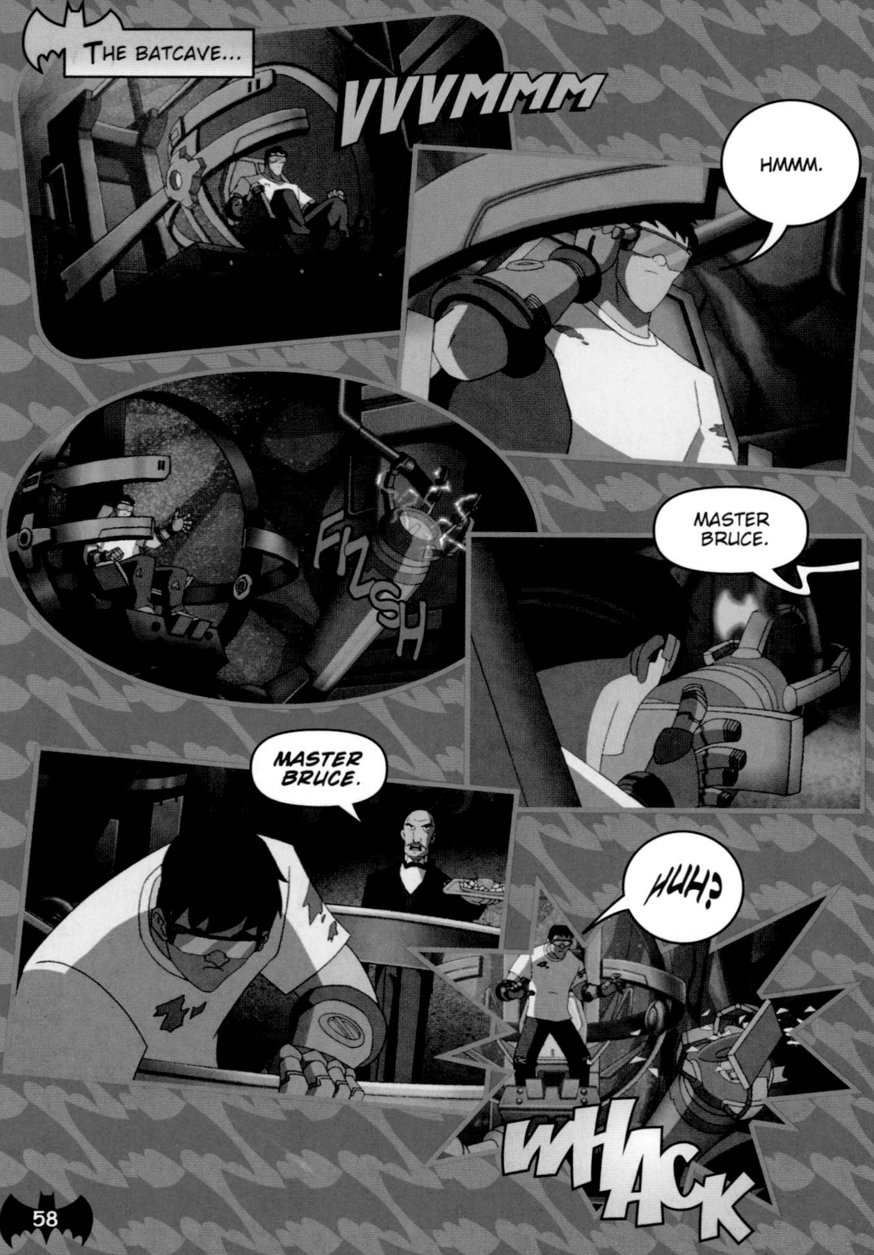
THE BATCAVE...
VVVMMM
HMMM.
FZZSH
MASTER BRUCE.
MASTER BRUCE.
HUH?
WHACK

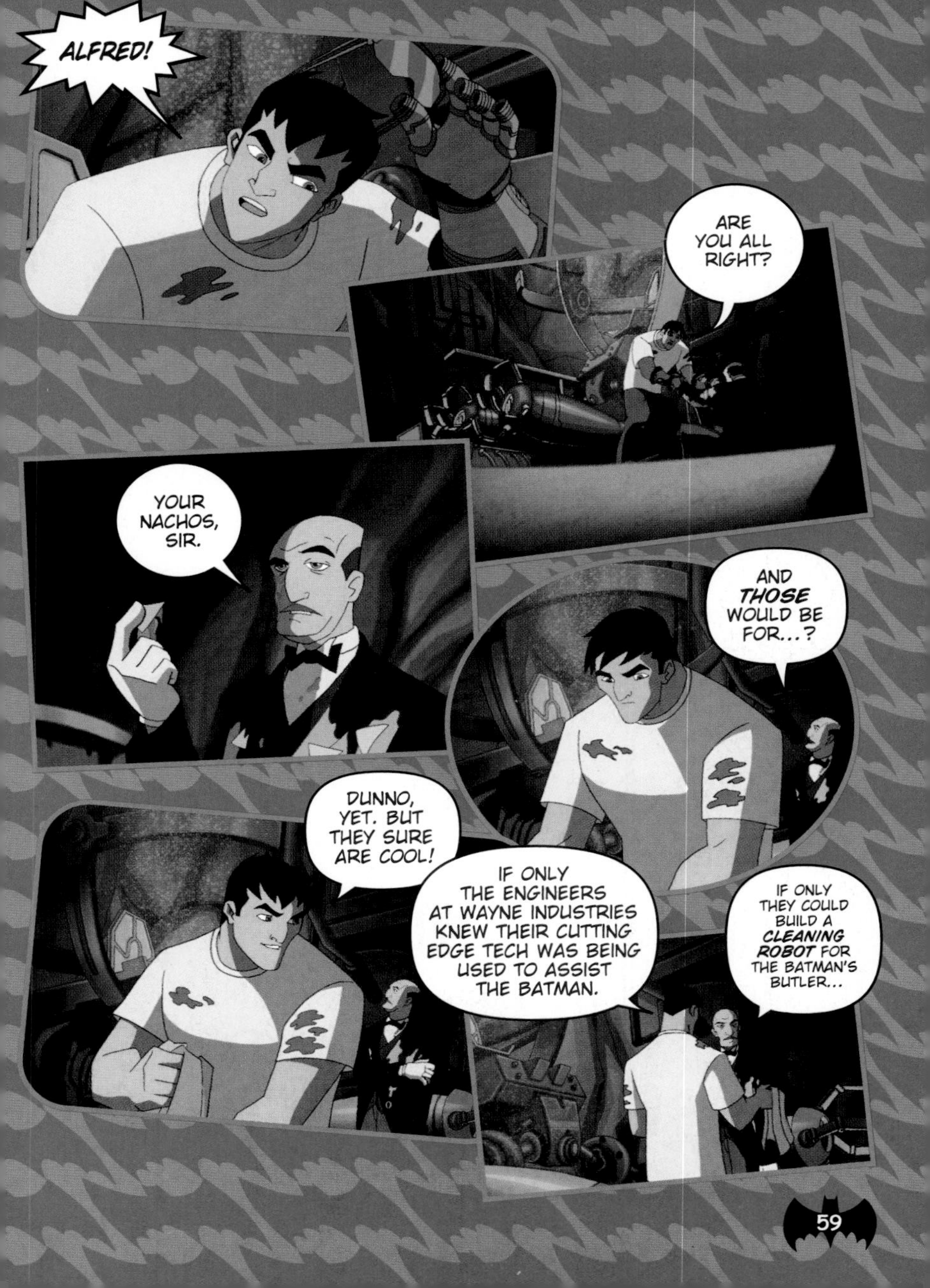

ALFRED!
ARE YOU ALL RIGHT?
YOUR NACHOS, SIR.
AND *THOSE* WOULD BE FOR...?
DUNNO, YET. BUT THEY SURE ARE COOL!
IF ONLY THE ENGINEERS AT WAYNE INDUSTRIES KNEW THEIR CUTTING EDGE TECH WAS BEING USED TO ASSIST THE BATMAN.
IF ONLY THEY COULD BUILD A *CLEANING ROBOT* FOR THE BATMAN'S BUTLER...

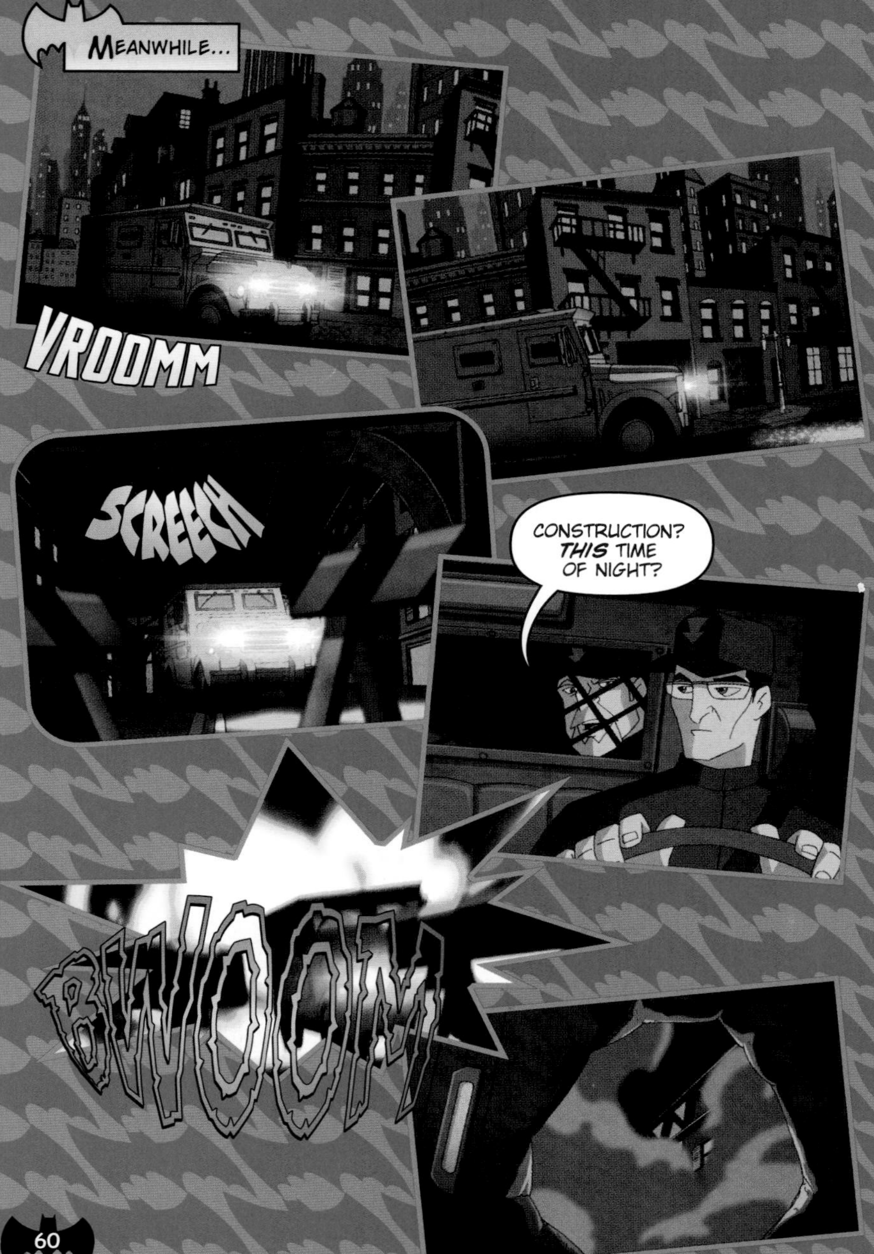
MEANWHILE...
VROOMM
SCREECH
CONSTRUCTION? THIS TIME OF NIGHT?
BWOOM

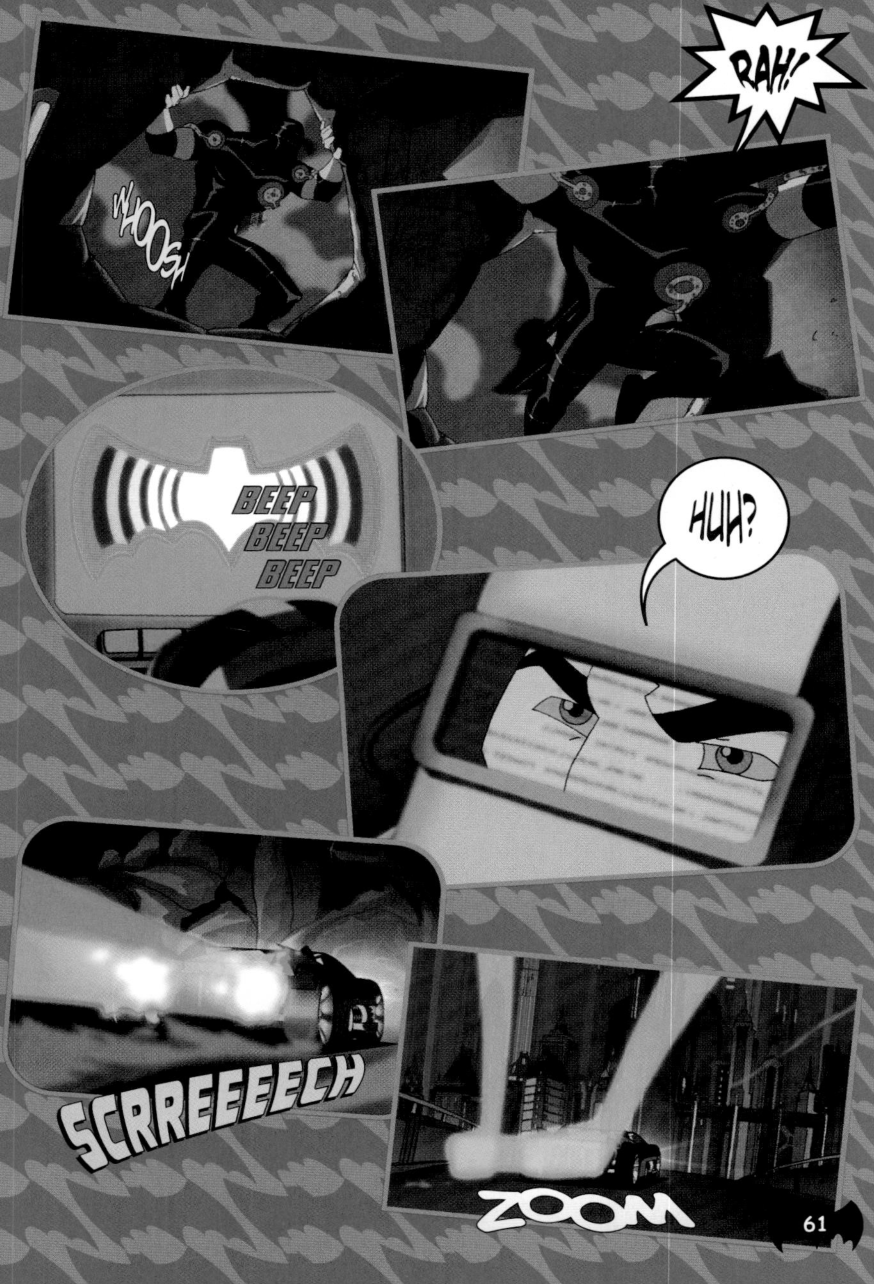
WHOOSH
RAH!
BEEP
BEEP
BEEP
HUH?
SCRREEEEECH
ZOOM

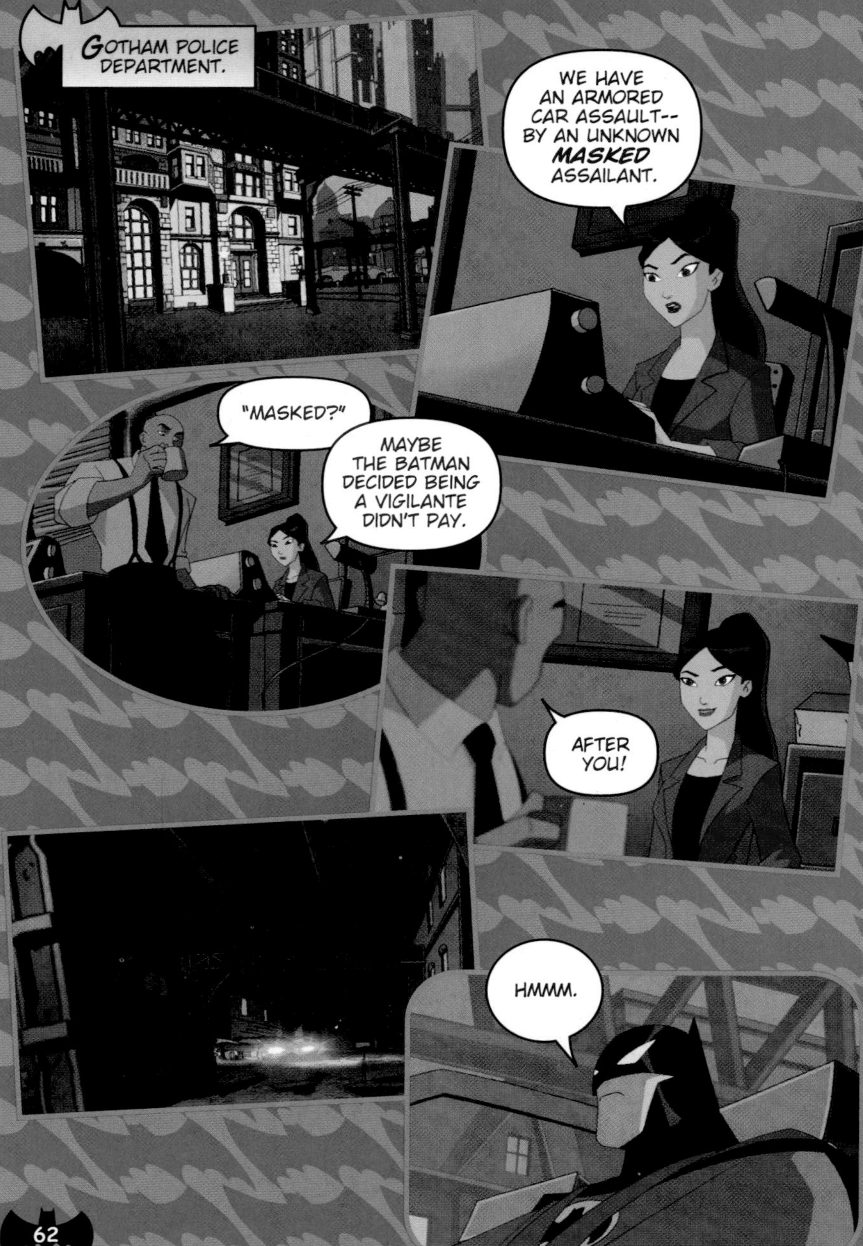
GOTHAM POLICE DEPARTMENT.
WE HAVE AN ARMORED CAR ASSAULT-- BY AN UNKNOWN MASKED ASSAILANT.
"MASKED?"
MAYBE THE BATMAN DECIDED BEING A VIGILANTE DIDN'T PAY.
AFTER YOU!
HMMM.

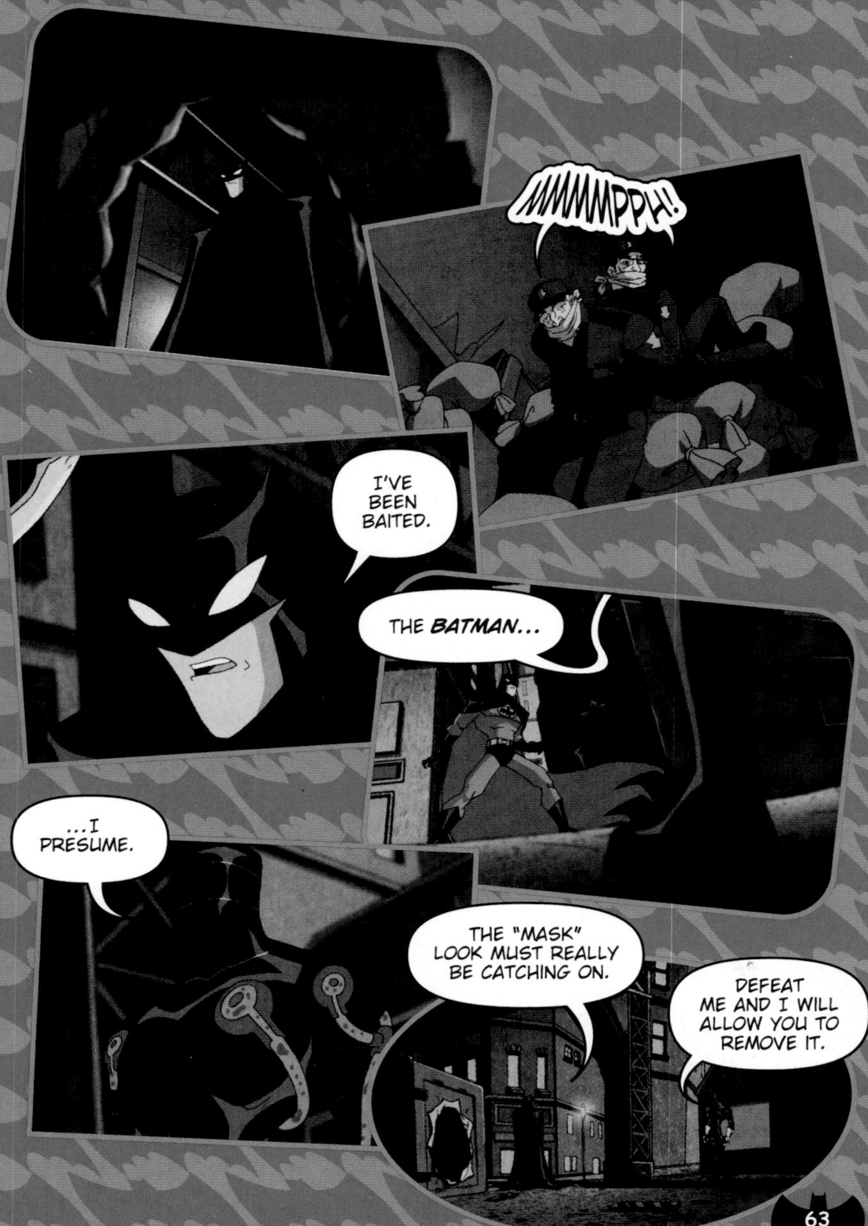
MMMMMPPH!
I'VE BEEN BAITED.
THE BATMAN...
...I PRESUME.
THE "MASK" LOOK MUST REALLY BE CATCHING ON.
DEFEAT ME AND I WILL ALLOW YOU TO REMOVE IT.

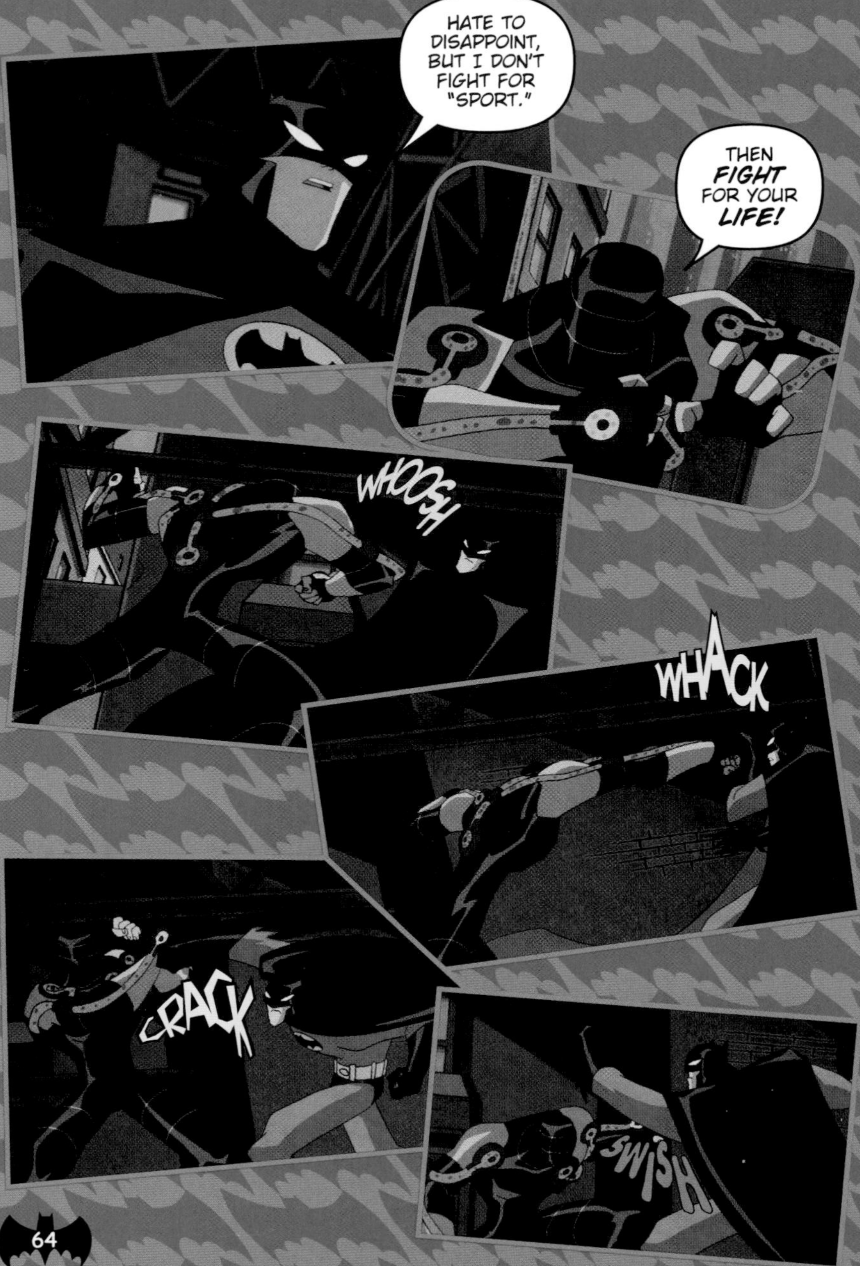
HATE TO DISAPPOINT, BUT I DON'T FIGHT FOR "SPORT."
THEN *FIGHT* FOR YOUR *LIFE!*
WHOOSH
WHACK
CRACK
SWISH

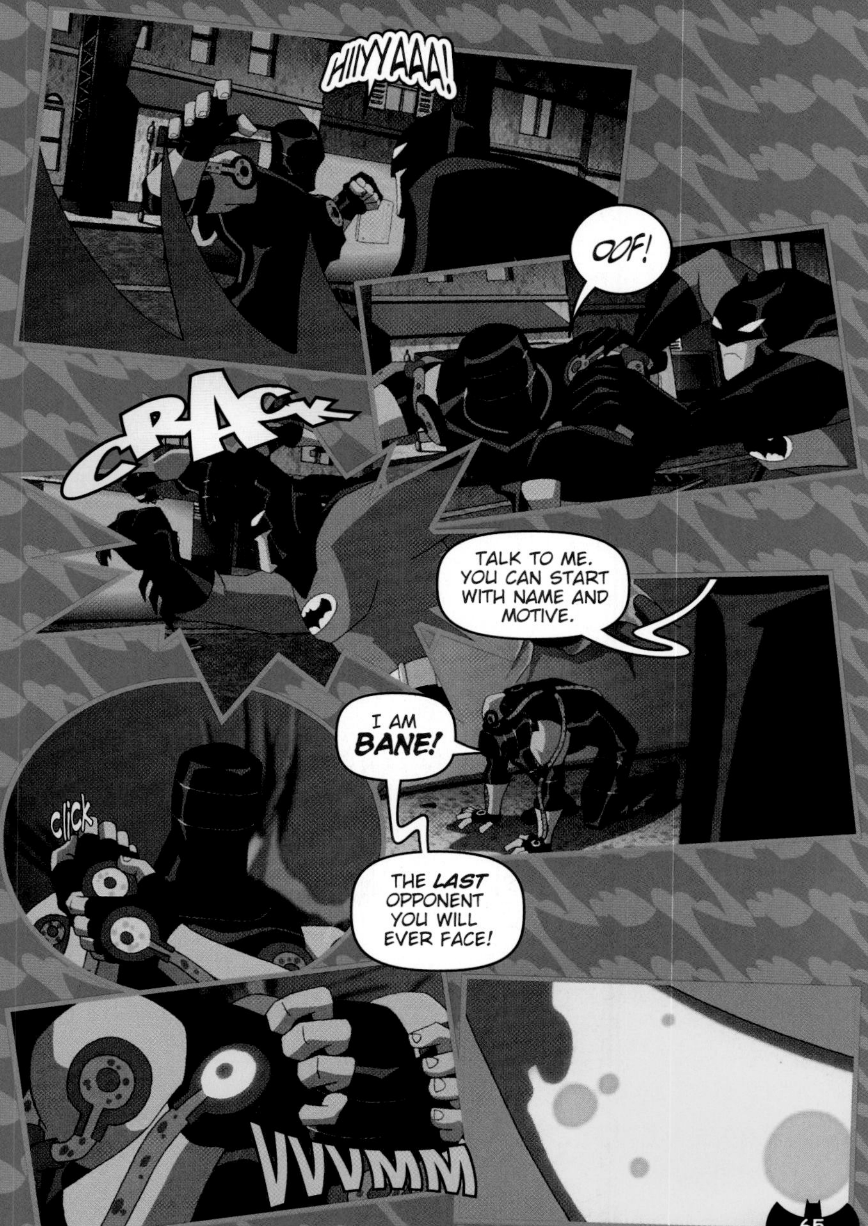

HIIYYAAA!
OOF!
CRACK
TALK TO ME. YOU CAN START WITH NAME AND MOTIVE.
I AM **BANE!**
CLICK
THE ***LAST*** OPPONENT YOU WILL EVER FACE!
VVVMM

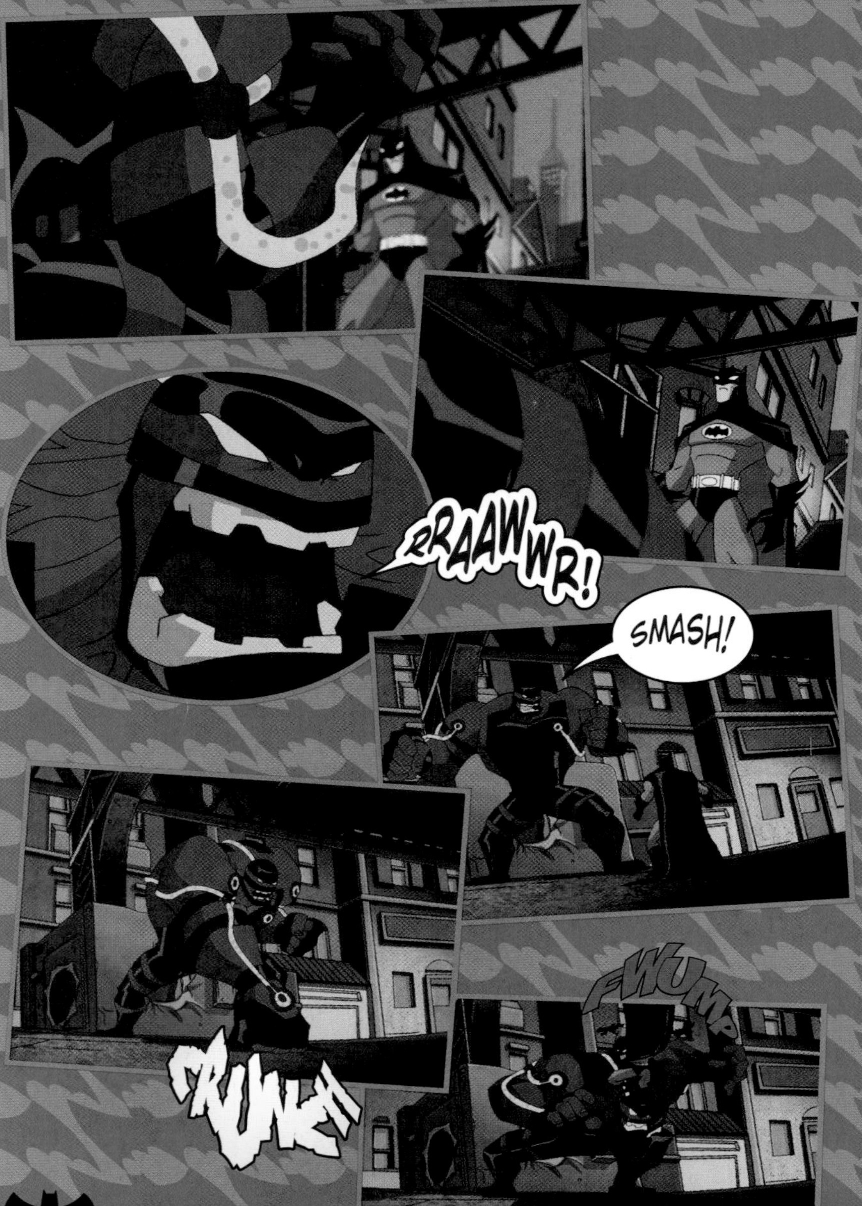
RRAAWWR!
SMASH!
CRUNCH!
FWUMP

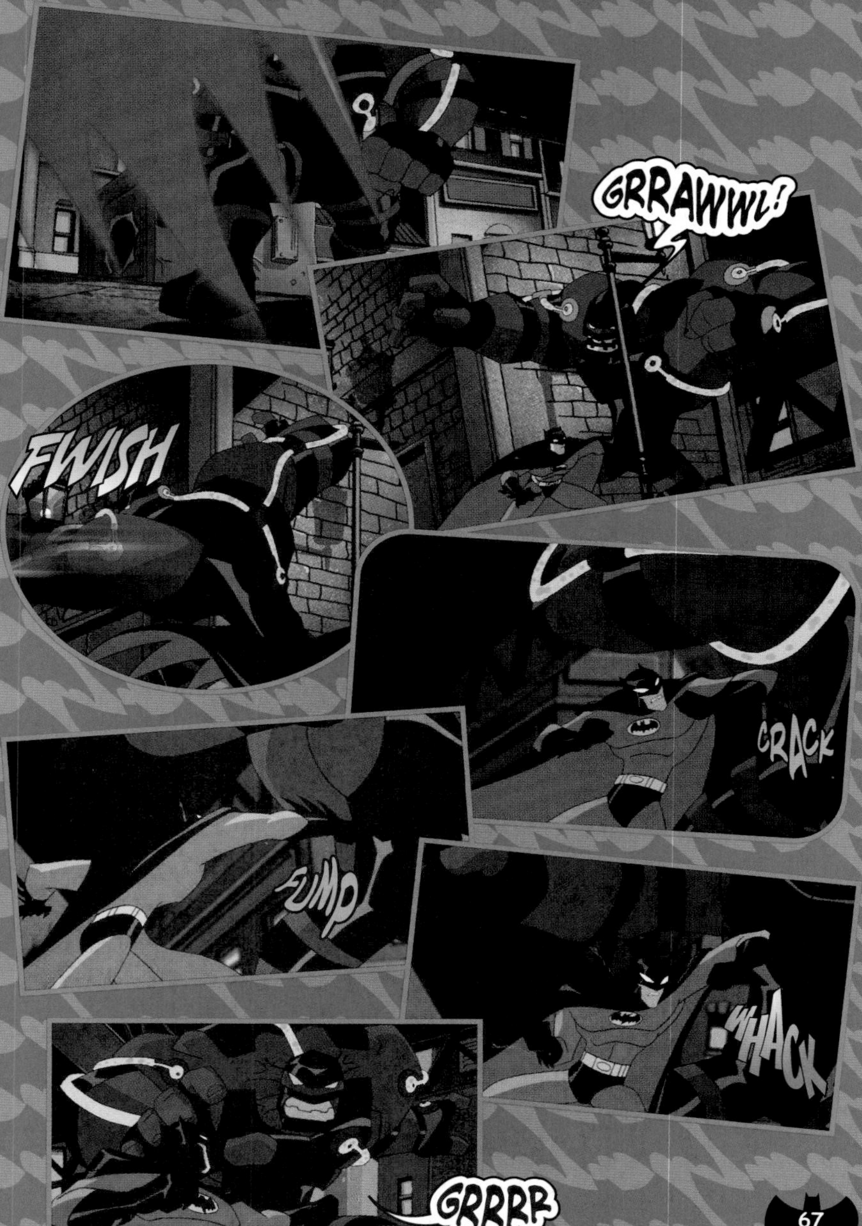
GRRAWWL!
FWISH
CRACK
FUMP
WHACK
GRRRR

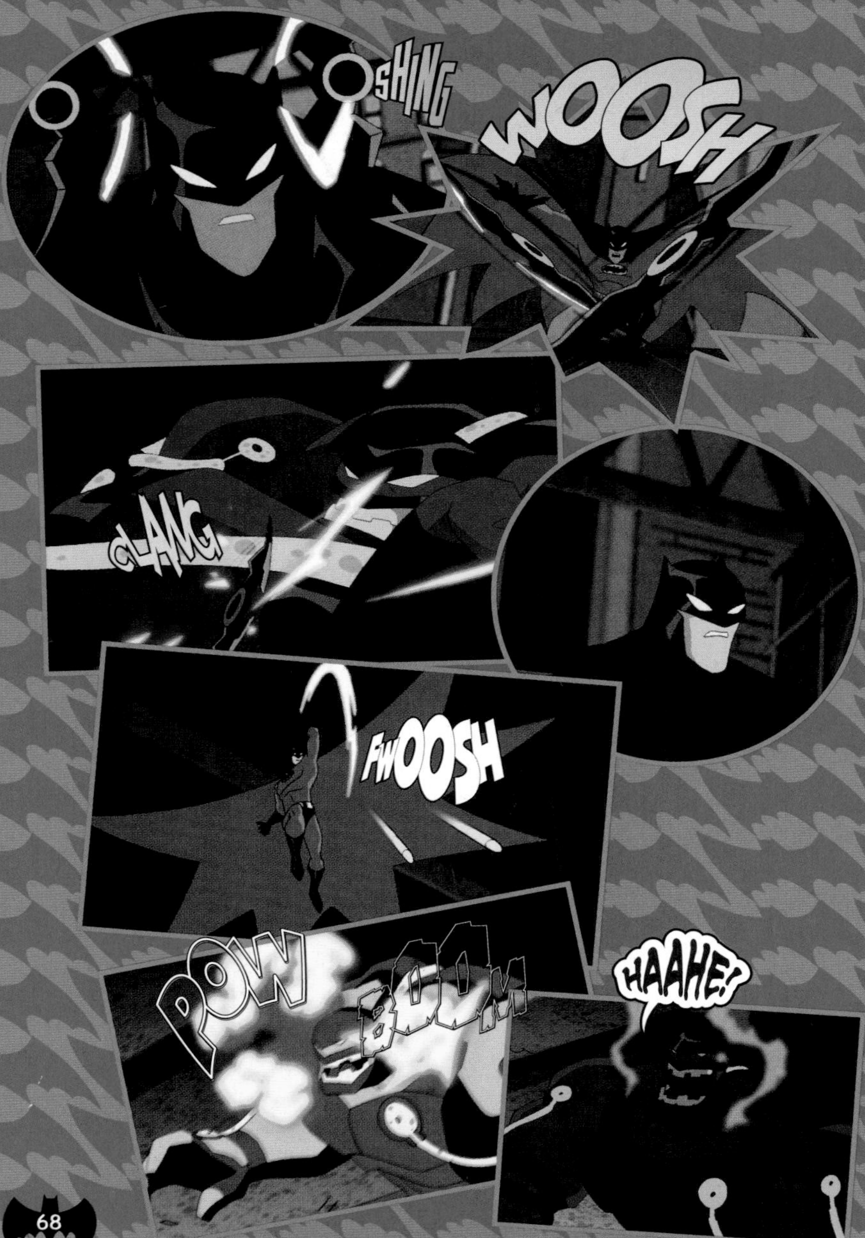
SHING
WOOSH
CLANG
FWOOSH
POW
BOOM
HAAHE!

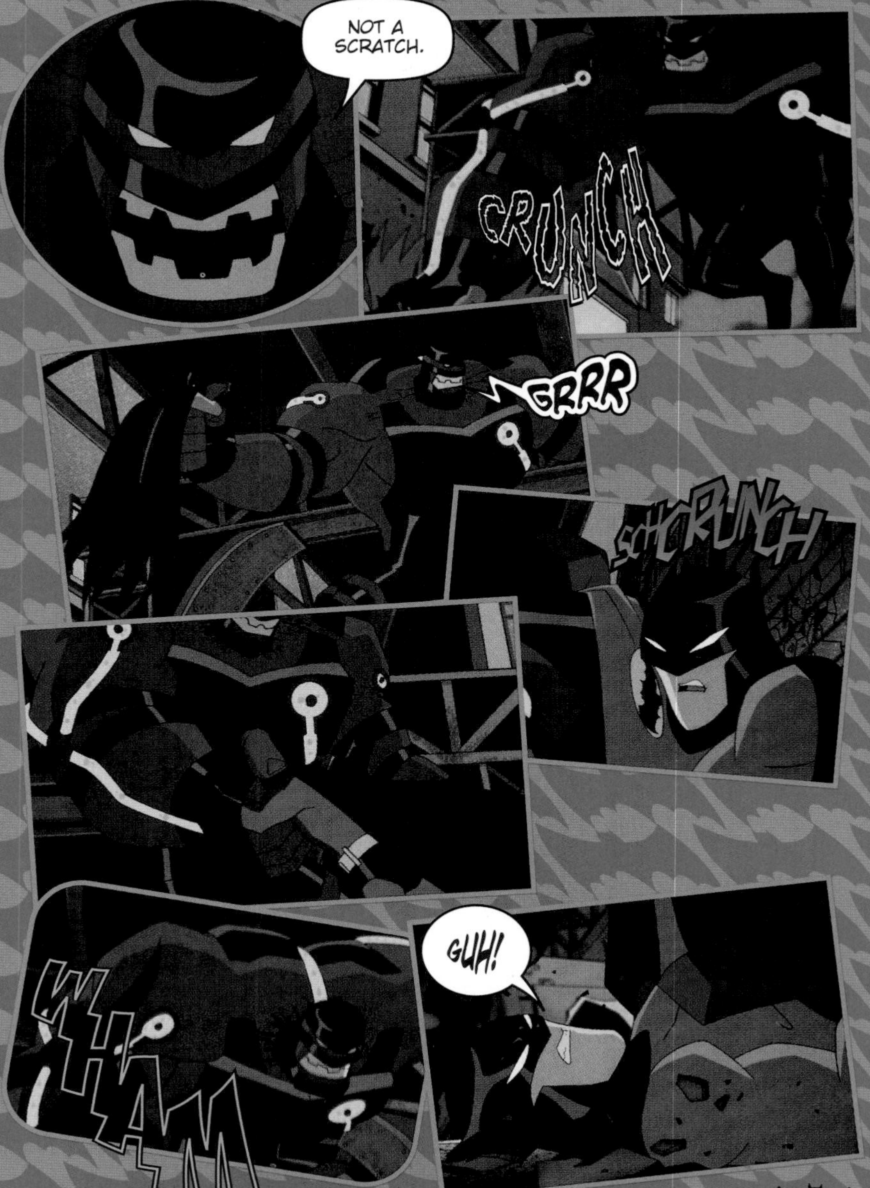
NOT A SCRATCH.
CRUNCH
GRRR
SCHCRUNCH
WHAM
GUH!

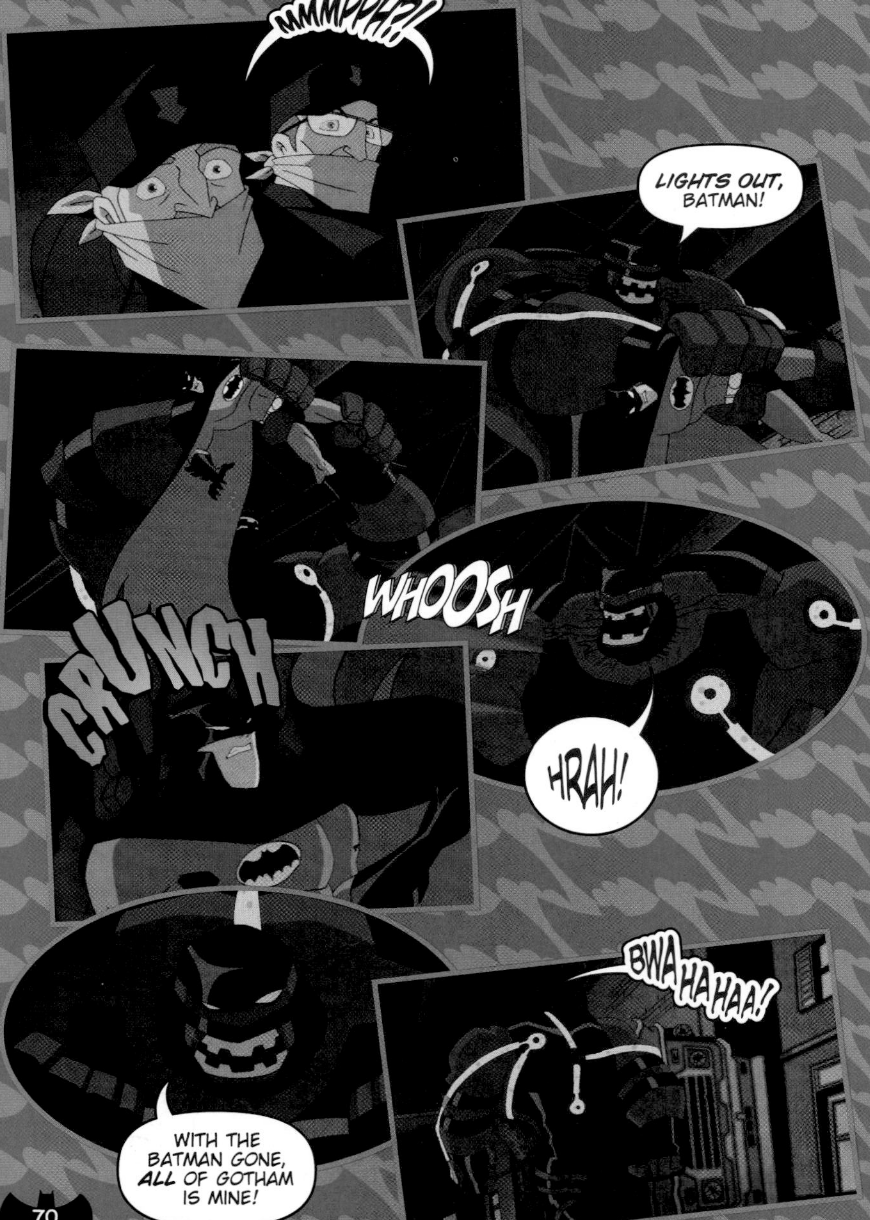

MMMPPH?!
LIGHTS OUT, BATMAN!
WHOOSH
CRUNCH
HRAH!
WITH THE BATMAN GONE, ALL OF GOTHAM IS MINE!
BWA HA HAHAA!

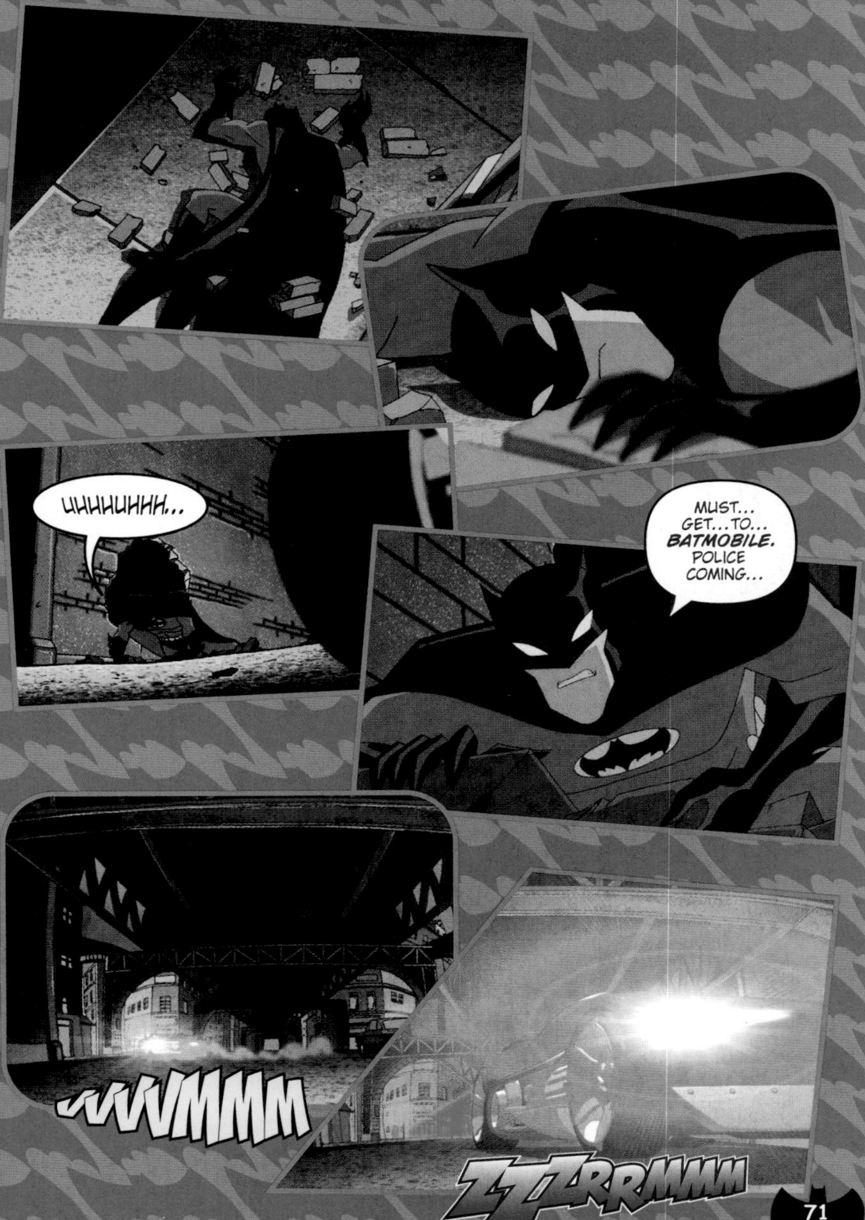
UHHHUHHH...
MUST... GET...TO... BATMOBILE. POLICE COMING...
VVVVMMMM
ZZZRRRMMMM

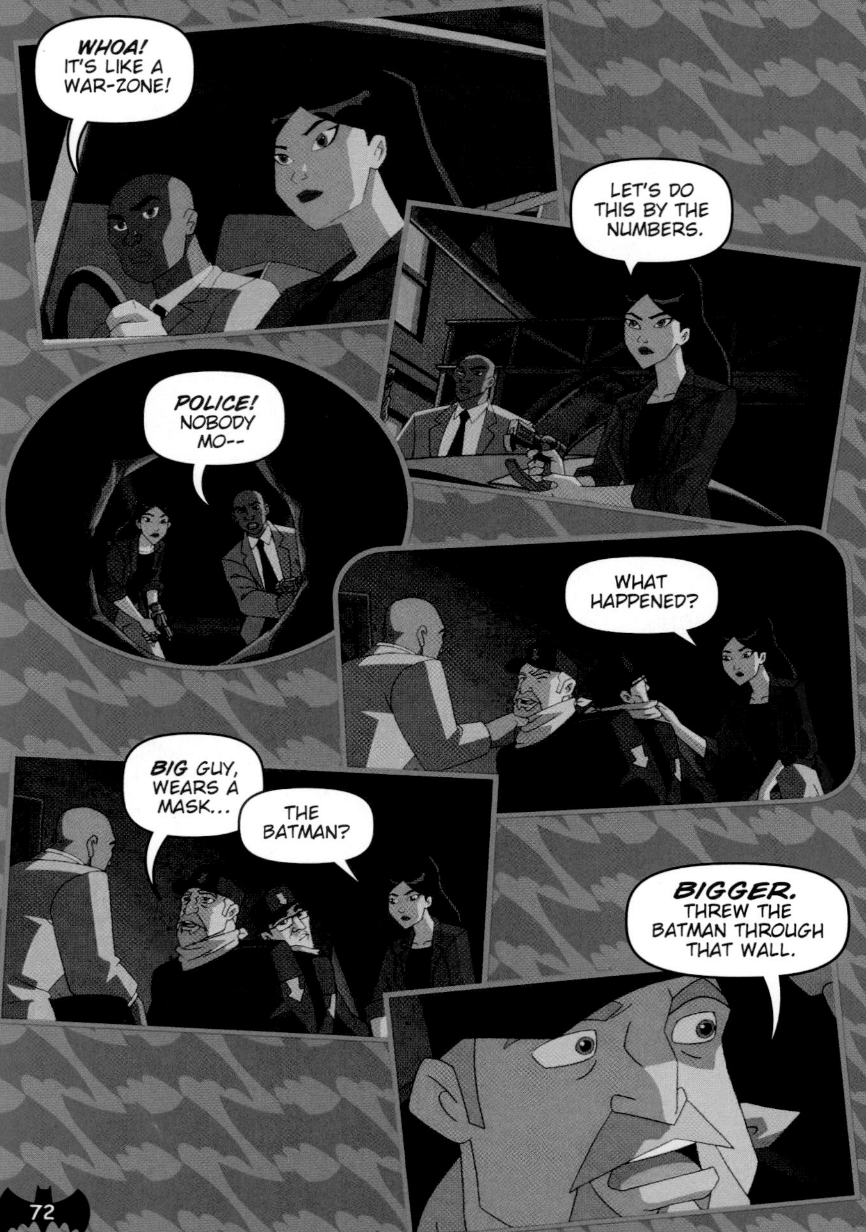
WHOA! IT'S LIKE A WAR-ZONE!
LET'S DO THIS BY THE NUMBERS.
POLICE! NOBODY MO--
WHAT HAPPENED?
BIG GUY, WEARS A MASK...
THE BATMAN?
BIGGER. THREW THE BATMAN THROUGH THAT WALL.

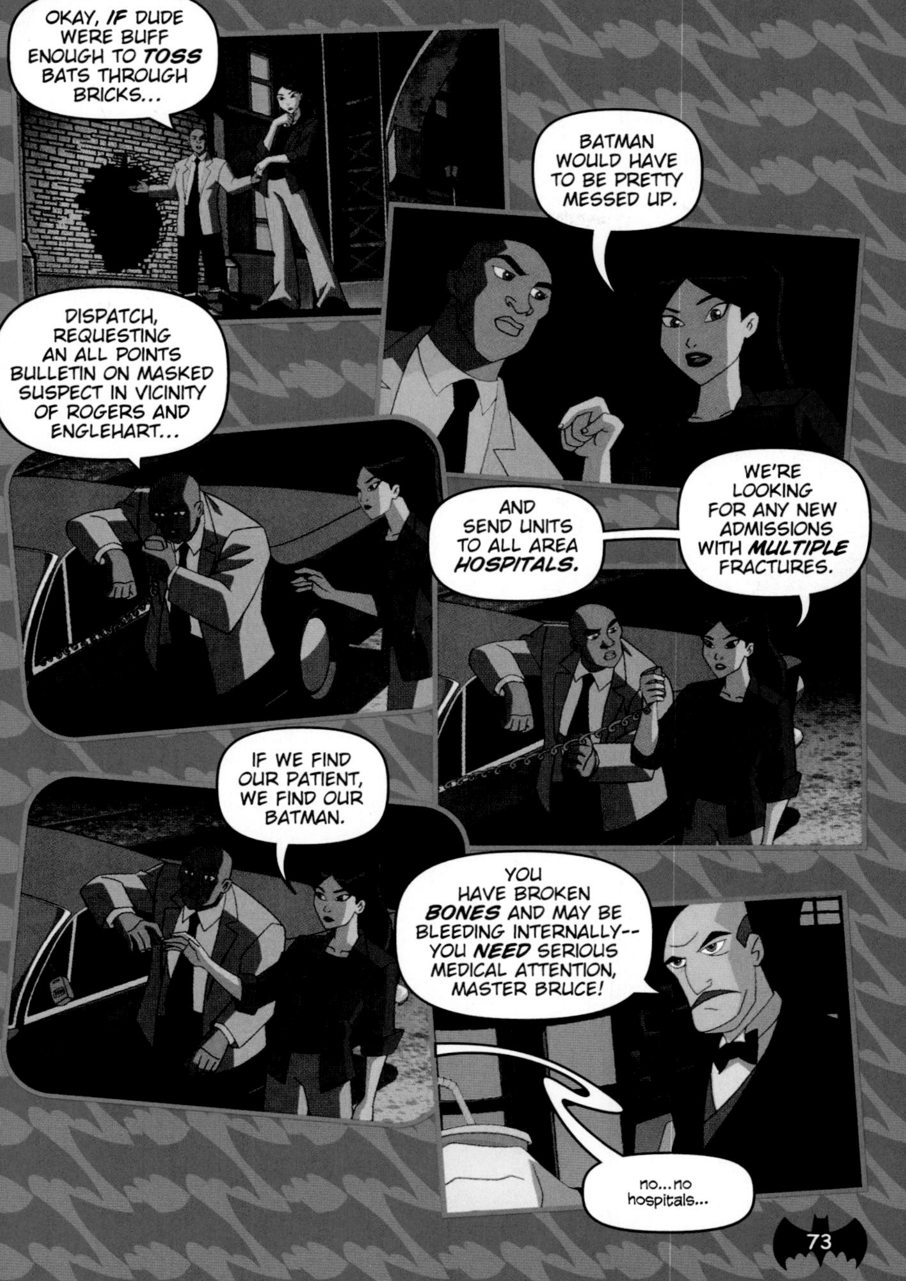
OKAY, *IF* DUDE WERE BUFF ENOUGH TO *TOSS* BATS THROUGH BRICKS...
BATMAN WOULD HAVE TO BE PRETTY MESSED UP.
DISPATCH, REQUESTING AN ALL POINTS BULLETIN ON MASKED SUSPECT IN VICINITY OF ROGERS AND ENGLEHART...
AND SEND UNITS TO ALL AREA *HOSPITALS.*
WE'RE LOOKING FOR ANY NEW ADMISSIONS WITH *MULTIPLE* FRACTURES.
IF WE FIND OUR PATIENT, WE FIND OUR BATMAN.
YOU HAVE BROKEN *BONES* AND MAY BE BLEEDING INTERNALLY-- YOU *NEED* SERIOUS MEDICAL ATTENTION, MASTER BRUCE!
no...no hospitals...

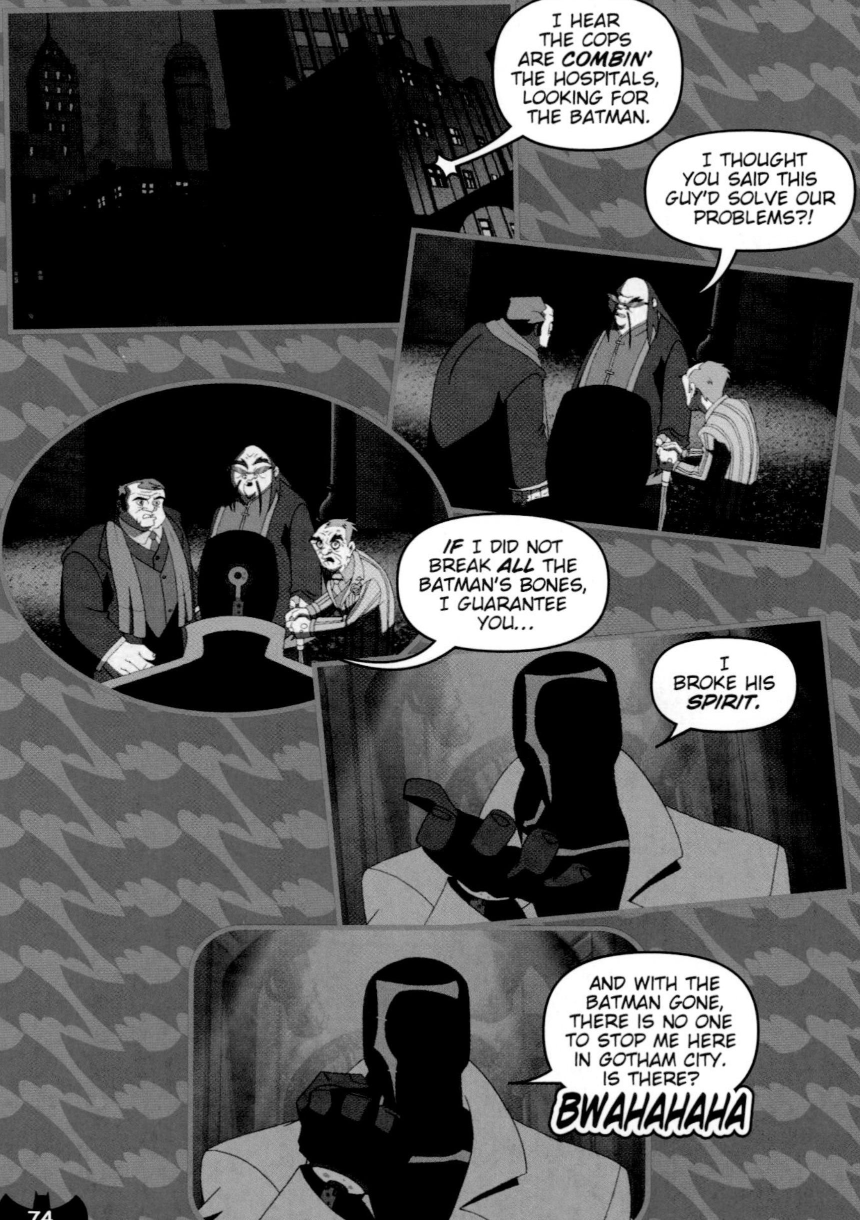
I HEAR THE COPS ARE COMBIN' THE HOSPITALS, LOOKING FOR THE BATMAN.
I THOUGHT YOU SAID THIS GUY'D SOLVE OUR PROBLEMS?!
IF I DID NOT BREAK ALL THE BATMAN'S BONES, I GUARANTEE YOU...
I BROKE HIS SPIRIT.
AND WITH THE BATMAN GONE, THERE IS NO ONE TO STOP ME HERE IN GOTHAM CITY. IS THERE?
BWAHAHAHA

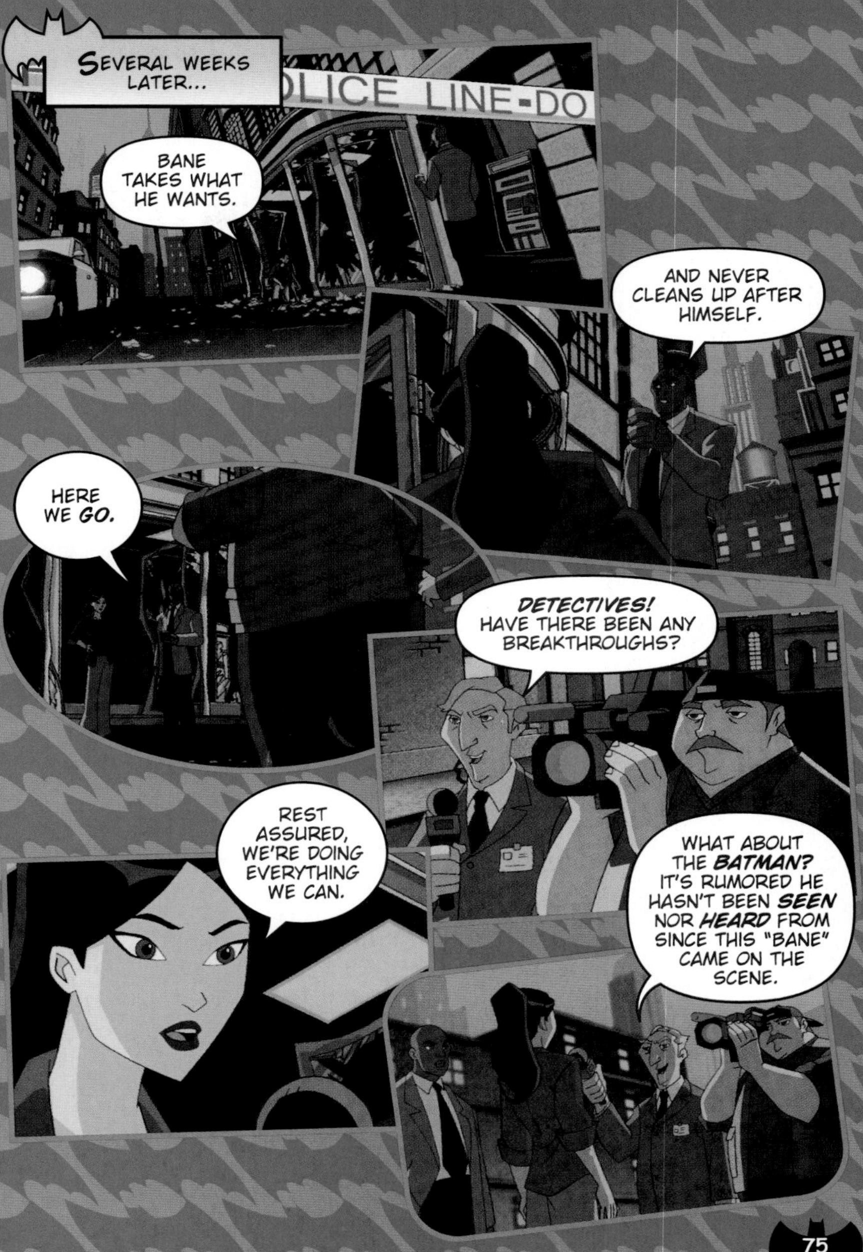

SEVERAL WEEKS LATER...
POLICE LINE-DO
BANE TAKES WHAT HE WANTS.
AND NEVER CLEANS UP AFTER HIMSELF.
HERE WE GO.
DETECTIVES! HAVE THERE BEEN ANY BREAKTHROUGHS?
REST ASSURED, WE'RE DOING EVERYTHING WE CAN.
WHAT ABOUT THE BATMAN? IT'S RUMORED HE HASN'T BEEN SEEN NOR HEARD FROM SINCE THIS "BANE" CAME ON THE SCENE.

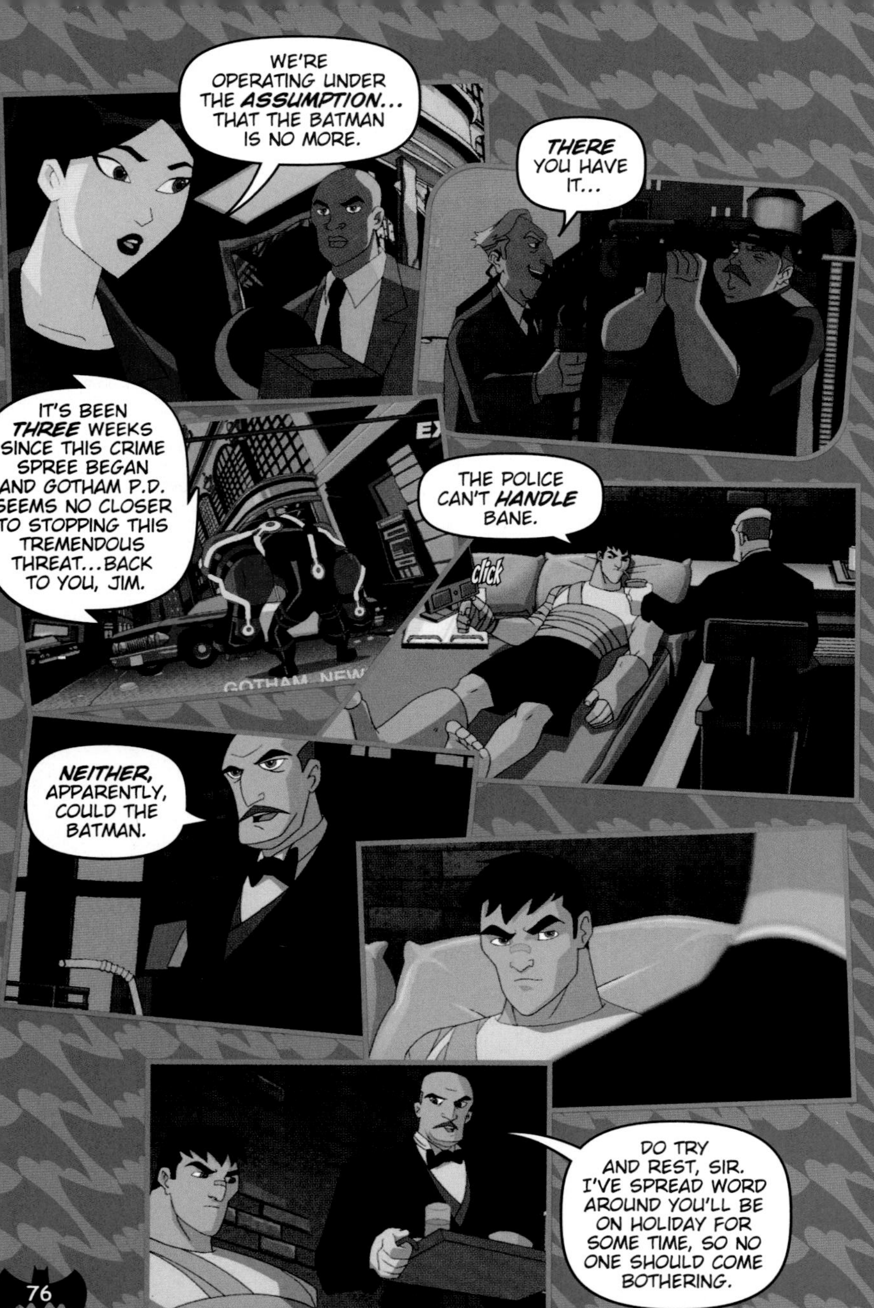
WE'RE OPERATING UNDER THE ASSUMPTION... THAT THE BATMAN IS NO MORE.
THERE YOU HAVE IT...
IT'S BEEN THREE WEEKS SINCE THIS CRIME SPREE BEGAN AND GOTHAM P.D. SEEMS NO CLOSER TO STOPPING THIS TREMENDOUS THREAT...BACK TO YOU, JIM.
THE POLICE CAN'T HANDLE BANE.
click
NEITHER, APPARENTLY, COULD THE BATMAN.
DO TRY AND REST, SIR. I'VE SPREAD WORD AROUND YOU'LL BE ON HOLIDAY FOR SOME TIME, SO NO ONE SHOULD COME BOTHERING.

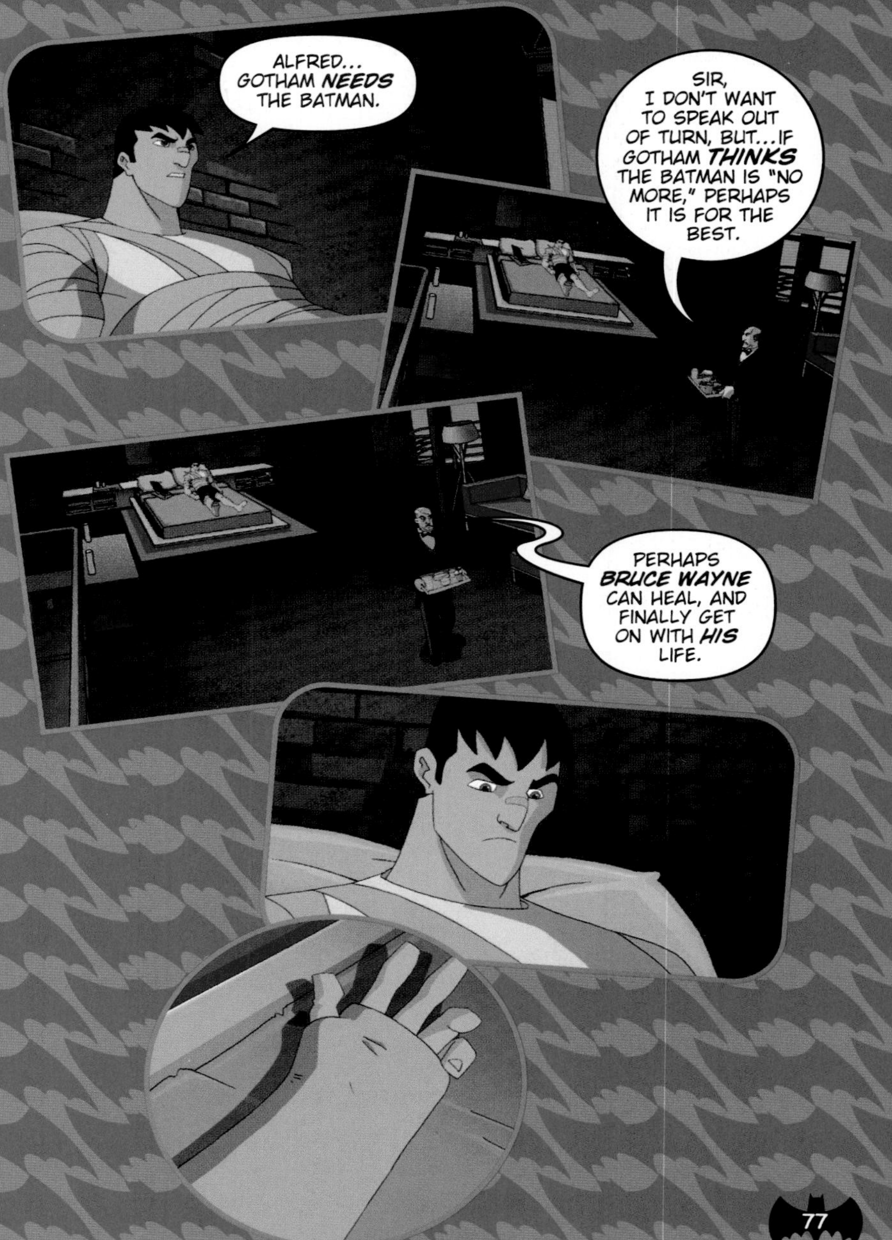
ALFRED... GOTHAM NEEDS THE BATMAN.
SIR, I DON'T WANT TO SPEAK OUT OF TURN, BUT...IF GOTHAM THINKS THE BATMAN IS "NO MORE," PERHAPS IT IS FOR THE BEST.
PERHAPS BRUCE WAYNE CAN HEAL, AND FINALLY GET ON WITH HIS LIFE.

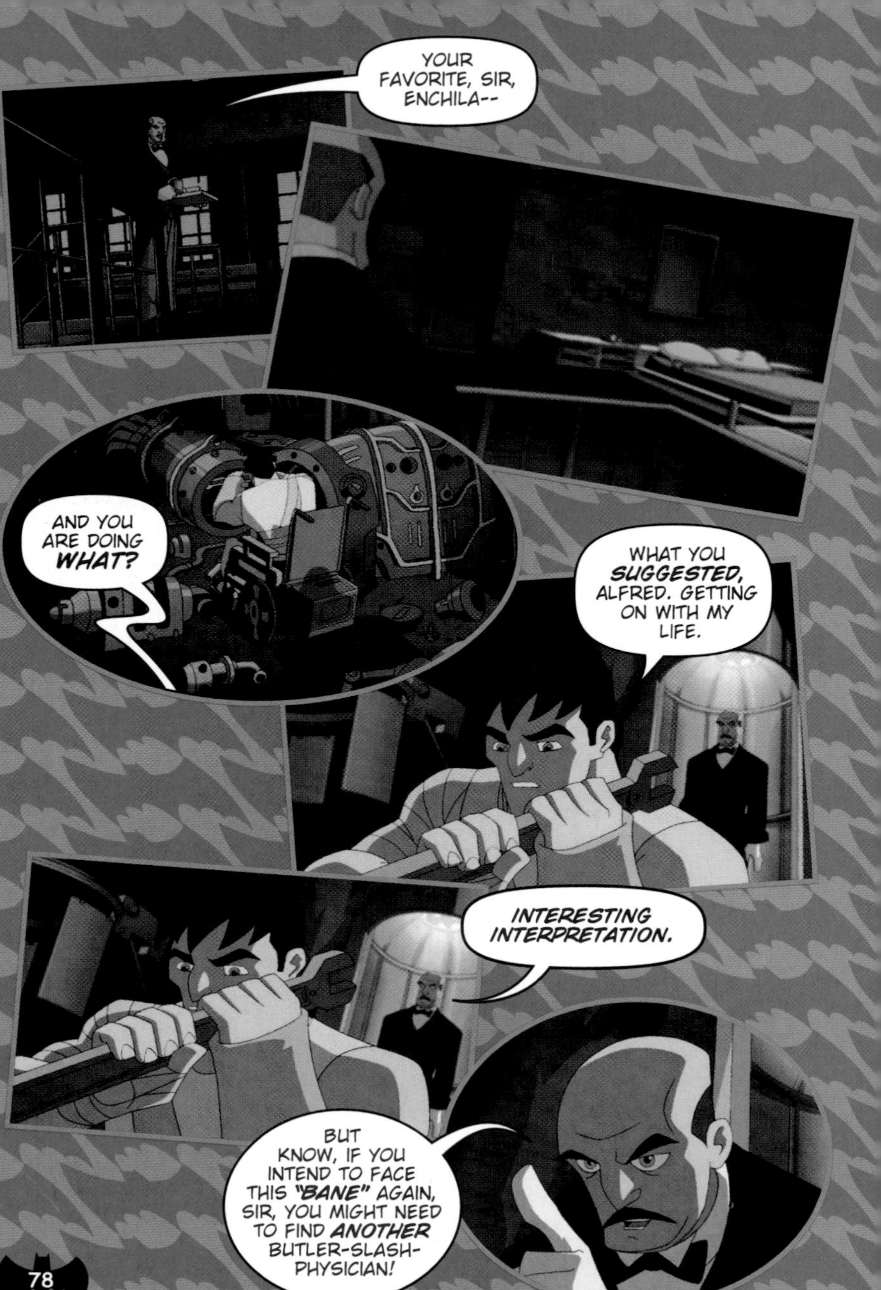

YOUR FAVORITE, SIR, ENCHILA--
AND YOU ARE DOING WHAT?
WHAT YOU SUGGESTED, ALFRED. GETTING ON WITH MY LIFE.
INTERESTING INTERPRETATION.
BUT KNOW, IF YOU INTEND TO FACE THIS "BANE" AGAIN, SIR, YOU MIGHT NEED TO FIND ANOTHER BUTLER-SLASH-PHYSICIAN!

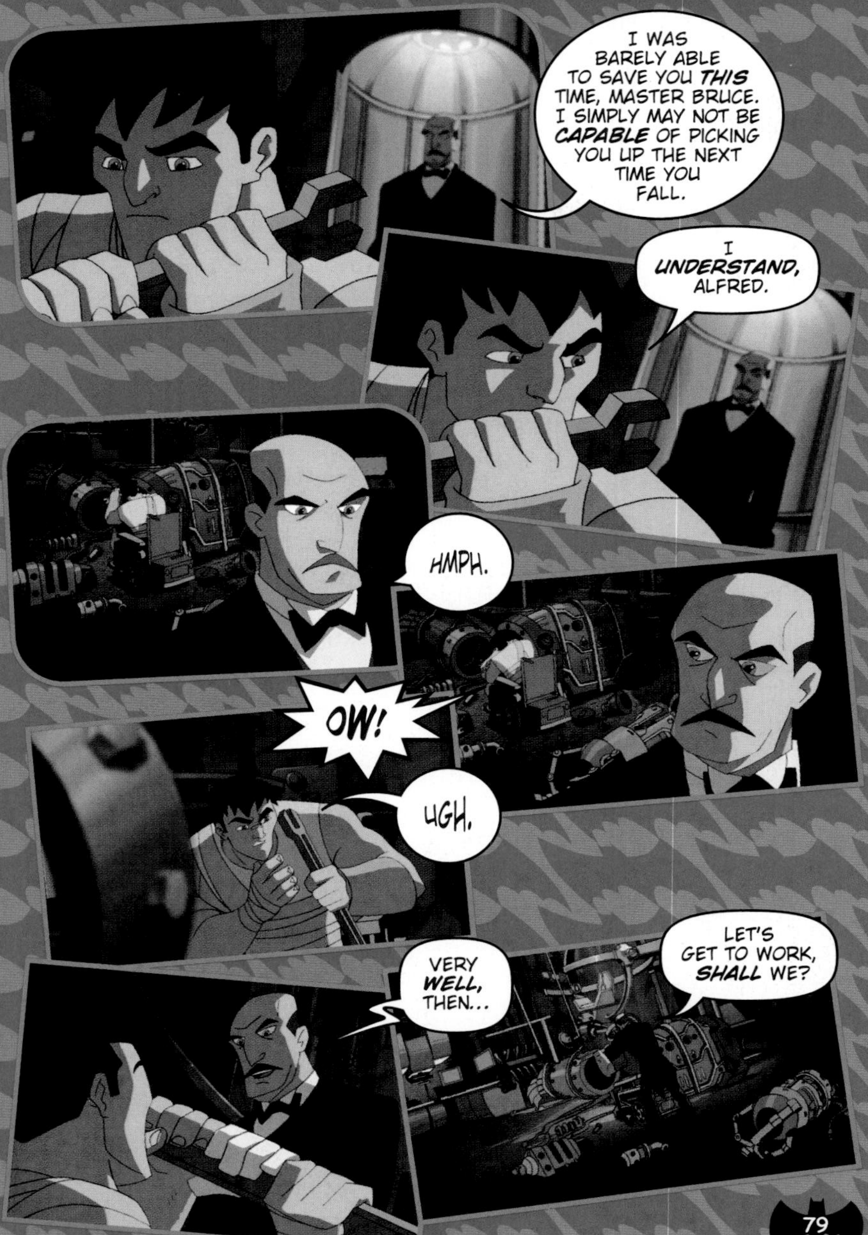
I WAS BARELY ABLE TO SAVE YOU THIS TIME, MASTER BRUCE. I SIMPLY MAY NOT BE CAPABLE OF PICKING YOU UP THE NEXT TIME YOU FALL.
I UNDERSTAND, ALFRED.
HMPH.
OW!
UGH.
VERY WELL, THEN...
LET'S GET TO WORK, SHALL WE?

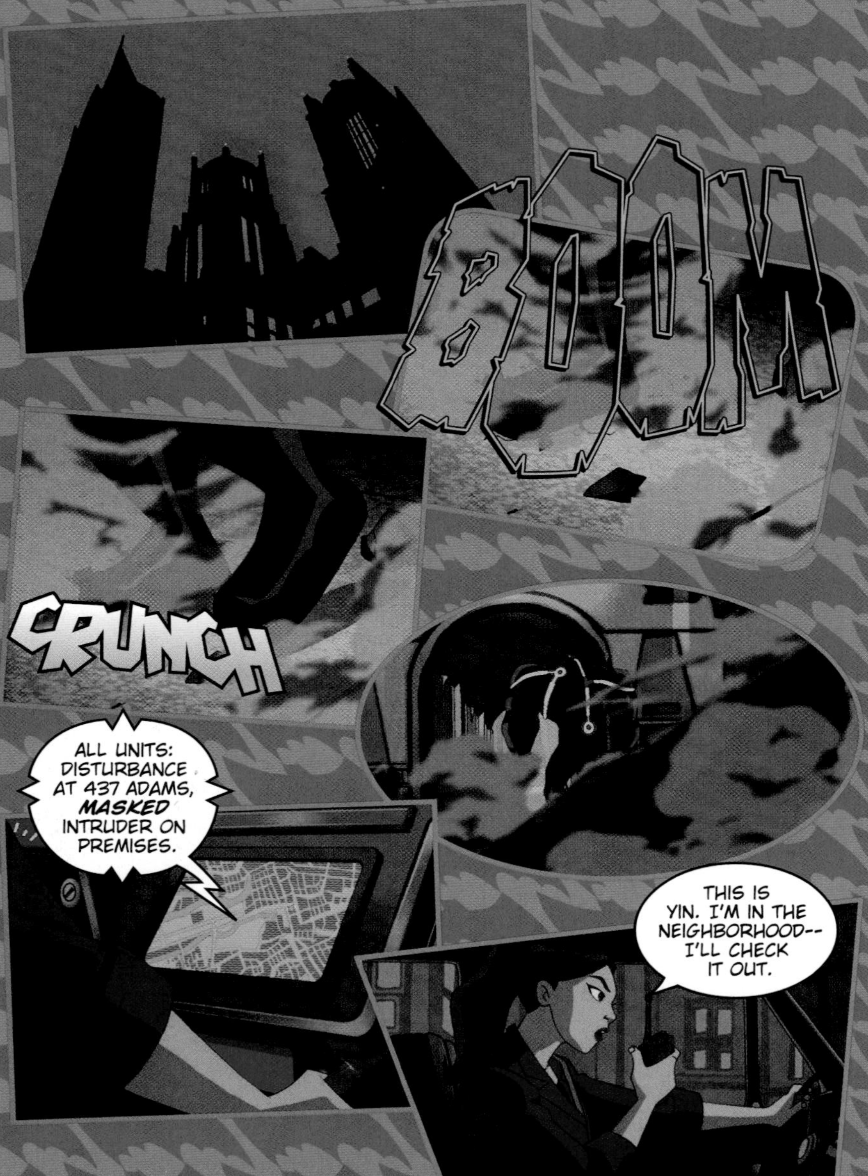
BOOM
CRUNCH
ALL UNITS: DISTURBANCE AT 437 ADAMS, ***MASKED*** INTRUDER ON PREMISES.
THIS IS YIN. I'M IN THE NEIGHBORHOOD-- I'LL CHECK IT OUT.

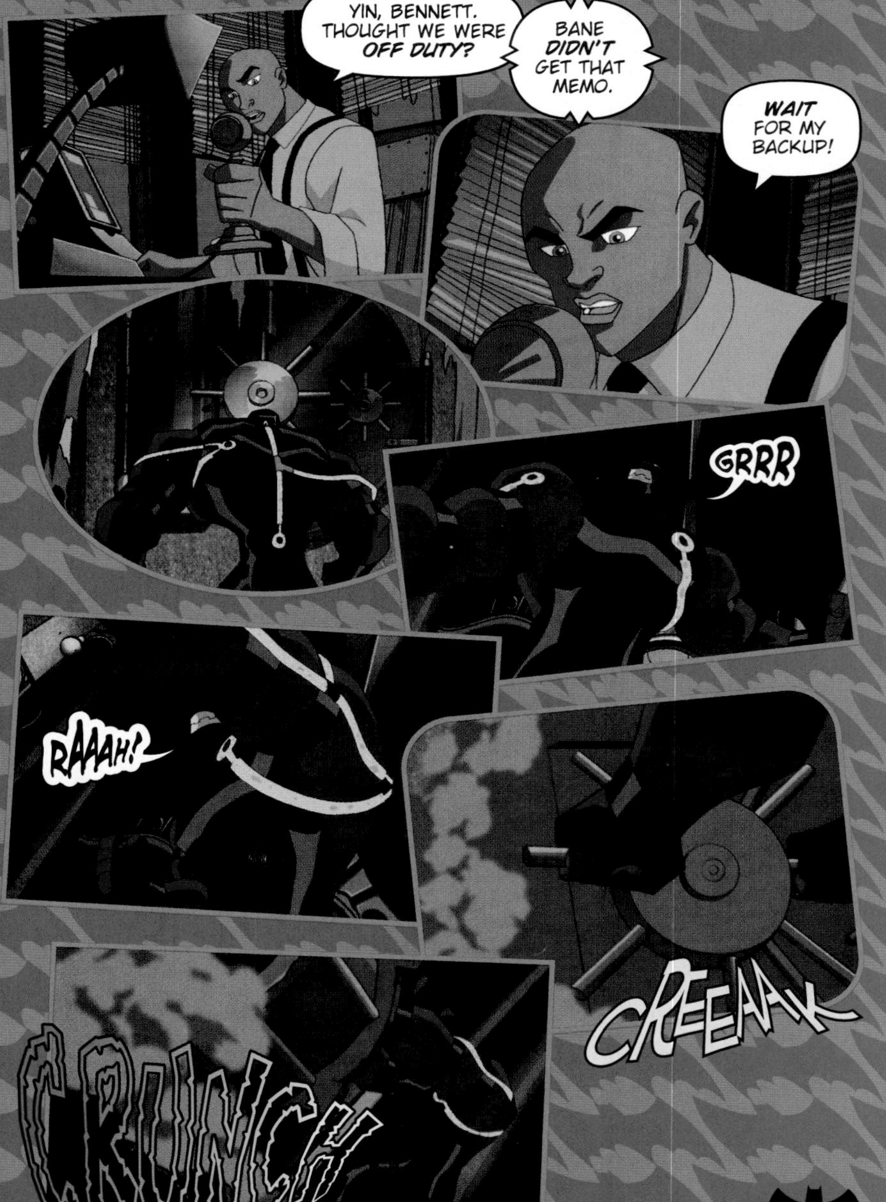
YIN, BENNETT. THOUGHT WE WERE OFF DUTY?
BANE DIDN'T GET THAT MEMO.
WAIT FOR MY BACKUP!
GRRR
RAAAH!
CREEAAK
CRUNCH

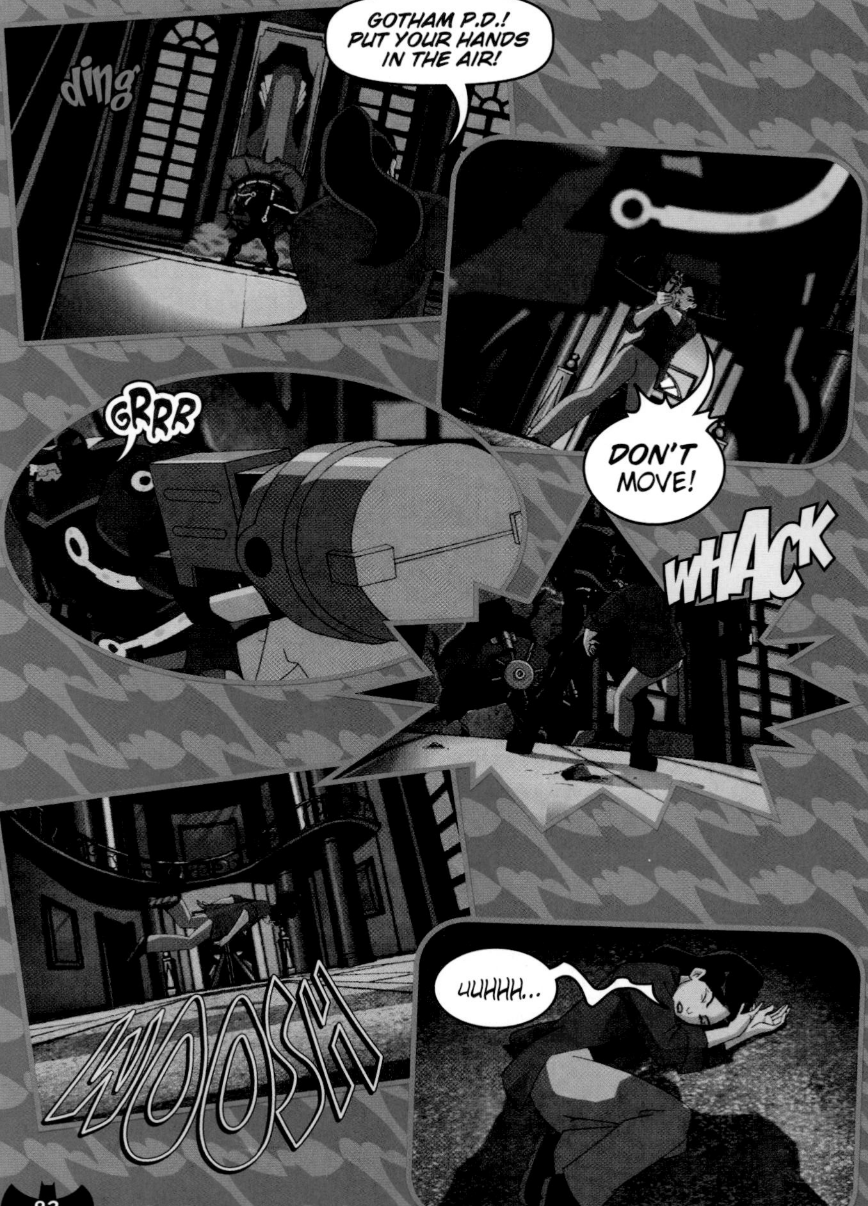
ding
GOTHAM P.D.! PUT YOUR HANDS IN THE AIR!
GRRR
DON'T MOVE!
WHACK
WOOSH
UUHHH...

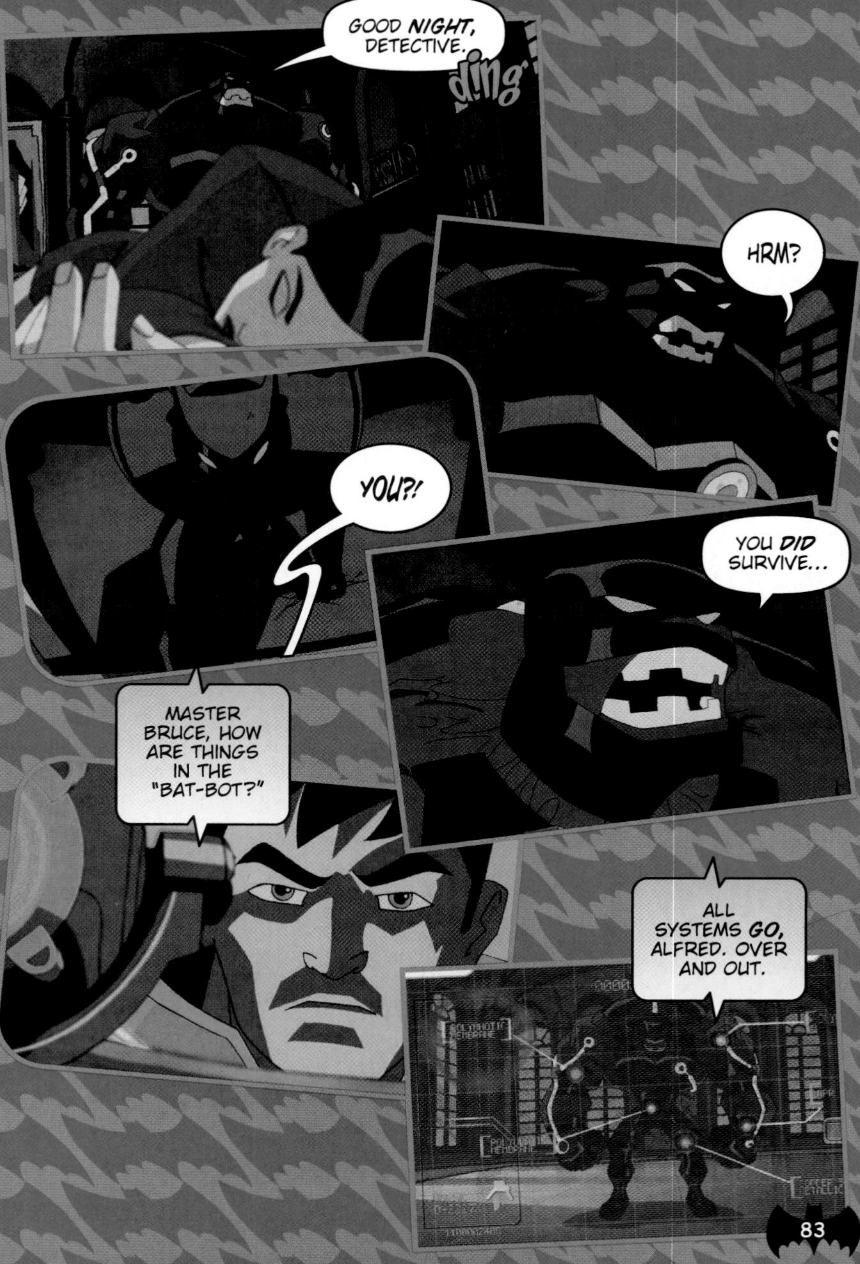
GOOD NIGHT, DETECTIVE.
ding
HRM?
YOU?!
YOU DID SURVIVE...
MASTER BRUCE, HOW ARE THINGS IN THE "BAT-BOT?"
ALL SYSTEMS GO, ALFRED. OVER AND OUT.

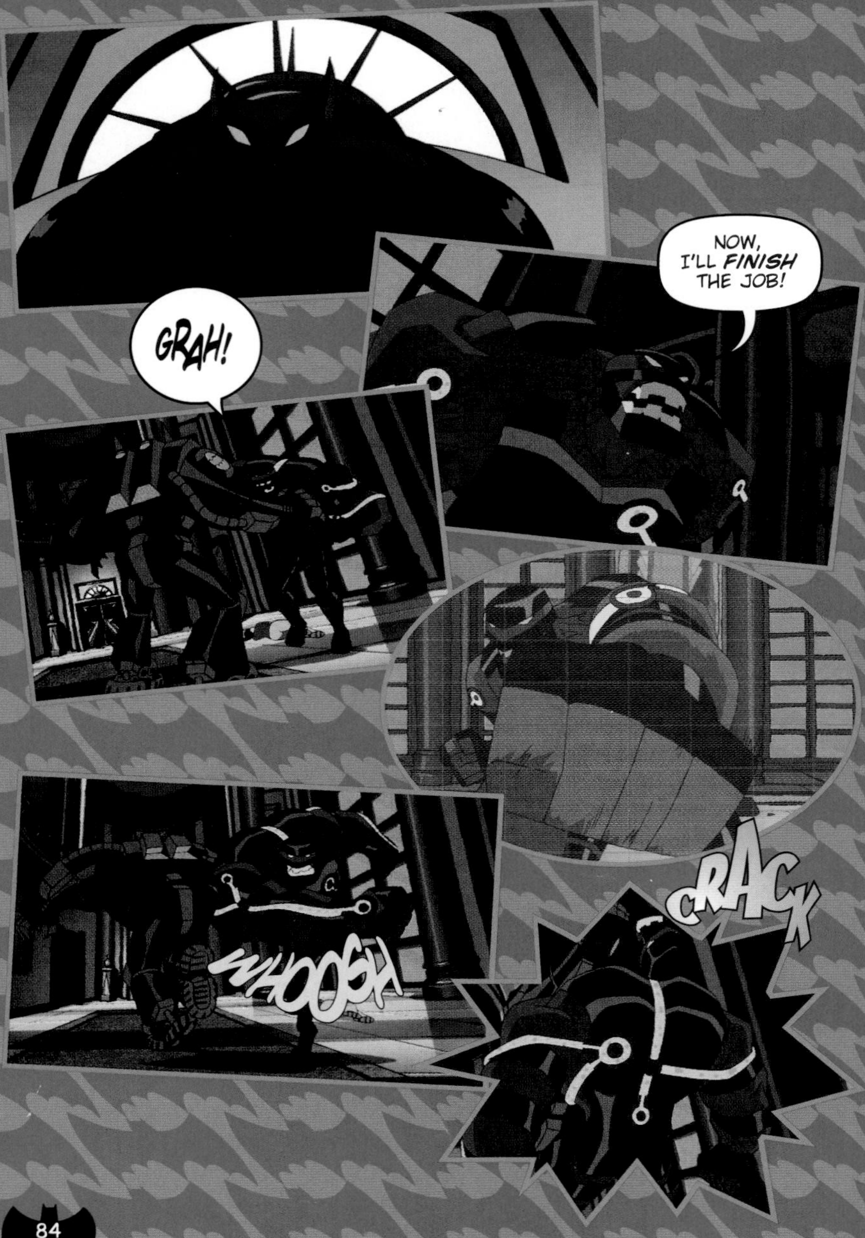
NOW, I'LL FINISH THE JOB!
GRAH!
WHOOSH
CRACK

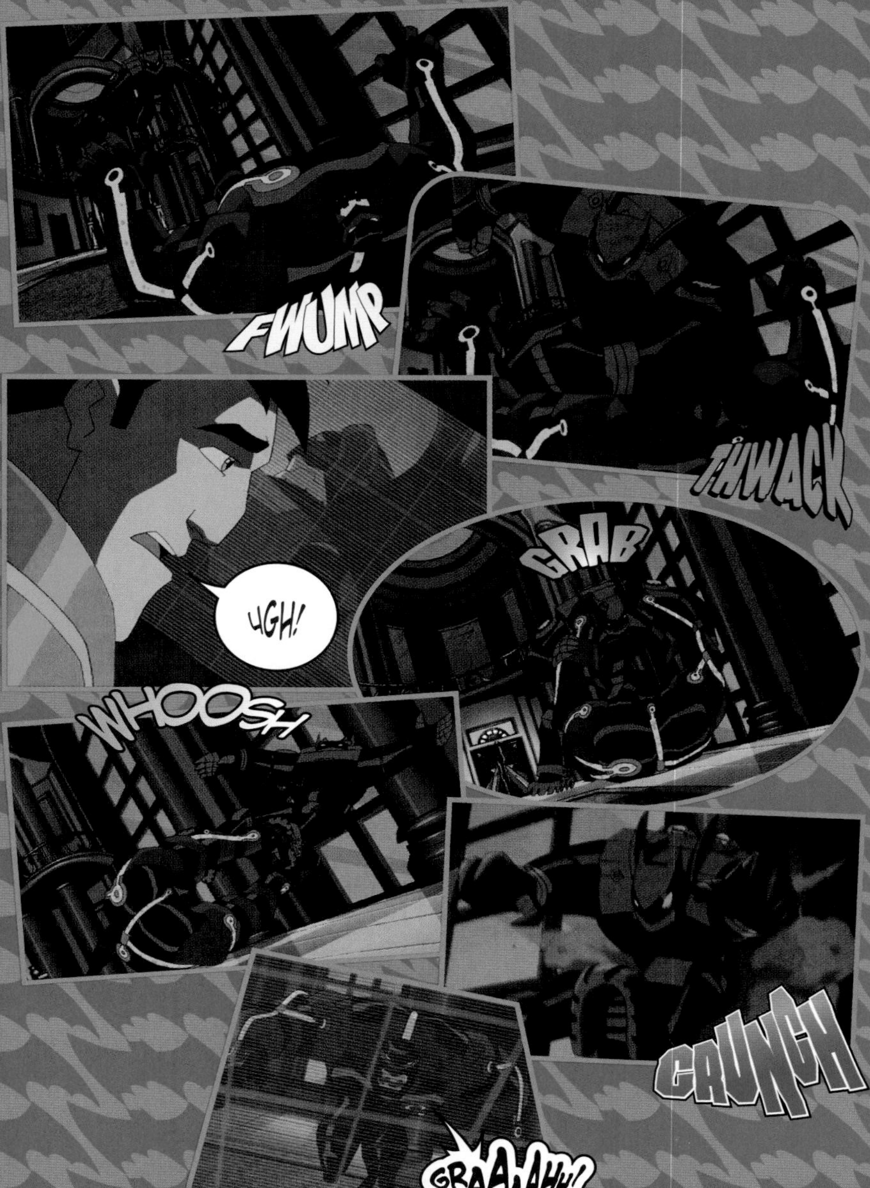
FWUMP
THWACK
UGH!
GRAB
WHOOSH
CRUNCH
GRAAAAAHH!

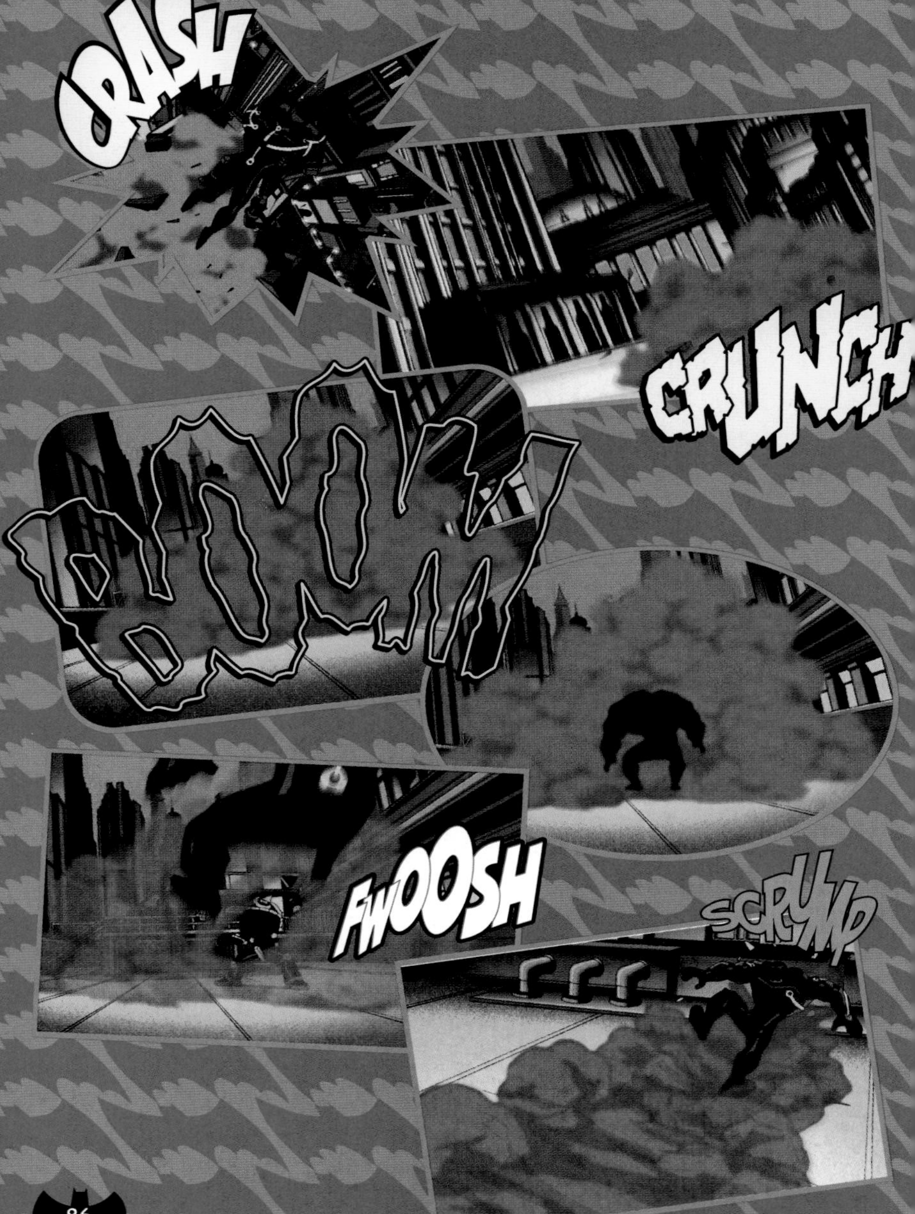
CRASH
CRUNCH
BOOM
FWOOSH
SCRUMP

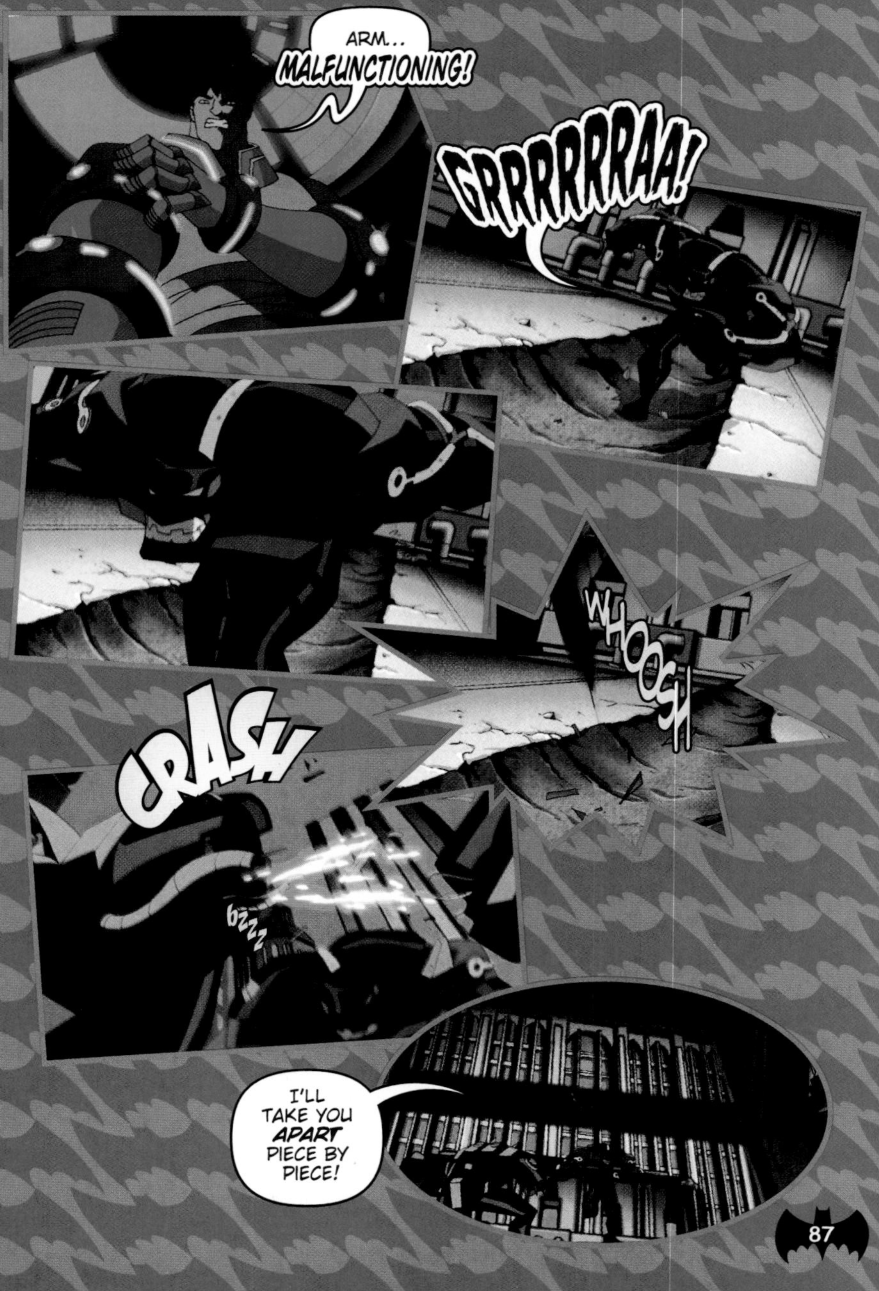
ARM... MALFUNCTIONING!
GRRRRRRAA!
WHOOSH
CRASH
bZZZ
I'LL TAKE YOU APART PIECE BY PIECE!

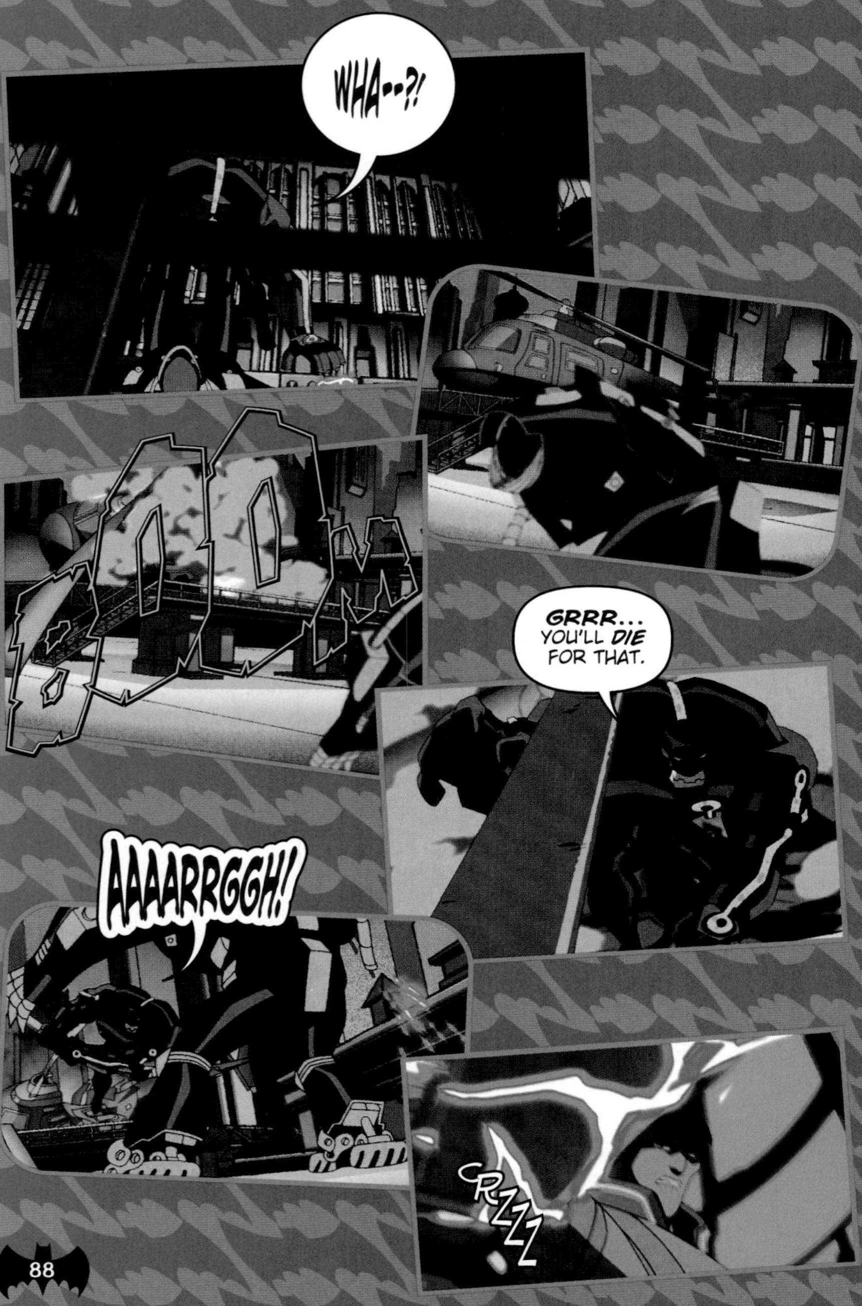
WHA--?!
BOOM
GRRR... YOU'LL DIE FOR THAT.
AAAARRGGH!
CRZZZ

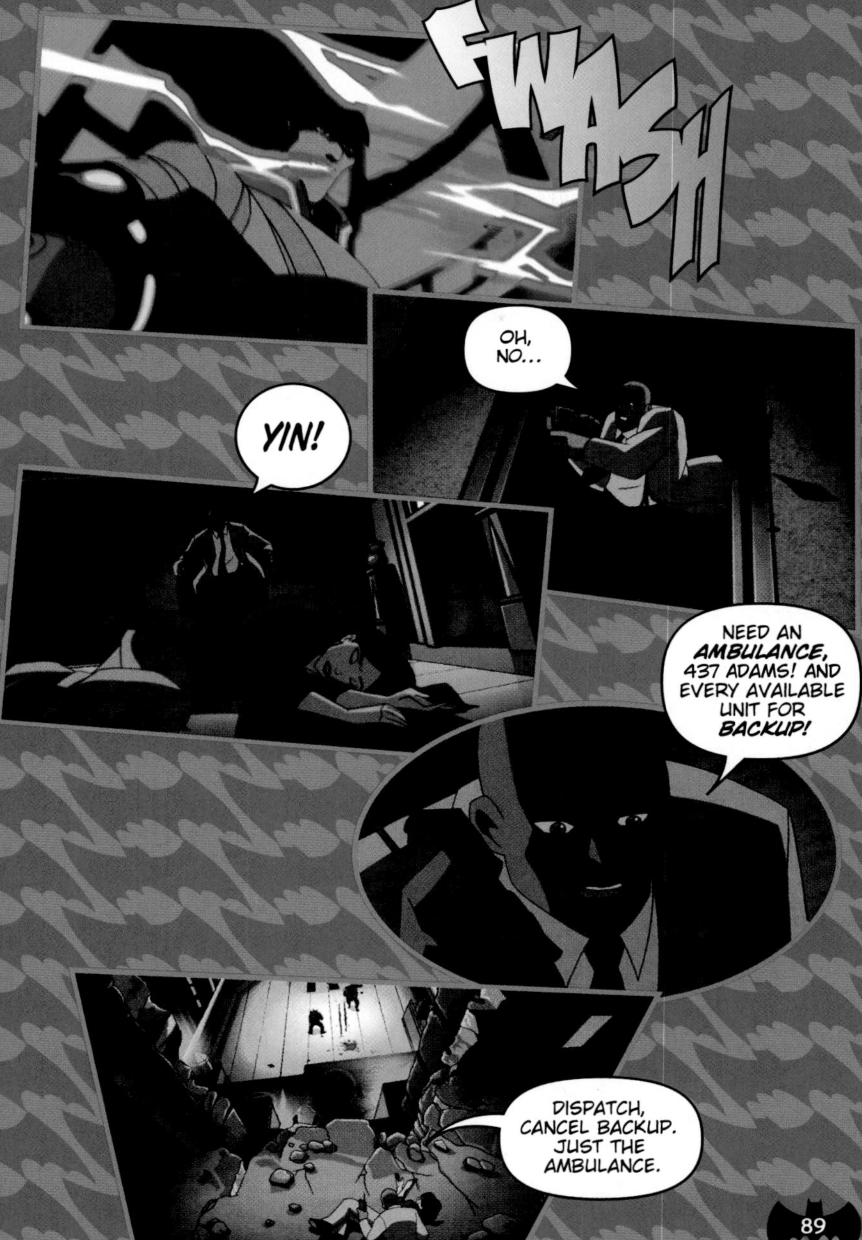
FWASH
OH, NO...
YIN!
NEED AN **AMBULANCE,** 437 ADAMS! AND EVERY AVAILABLE UNIT FOR **BACKUP!**
DISPATCH, CANCEL BACKUP. JUST THE AMBULANCE.

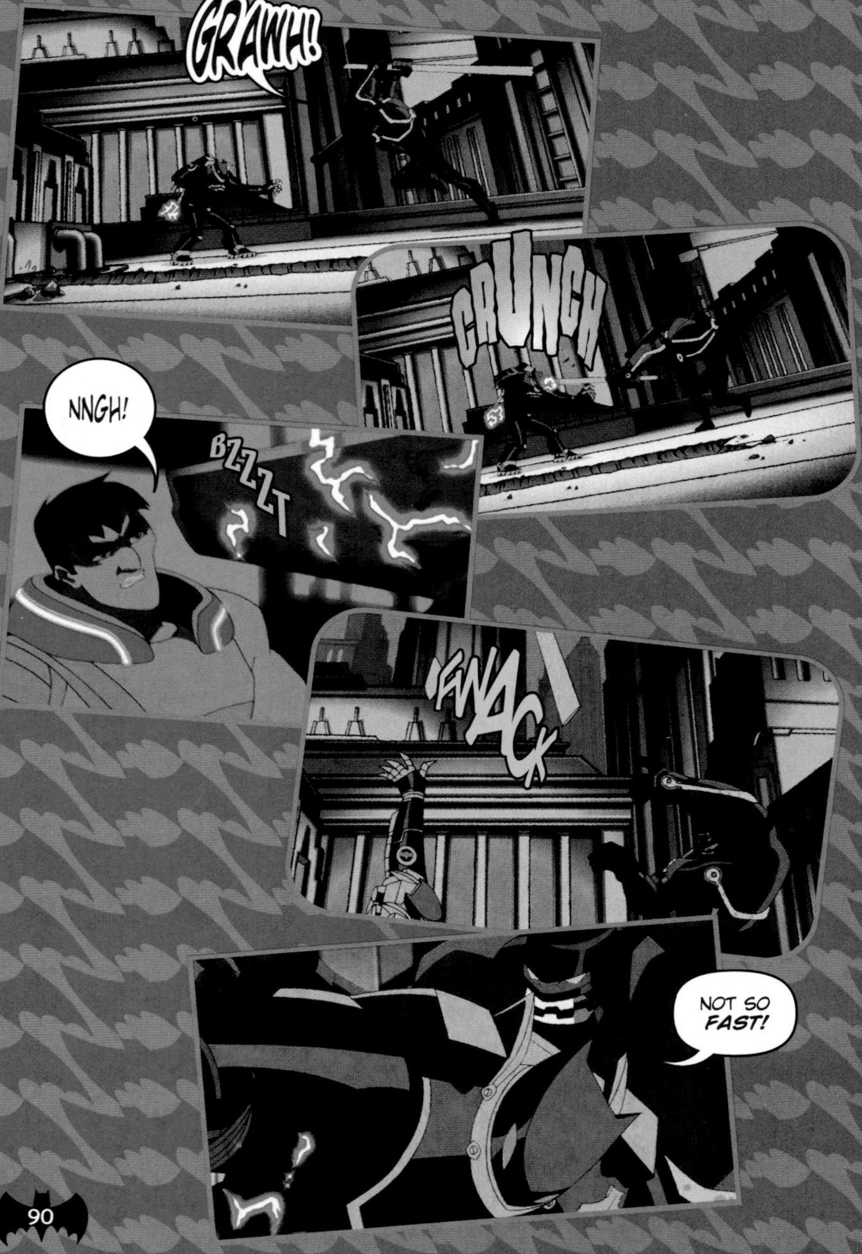
GRAWH!
CRUNCH
NNGH!
BZZZZT
FWACK
NOT SO FAST!

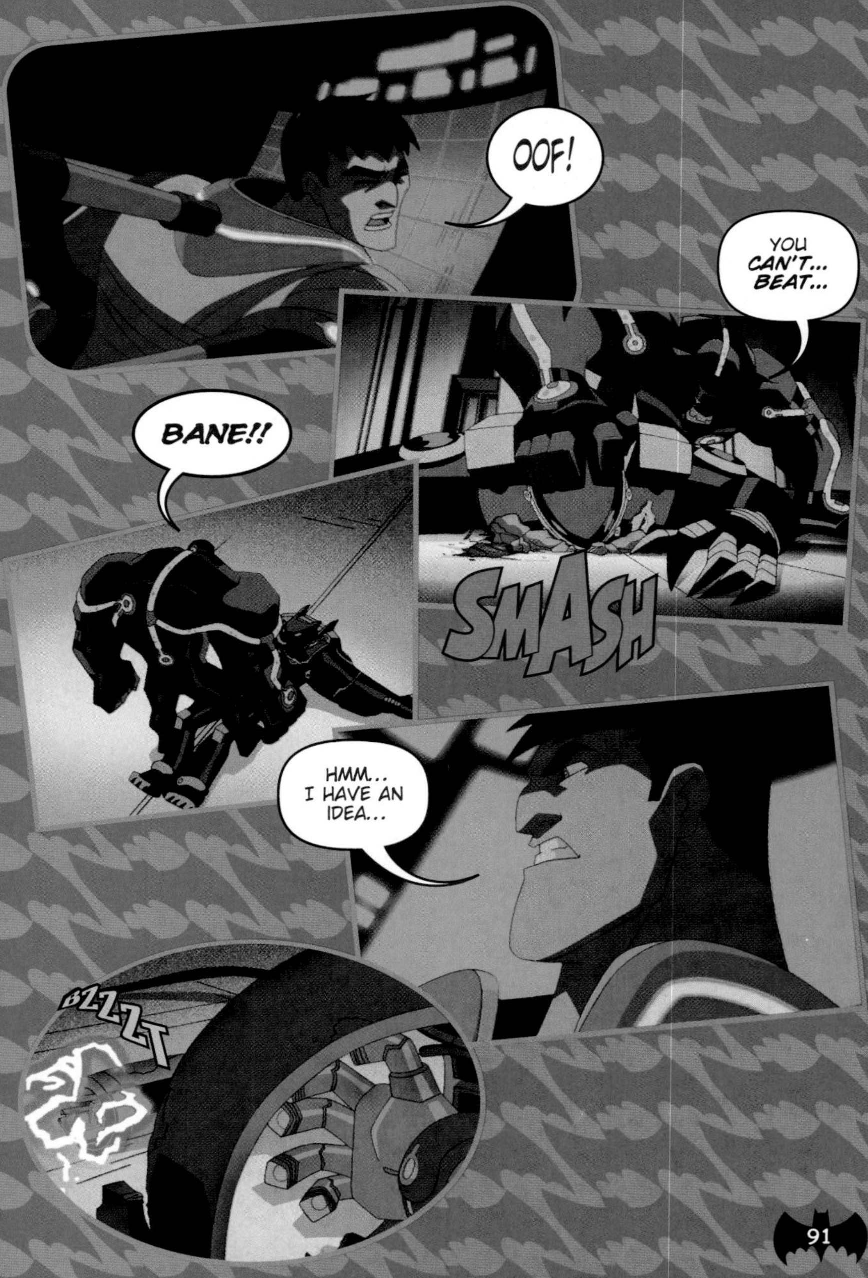

OOF!
YOU CAN'T... BEAT...
BANE!!
SMASH
HMM... I HAVE AN IDEA...
BZZZT

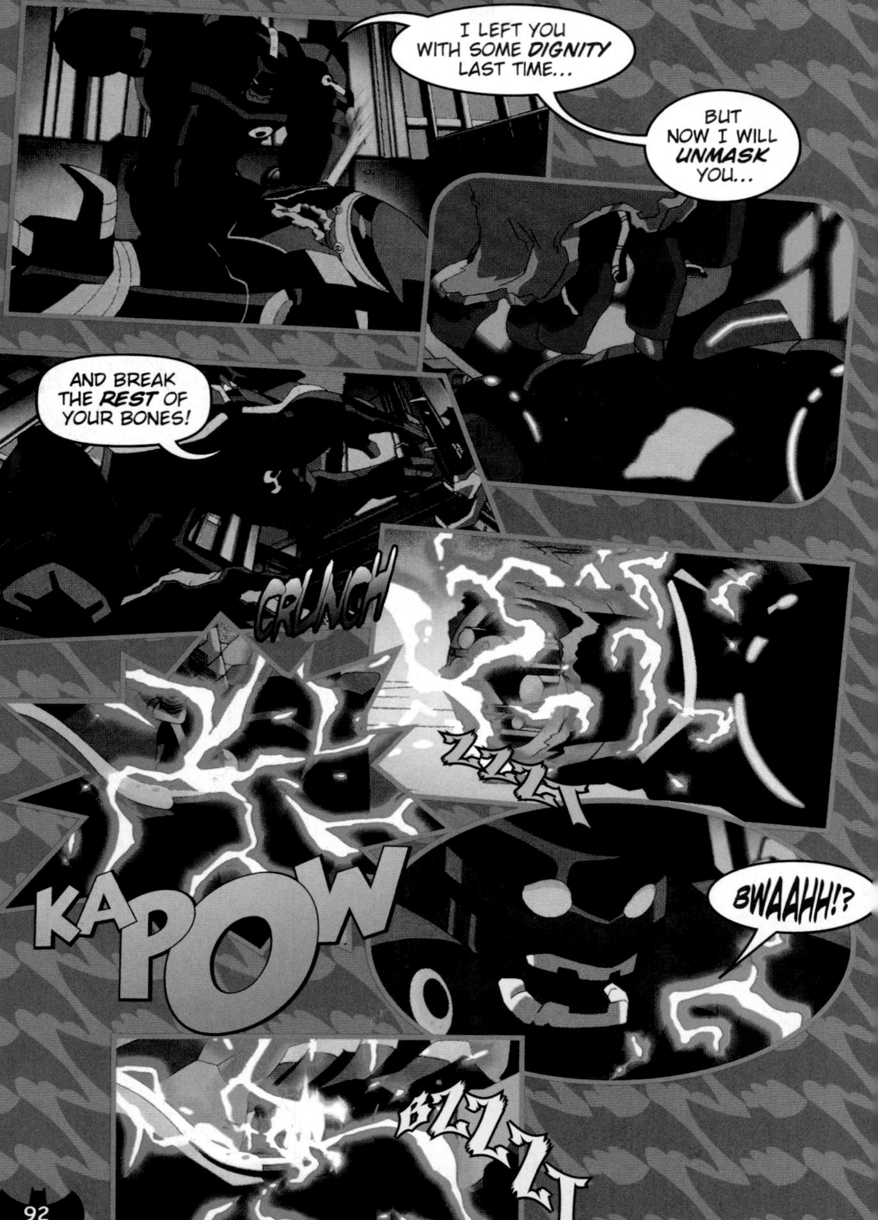
I LEFT YOU WITH SOME DIGNITY LAST TIME...
BUT NOW I WILL UNMASK YOU...
AND BREAK THE REST OF YOUR BONES!
CRUNCH
ZZZT
KAPOW
BWAAHH!?
BZZZT

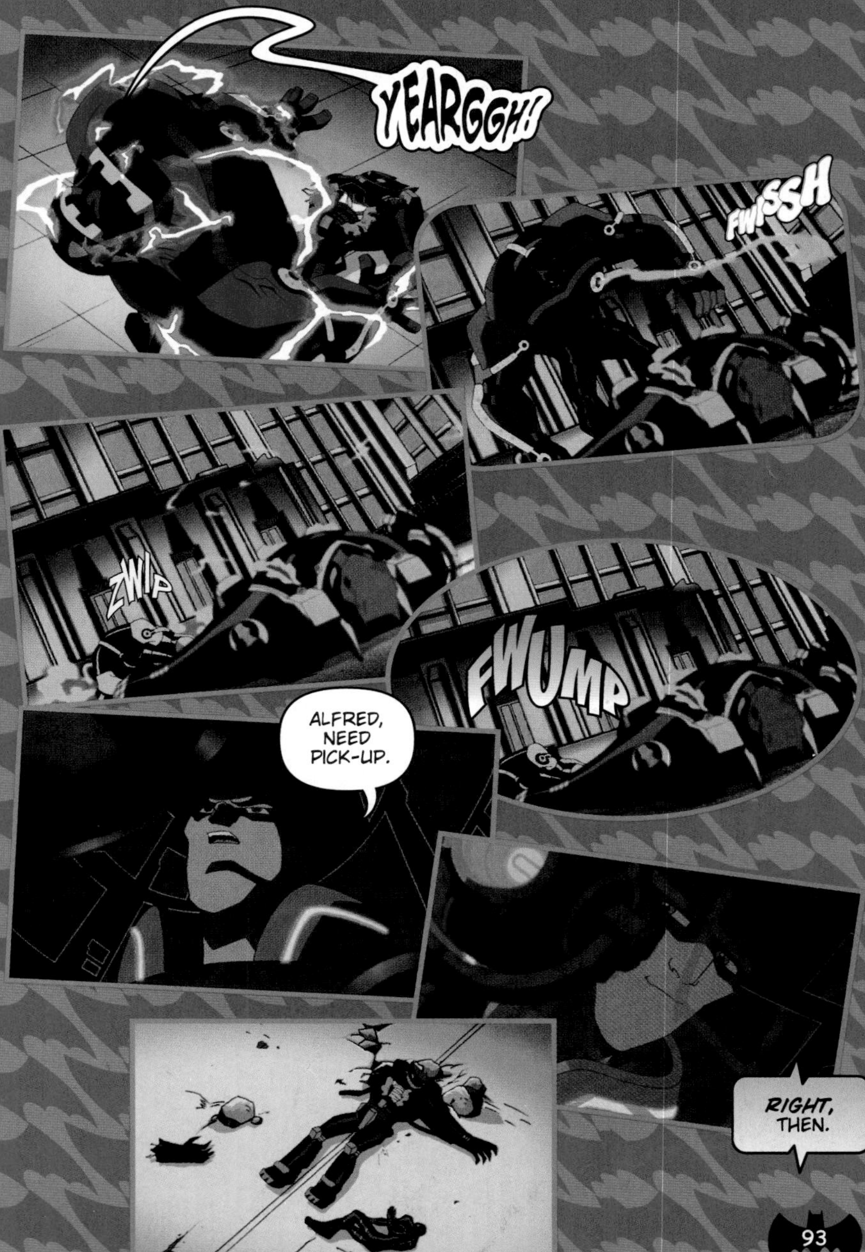
YEARGGH!
FWISSH
ZWIP
FWUMP
ALFRED, NEED PICK-UP.
RIGHT, THEN.

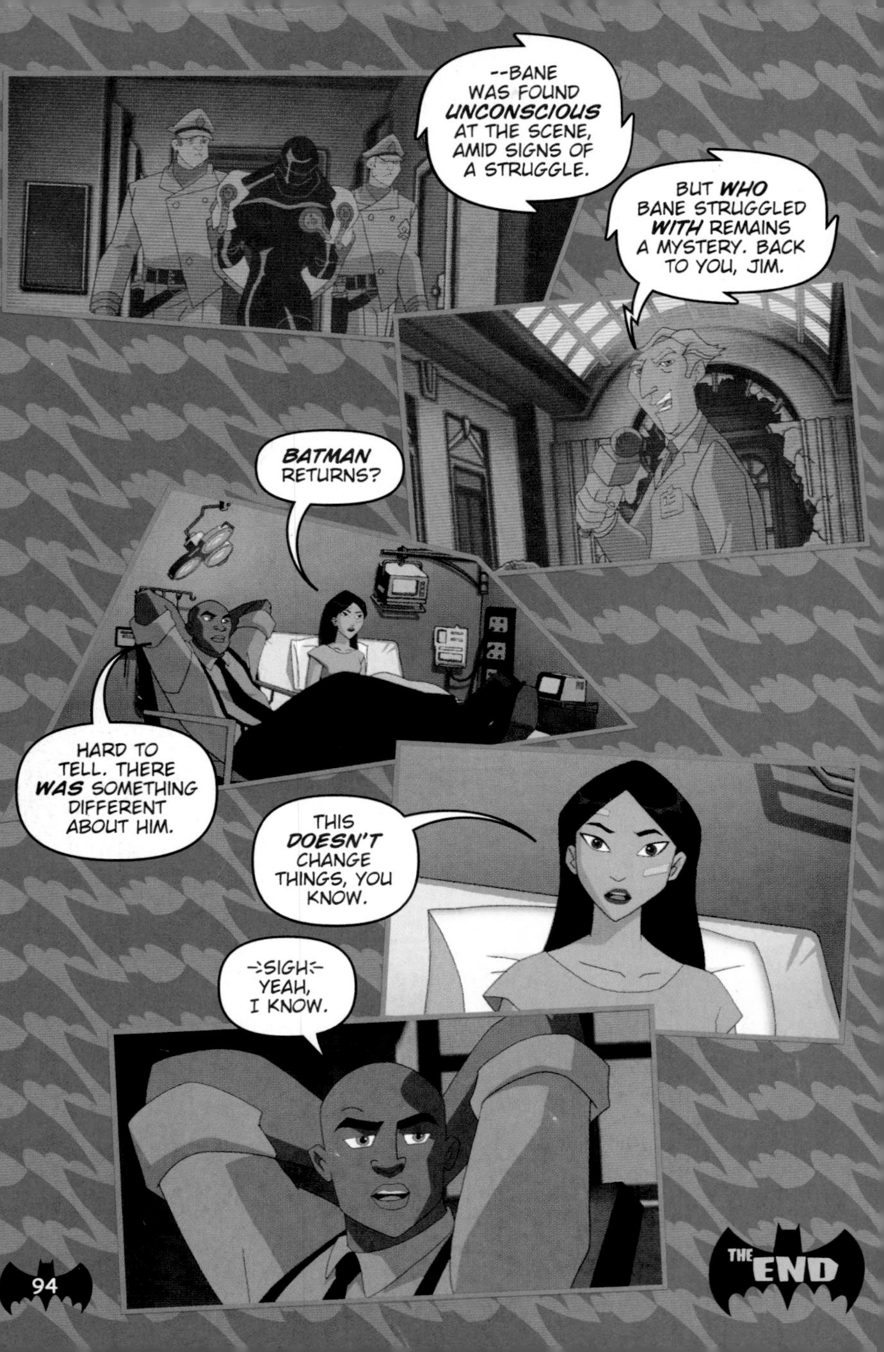
--BANE WAS FOUND *UNCONSCIOUS* AT THE SCENE, AMID SIGNS OF A STRUGGLE.
BUT *WHO* BANE STRUGGLED *WITH* REMAINS A MYSTERY. BACK TO YOU, JIM.
BATMAN RETURNS?
HARD TO TELL. THERE *WAS* SOMETHING DIFFERENT ABOUT HIM.
THIS *DOESN'T* CHANGE THINGS, YOU KNOW.
-SIGH- YEAH, I KNOW.
THE END